THE NOBODIES

THE
NOBODIES

ALANNA
SCHUBACH

**BLACK
STONE**
PUBLISHING

Copyright © 2022 by Alanna Schubach
Published in 2022 by Blackstone Publishing
Cover and book design by Zena Kanes

Printed in the United States of America

First edition: 2022
ISBN 978-1-6650-9577-8
Fiction / General

Version 1

CIP data for this book is available
from the Library of Congress

Blackstone Publishing
31 Mistletoe Rd.
Ashland, OR 97520

www.BlackstonePublishing.com

1

REUNION

(2005)

Jess reentered her life without ceremony. She just walked up the street while Nina was taking out the trash. It was 10:00 a.m. and she came from the east, her features shadowed, but there was no question it was her. Nina recognized the walk: a trace of masculinity in the set of her shoulders, arms slicing wide arcs through the air. Nina had never quite been able to imitate it.

As Jess drew nearer she came into focus. Her hair was longer than Nina had seen it before, and darker. Her eyebrows were plucked thin enough to be more like suggestions. She was still small, but dense, a collapsed star. The world slid toward her.

Nina's first instinct was to run. She was undefended—she needed time to prepare. But where was there to go? Jess was almost upon her. Nina was painfully conscious that she had just touched the befouled lid of the trash can, that she was wearing the T-shirt she'd slept in, which had green lettering that read YOU WOULDN'T LIKE ME WHEN I'M HUNGRY. She wiped her hands on the back of her jeans, as though she could wipe away their trembling.

Then Jess was there. Her lips stretched wide, seemed to flick on a light behind her eyes. "You look the same," she said. Nina took a step away from the garbage and Jess drew her into a hug. She hoped Jess couldn't feel the thrum of her heart as their bodies touched. There was the familiar smell of shampoo and something new, chemical, like turpentine.

They parted. Jess took in the shirt. "I was worried," she said, "that I wouldn't recognize you."

Nina unstuck her tongue from the roof of her mouth. "You look amazing," she said, which sent Jess's eyes mercifully away, down toward her feet. "What—I mean—" *What are you doing here?* was too cold. "What brings you here?" she said, and wished immediately she could shove the strange phrase back down her throat.

Jess laughed. "I missed you," she said. Her voice was richer somehow, thickened by the five years since Nina had last heard it.

Nina swallowed the urge to ask if this meant all was forgotten, made right. She had believed what she needed, what she deserved, was an apology, a reckoning. For everyone who claimed to care for her to feel, saturated in every cell, her devastation. But Jess's three words, like a charm, dissolved the desire completely.

***

You should see *my* place, Jess told her, as Nina apologized for the apartment. It was a duplex, with none of the glamour the word suggested. Nina's room on the basement level was raided by mice; the freezer overfilled with frost they had to hack away at each month. The living room, all but crammed by the couch, faced the busy East Village street, and sometimes at night people would stop and peer in. Nina guided Jess around the tiny space, murmuring; Eleanor was still asleep, her door closed.

"Show me your room," Jess said.

The single bed with its unwashed comforter flush against the wall, the dull blue carpeting, the slice of sidewalk visible through the window only if you craned your neck. Nina wished again she'd had time to prepare, to clean, so that she could have reunited with Jess from a position that projected power, evinced a life that said, *I've hardly thought of you at all.*

She had imagined the scene of this reunion many times. In it she was elegant and remote, thinner, in an expensive, form-fitting dress and heels; in it Jess shakily confessed that upon reflection, Nina had been in the right, she could see now that Nina had only been trying to protect her. Other times she told herself they would never speak again. She vacillated between the two possibilities with a masochistic compulsion.

Jess peered at the framed photos over the desk as Nina's heart thrashed in her chest. In this state, she'd never be the aloof sophisticate of her imagination. Her teacher, Avi, could slow or speed his heart rate at will; he'd demonstrated once for them with a cardiac monitor, claimed they'd all be able to do the same before long.

"Where was this?" Jess said of one image.

"Tokyo."

"You went to Tokyo?"

"Second semester of junior year," Nina said. "I got more adventurous."

"Apparently!" Jess sounded as proud as a parent. She sank onto the bed and Nina took the only other seat in the room, in the office chair. "I dropped out of Hunter after sophomore year. I should've stayed long enough to do a study abroad."

Nina had heard; Jess's entrance and exit both caused their respective stirs, sent gossip swirling among their former high school classmates. It was hardly a surprise Jess couldn't stick with it—she'd had no support. She still remembered what Jess's mother had said when she thought she was speaking to her daughter: *I'm supposed to believe you'll go off to college and magically turn into a brilliant person?*

Her eyes traced Jess, as though the wages of her childhood might have become visible on the surface of her skin. But Jess faced away, eyes lingering on the photos. "Wow," she said. Then she looked at Nina. "I guess you want to know why I'm here." And before Nina could respond and finally seize the answer as to whether Jess forgave, whether she wanted Nina's forgiveness, she continued, "And how I got your address."

Nina nodded. Every object in the room, every sandal and pillow and paperback, was charged with the strangeness of Jess sitting inches from her after all this time.

"My mom's dating a private investigator."

"Anita?" Nina said. And then: "You investigated me?" But she was flattered and relieved that it hadn't been her alone who lived with the small and wounded voice that hissed: *What is she doing right now?* At last her heartbeat was easing.

Jess picked at the bedspread. "Are you telling me you never tried to look me up?"

"No, I did." It seemed safe now to admit it. "I missed you, too."

Jess smiled, still looking down. It was her victory smile, the private glow that came into her face whenever she landed a blow on the deserving.

"So what's new with you?" Nina asked, absurdly, but she succeeded in bringing Jess back to a place of neutrality.

"I'm an intern at a photography studio. The one that got famous for covering 9/11," Jess said, now stroking the bedspread with her fingers. Then, as though the two were related, "And my dad died."

The announcement struck Nina as another victory: it was monumental. And here she had bragged about a semester abroad. "Oh my God. I'm so sorry."

One of Jess's shoulders rose and fell. "I hadn't seen him in so long. You know how I tried to find him when we were little."

They had tried together. There were recordings—the cassettes still stashed somewhere in Nina's childhood home—of their attempts, their girlish incantations of his name.

It was in the studio darkroom, Jess continued, that she got the call. She was plunging photo paper into the developer, shaking loose from blankness the beginning of an image. (That, Nina thought, was the chemical odor she'd noticed.)

Her phone rang and she'd answered, using tongs to pull the paper out of the developer and slide it into the stop bath. On the other end was a stranger, a man who told Jess that he had been appointed by the New Mexico bar association to execute her father's will, and it was his duty to inform her that as sole heir she could come and look through his things and claim what she wanted before the rest was put up for auction at an estate sale.

"Wait," Jess said to the stranger on the phone. The photo languished, blackened. "Does this mean he's dead?"

There was a long inhale at the other end of the line. In a drab office in a Santa Fe strip mall, a young attorney was now tasked with sharing the worst news a person could be given. He was sorry, he said, but yes, Mr. Garcia had passed away from what they suspected was cardiac arrest. Friends had overseen his burial; they hadn't even known he had family until they found a will among his papers, in a file cabinet in his apartment.

Jess sighed after sharing this and turned her face to the window. All their attempts at contact had failed, Nina thought. In fact, he had nullified her. And perhaps that was the reason for the reunion—for Jess to return to the person for whom she was most real, more than real.

Jess had asked the lawyer if she could call him back. At first she didn't feel anything. She was like the photo paper after it was exposed but before it was dunked in the developer, when there was something hidden, waiting to be brought forth.

"I'm sure it takes a while for news like that to hit you," Nina said. If there were a time to touch Jess, to lay a hand over hers, this was it. But a queasy resentment was rising in her chest. After all this time, a dead man was lodged inside their conversation. He left no room for Nina's questions: Why had Jess ended things the way she did? Did she see now that Nina had only wanted what was best for her? And did she miss their power the way Nina had, its absence carving a void within her?

"So I flew to Santa Fe," Jess said, "even though it cost me a fucking fortune."

There she went to the storage facility where her father's things were being held. The objects inside the freezing locker struck her as innocent—innocent of his coming death, which must have been sudden; redolent of his expectations for a longer time on Earth than what he'd gotten. There was a datebook in which she read his schedule for weeks into the future. He was in a bowling league that met on Wednesday nights, and he'd planned to go to the christening of a baby named Adriana later that month. Jess felt comforted, though she didn't know why, that her father's life hadn't been empty.

She claimed for herself only one thing. There wasn't anything else in the locker that appeared to be of much value. And she was getting colder and colder.

It was a portable radio. She remembered him bringing it to the community pool where he had sometimes taken her on his days off from work, watching her swim as he lay in a lounger listening to Phoenix Suns games. It was funny, wasn't it, he'd asked her once: a short Mexican guy like him loving basketball? She hadn't understood why that would be funny. He seemed huge to her.

The radio was long obsolete, and Jess thought maybe he'd kept it because it reminded him of a little girl splashing, entreating him to come in and play. So it came back with her to New York and took up residence on the top of her dresser.

"Here's the weird part," Jess told Nina, as though everything about this visit weren't strange. The first night, she said, the radio began emitting a smell. It actually woke her, it was an odor with layers: mothballs woven in with sulfur and boiled broccoli, old garlic, and beneath all that, so she'd only catch it on every fifth or sixth inhale, shit. It was as though the radio had absorbed the smell of his death and held it tightly until now.

"You know, he was dead for like a week before anyone found him," she said. To Nina this seemed a just ending for him, but she shuddered. Back, already, to trying to respond in the way Jess would want.

Jess had opened the window and put the radio on the fire escape, and when she checked in the morning, the odor was gone.

She decided it must have been a bad dream, and brought it back inside. But the next night what came out of it was noise, what machinery might sound like if it could speak, a deep, electric voice that yanked her from sleep with her own name. *Jessica. Jessica.*

Her father, some part of him, was inside the radio. She couldn't get rid of it, but she didn't want it either; it was cursed. She thought Nina might know how to help.

"You believe me, right?" There was a faint vertical line of worry between her eyebrows. That was new, too.

Nina nodded.

"I knew you would," Jess said, but her body sagged with relief. The room around them had grown very warm. "We, of all people, know that crazy things are possible." She flopped back onto the pillows. "I don't have time for this. If he wanted to get to know me, he should have done it when he was alive."

Was this why Jess had come back—only so that Nina could bear witness, offer assistance? Through a fog of disappointment, Nina scooted her chair across the floor until she was beside the bed. She looked down at Jess. "Don't you want to see," she said, "if we can still do it?"

***

Jess sat up, wordlessly, and ice water seemed to pool inside Nina's chest. This had been the worst possible response, she saw. Proof that throughout Jess's story she'd only been waiting to take back what she wanted.

But Jess said, "I didn't just come about a radio."

It was like the moment before first kisses, faces close, waiting in the anteroom that opened onto the inevitable.

At the same time, they shifted their weight toward one another until their foreheads touched. Nina had thought she would never feel it again, but here it was, same as always: the sunburn-like tingle that covered all of her at once, and the pull, pleasant but urgent, insistent, which she'd never dared or wanted to resist, a tugging along her entire surface. And as she answered it, the gates of her body swung open. She hung for that smallest moment nowhere, inside nothing, her self—whatever it was— suspended over a void, before she was welcomed back into the home she remembered and had believed, in despair, she would never reclaim; that wasn't Nina's but took her in without hesitation, clamped itself around her. She was back inside Jess's body.

There was, again, that first destabilizing moment of seeing herself from the outside. Reflections lied, photographs and videos lied. They didn't communicate the warmth of her own body and its breath, let her see the life pulsing it upright. Inside Jess, she groped blindly, trying to find what had changed over the five years.

Jess raised her hands, Nina's hands, and turned them over, skimming them down her face. "You're *not* the same," she corrected herself.

Their possessions of one another, she saw each time, were approximations. No matter how close they were, Nina's version of Jess's half-shrug lacked its usual potency, failed to provoke in others the thudding in their chests, the terrible certainty that they were disappointing somehow. And as Nina, when Jess crossed her arms over her chest, folding the tenderest parts away from view, her movements held a trace of mockery.

But no one, not Nina's parents, not her friends, not even Zachary—who had come closest to guessing their secret, which wasn't very close at all—understood that what they were seeing was only an impersonation: that the real Jess, the real Nina, was somewhere else.

***

Nina tried to scan the body she was in, but her mind darted from one corner to the next, and it was impossible to measure what might be different. The palms were dry, peeling from the photographic chemicals, and the long hair was heavy down her back.

"Sometimes I wondered if I imagined it," Nina said. "But deep down I knew I didn't."

Jess said, "We did too much damage for it not to be real."

2
THE CANDLE ROOM
(1992)

There was a house across the street from the elementary school whose owners outdid themselves each autumn, with ever more baroque Halloween decorations, and on the early October morning that Nina and Jess first met, there was already a half-buried skeleton in the front yard, one hand outstretched and clawing at the air.

At the front of the classroom Ms. Brandon clicked through slides for her science lesson, somehow making the birth of stars boring. Then she broke off, looking through the doorway and into the hall.

"Come on in," Ms. Brandon said, and a girl stepped into the room. Behind her, still half in the hallway, a woman stood, arms crossed over her middle to shield it from the rising murmur of the children. This was Anita, Jess's mother, who, Nina would soon learn, always smelled of hairspray, smoke, and spearmint.

From the threshold, Anita waved to her daughter, then vanished.

Ms. Brandon beckoned the girl to stand beside her and face the students. She placed a proprietary hand on her shoulder. "This is Jessica Garcia," she said. "She just moved here from Arizona."

"Is she a new student?" Fallon asked.

"Obviously," Ms. Brandon said. Giggling started in the rear corner and radiated outward.

Jessica Garcia had dark hair, dark eyes; dark enough that Nina could not distinguish between iris and pupil, which gave the impression that the new girl was from not another state but another world.

"Why don't you introduce yourself?" Ms. Brandon said.

The laughter died down. Jessica Garcia's dark eyes moved over their faces, and all the children went quiet. It was as though this stranger had been summoned to judge, that she was scanning their souls, that soon she would pronounce her verdict on every one of them.

"No," the girl said. A ripple of sound, somewhere between a gasp and a chuckle, started up again.

Ms. Brandon's colorless lips sagged. "Well," she said. "She's shy."

Jessica Garcia's thick eyebrows drew together. She did not need to tell any of them that she was not shy.

"Everyone from Steven Hirsch on, move over one seat," Ms. Brandon said. A riot of metal chair legs scraping against linoleum, books and pencils, candy stashes and intricately folded notes extracted from the dark compartments of desks. Jessica Garcia watched them and Nina watched her. At the end of it, there was an empty spot to her right. Garcia and then Glass.

Before she could be directed, the girl hoisted her backpack onto her shoulders, walked over, and slid into the space beside Nina. At the front, Ms. Brandon stood with the rigidity of a telephone pole, waiting for them to hush. Then she clicked the projector back on.

Beneath the teacher's drone, Nina heard the patter of sneakers against floor. She glanced over and saw Jessica's legs jiggling under the desk. She was young enough to believe she had been selected, not by Ms. Brandon or the vicissitudes of the alphabet but perhaps by the universe itself, to serve as guide to this outsider. That from the clouds a great hand had reached out and pointed: *You.*

She leaned over to the girl. Whispered, "I'm Nina."

***

All through the morning, the new girl managed to cleave to her without making it apparent that she was doing so. When they walked to gym class, Jessica was right behind her, dragging an index finger along the dusty grout between the pale green tiles of the walls. When Nina turned to warn her of how Mr. Vitale, the bald and bearded teacher, favored the boys, Jessica feigned surprise, blinking as though her nearness to Nina was mere coincidence.

At lunch they were finally separated: Nina had brought food from home, and she carried it to the usual table where she sat with Raymond, a chubby boy hounded by the other children ever since they first heard his high, clear singing voice in music class. She eyed Jessica as she took a spot on the line to buy lunch, right behind Fallon and Mara, and wished she could tell the new girl she had other friends in another class, ones more palatable than Raymond.

"Arizona's like the desert, right?" he said. "I wonder what they're telling her."

She looked over and saw they were speaking to her, hissing, maybe, about the misstep it would be to ally oneself with Nina and Raymond. Jessica's eyes flitted their way. But ten minutes later she emerged from the hollow in the cafeteria wall and walked toward their table. She sat, looking down at her damp piece of breaded chicken and undercooked French fries.

"What did Mara say to you?" Raymond asked.

Jessica looked up. "Mara?"

"That girl talking to you," Nina said. "The blond girl."

"She wanted to know if I like Mariah Carey."

"Oh," Nina said. She felt strangely disappointed. "Do you?"

Jessica shrugged.

"I like her," Raymond said. "Mariah Carey, not Mara." He glanced around to see if any lunch ladies were hovering. "Mara's a bitch."

Jessica's face didn't change at the utterance of this forbidden word: it was still, waiting for more.

"Especially to Nina," Raymond continued. "She tripped her the other day when we lined up for art."

Heat gathered beneath Nina's eyes. Now the new girl would know her mistake. Jessica poked at her chicken with a plastic fork, presumably flooded with regret.

"Are you nine?" she suddenly asked.

Nina nodded.

"Me too. It's the worst number."

"What do you mean?" Raymond said.

"I mean it tastes bad, it smells bad, so of course being nine sucks."

"Numbers have tastes?" Nina said. She wondered if this was an Arizona thing.

Jessica said, "To me they do."

"So what does nine taste like?"

Jessica wrinkled her nose. "A chicken carcass that's been sitting in the garbage for days."

Raymond said, "Are you for real?"

Something under Jessica's face changed, like tectonic plates shifting beneath the surface of the Earth. "Are you calling me a liar?"

"I believe you," Nina said quickly, desperate to learn more about the numbers. "I have that too."

Raymond, cowed, drank his milk, didn't mention that somehow this had never come up.

Jessica's face relaxed, and she smiled a little. Up close, her eyes were a rich brown color, less alien. They locked onto Nina's.

The girls cataloged throughout the lunch period, neglecting their own food in favor of mapping the flavorscape conjured by different numbers. One was icy but practically tasteless, a Popsicle with all its juices sucked out. Four was Hatch green chile; Nina pretended to know what this meant. Because six was orange and ten vanilla pudding, sixteen was Creamsicle, Jessica's favorite. If she was ever punished by being denied dessert, she'd just go to her room and turn the numbers over and over in her mind until its citric sweetness filled her mouth.

Nina tried to conjure the taste herself. She closed her eyes and envisioned an enormous, glowing *16* floating out of the darkness, dripping sugar, but there was only a ghost of tartness on her tongue.

"Do you think that means sixteen will be a good year?" Nina asked.

Jessica thought for a moment. She chewed a French fry. "If we're still alive," she said.

Raymond, who had long evicted himself from the conversation, shook his head and stood to carry his lunch bag over to the garbage can. The cafeteria continued to roar around them. It was like flipping back and forth a page in a book: Nina felt at once confounded by the idea that they could both, in seven years' time, easily be dead, and then sheltered beneath the warm hug of the *we*, delighted that this new girl, who'd turned out to have magic, already thought of them as united.

***

Knowing the taste of numbers was the first secret they shared, the first entry in their common language. That Nina was feigning the ability didn't seem to matter. They were linked by it, and the more they cataloged the more it came to exist outside them, rising to a high wall behind which they shared a private courtyard. When Mr. Vitale, in gym class, berated Raymond for doing push-ups like a girl, Jessica looked over at Nina and mouthed, *forty-nine*, an especially repulsive number, redolent of trash steaming in the summer sun. When Mara passed out invitations to her tenth birthday party, dropping the cards from a great height upon each student's desk, skipping over Nina, Jessica, Raymond, and Todd, a boy missing the pinkie finger from his right hand, Nina told her none of them had wanted to attend, anyway, because she smelled like a dead animal. It was the first time she had struck back, and she noted with satisfaction how Mara flinched and began to protest, until Jessica drowned the girl out with such a fusillade of cackles that Ms. Brandon made them all stay behind in the room during recess.

Nina had never been punished in this way, and she imagined Ms. Brandon calling her parents to inform them that their daughter had been caught tormenting another student; she imagined their confusion and disappointment. She felt no remorse, only the impossibility of explaining to them the justice of what she had done. They couldn't know how at the start of the school year the classroom hierarchies had cemented themselves, the girls sorted according to a set of rules about clothing and hair that they, but not Nina, were somehow privy to, blocking out all potential for connection—until Jess had arrived.

Their punishment was to sit with the lights dimmed, heads resting on their desks, for the entire period. Nina studied the new angles that materialized from this new vantage. The blackboard at the front of the room became the ceiling, the chalked words mysterious encryptions; the windows onto the outdoors where her classmates swarmed—the handball court, the netless basketball hoops, the yellow grass of the soccer field, the playground where they were now too old to do anything but sit on swings with affected disinterest—a bright netherworld she slid toward.

Something landed in her lap. Nina looked down and saw a piece of notebook paper folded tightly into a square. Beside her, Jessica, her head similarly sideways, smiled.

At the front of the room, Ms. Brandon was reading a paperback, occasionally licking a fingertip before lifting a new page. Nina looked down into her lap and unfolded the square.

Dear Nina, I keep having this dream, Jessica had written. *It's just me in a room full of candels. It's really pretty and calm. Last night you were there for the 1st time, but your eyes were closed. I think if you opened your eyes you would really be there. Jess*

Nina knew that her new friend was called Jess only by people with whom she was close. Now, she had been invited to use the single syllable, to join the ranks of the favored.

She silently extracted a pen from her desk. Leaning against her thighs for support, Nina wrote below the message, *Dear Jess* (a warm thrill shot down her spine), *Do you mean if I opened my eyes we would be in the same dream? Nina*

After the furtive exchange and more of Jess's scribbling the note was returned. *Ya. Tonight when you're falling asleep you have to concentrate on waking up inside the candel room.*

Nina wrote, *I think I can do it. I sort of remember having a dream last night where I felt really warm but I couldn't see anything, so I must have really been there like you said.* It felt true, much in the way it did when she described for Jess the way numbers tasted to her. Already the candle room was surfacing from the muck at the bottom of her mind. The dream-things that dwelled there she usually tried to avoid probing, but now she could see narrow contours, stacks of soft pillows, melting wax, and her friend, sitting across from her, holding Nina's hands in her own, smiling.

You were there, Jess replied, underlining it for emphasis.

Then the bell rang, and children, red-cheeked, smelling like cold, began shuffling back into the classroom. Ms. Brandon extracted her long, bony limbs from behind the desk and turned on the lights. Jess and Nina lifted their heads and looked at each other, grinning. They had a place now beyond the reach of any punishment from the terrible repertoire of grown-ups.

***

She tried very hard to reach the candle room. She consulted *A Child's Compendium of the Universe,* the entry on **Astral Projection**, which began: "A type of out-of-body experience (OBE) in which the dreamer, conscious that he is dreaming, may send his spirit out of the bounds of his physical form to any place in the Heavens." There was a simple line drawing beside the text, of a man sleeping on his back in bed, a ghostly double hovering just above him, about to lift. The way the *Compendium*'s drawings mimicked diagrams from her school textbooks lent them an aura of scientific veracity, the sense that with close study each entry might sharpen into clarity. The book's spine was broken, had already gone floppy with use by the time Nina's mother had gifted it to her, a find from a stoop sale on a visit to the city. It was old. It had the smell of years in it. Nina kept it hidden in a drawer, beneath her underwear.

Uncertain she'd understood what she had read, Nina nevertheless attempted astral projection when she went to bed that night. She had, before falling asleep, focused on envisioning the candle room Jess had described, on curling her body tightly into a ball, preparing to hurtle herself through the ether and into the magical place, but when she woke in the morning her dreams were like wisps of smoke.

Jess would probably ask, when Nina went to visit that day, why she hadn't showed, so she slid the *Compendium* into her backpack to bring with her, hoping that if they consulted it together they might unlock the secret to reaching the astral plane.

But a first-time visit to a new friend's house meant—before you could explore its unfamiliar odors and angles, its peculiar governance—subjection to a gauntlet of tedium. Parents had to yammer while skimming a custodial hand over your head, vetting each other, each other's homes. And upon pulling up at Jess's house, which to Nina's mild disappointment was only a vinyl-sided split-level like all the others, Nina's mother announced that she wanted to meet Jess, about whom she'd heard so much over the past month.

At the front door Nina rang the bell, and then there stood Anita, whom Nina had seen a sliver of on that first day when Jess arrived in the classroom. She said hello, leaning her slim body against the doorframe; her lips, a deep crimson, spread wide. Nina looked up at her mom, who seemed startled by Anita's unmotherliness.

They introduced themselves and shook hands. There was a pause, and then Anita said, "Well, Jessica just *loves* your daughter. All we hear about is Nina. I feel like I'm meeting a celebrity!"

As if summoned, Jess materialized in the doorway behind her mother, out of the dimness of the home beyond. She reached out an arm to tug at Nina. "Come on," she said, and yanked her inside. They entered a foyer whose floor was lined with thick brown carpeting; there was a pile of shoes against the wall, and a smell of coffee and smoke over the real smell, the unshakable underaroma specific to each house, each clan. "See ya," Jess called over her shoulder to the mothers, who suddenly seemed so ignorant and locked out, not just of the house but of everything, that pity rose in Nina's throat. Before the women could respond, Jess pulled her up a flight of stairs and into her bedroom, and slammed the door.

Jess's room was smaller than Nina's, dimmer and fuller of things.

It had the feeling of a hideaway and immediately Nina began imagining how to make her own bedroom more like it. The walls themselves could only be seen in punctuated white strips, otherwise papered with magazine tear-outs and Polaroids and collages, artist unknown. There was a bookcase whose shelves were crammed with disorder, stuffed animals, bright feather boas, jewelry boxes of varying shapes; each object seemed to hold only more objects so that the room felt at once cramped and bottomless. On the floor, puddles of clothing, on the bed, a pile of throw pillows, on the dresser, tubes of lip gloss squeezed flat and an empty, elegant perfume bottle that looked culled from the possessions of someone's grandmother.

Out of this chaos Jess began extracting and showing her things. First a plastic ring adorned with a clear bauble, which, she demonstrated to Nina, if you held it at the right angle revealed a tiny pink rose embedded within.

"This was a present from Javi," Jess told her. "Javier. He was my boyfriend back in Phoenix." Before Nina could ask for more information Jess plucked the ring from her fingers and tossed it aside, replacing it with a square autograph book with a blue plastic cover. "Everyone signed this for me when I found out we had to move to Long Island," she said, and Nina had a few moments to flip through it, spot the fine script of teachers and the doodles of friends before Jess thrust upon her something else, a crude doll with a puffy white body and uneven stitching, through which some cotton protruded. A sour face had been drawn in black marker on it, and several pins protruded from its throat.

"It's a voodoo doll," Jess said. "I made it of this girl Karolina after she tattled on me and Javi for passing notes in class. I went home that night and—" She made stabbing motions.

"Did it work?" Nina asked.

"Three days later she came down with strep." Jess stroked the doll's stringy yellow hair, mockingly. "Poor Karolina," she said. Then her dark eyes lifted to Nina's face. "We can make one for Mara, if you want."

"Oh," Nina said. Violence had slipped into the room; one of the collages, it occurred to her, looked spattered with blood. "She hasn't been that bad lately."

Jess shrugged. "She still deserves at least strep."

Nina spotted a blue-and-yellow tape deck among the detritus on top of Jess's dresser, with a microphone attached to it by a twisted cord. "What's that?" she said, pointing.

Jess jumped to her feet and retrieved it. "We can record ourselves," she said, unwinding the microphone. She pressed play and a tape began: En Vogue, "Free Your Mind." "I usually just sing along with stuff, though," she said, and then began to do so, unaware of or unbothered by how her voice warbled.

She held the microphone out to Nina, who leaned away, dazed, still, from all that had been shown her. "Why don't we make a radio show?"

"Yes!" Jess dropped the microphone. "So like, we say intros to the songs?"

Nina knew little more of pop music than what she and Zachary caught on MTV while their mother made dinner. "We could do a show about how to taste numbers," she said.

Jess frowned. "I don't know how to teach that."

"It could be about *all* our powers. Like how to get to the candle room, or make a voodoo doll . . ." As she spoke she realized these were not her powers, but Jess did not correct her. Her eyes brightened and she snatched up the microphone. "I want to tell the story of how I got back at Karolina."

Nina nodded. Jess began again, chronicling the girl's misdeeds, her rightful hexing. Finally, she turned the microphone toward Nina. "Talk about Mara and what we're going to do to her."

Maybe it was the room, how it seemed like a secret lair, locked away from the domain of green lawns and mothers and consequences. The venom spilled easily from Nina's lips, and she devised a punishment far worse than a bout of strep throat. She would lure Mara's astral body to the candle room, promising that Mike Conti, whom everyone knew she had a crush on, was waiting for her there; then, she'd shove Mara in and slam the door shut, locking it with a deadbolt and chain from the outside. Mara would be unable to get back to her physical form, to wake up. To everyone in the daytime world, it would look as though she had fallen into a coma; they'd never know she was trapped in a room on the dream plane, wasting away.

Jess stared at Nina for what felt like minutes. Somewhere, far off, it sounded like Anita was washing dishes.

Finally, she reached out and took the microphone. "Nina, you are so smart," Jess said into it, wonderingly. And then, addressing an assembly of silent listeners: "Nina Glass, everyone." She dropped the microphone and applauded.

"I got the idea from this," Nina said, and pulled the *Compendium* from her backpack. She lowered it gently into Jess's lap and opened it to astral projection. From the pages came the whiff of age. Jess began reading silently, her index finger skimming over the text, and then there was a knock on the door.

Anita leaned in, keys jangling in her hand. "Girls, can I get you anything from the store?"

Jessica shook her head wordlessly as she closed the book.

"Back in half an hour," Anita said.

Jess perched, waiting, until she heard the front door close, and Nina hoped they would be returning to the book, that Jess would register its opaque authority, its potential. But her friend had still more to show. "Come here," she said, and led Nina across the dark hallway and into another bedroom. There was a wide bed in the center; Jess took Nina's hand and pressed it into the mattress, which trembled like soft skin and gurgled in response. "Waterbed," Jess said, and giggled. She flopped backward onto it, let it slosh her about. Just as quickly, she leaped to her feet and went to an armoire, opened its doors, and then pulled out a shelf. She extracted a little plastic bag and waved it under Nina's nose; it smelled of pine and skunk.

"What is that?"

"Rob's pot," Jess said. "He thinks I don't know."

Nina had a vague idea of what this meant. "Did you ever do it?"

Jess snorted. "No. Do you think I want to become as dumb as my stepdad?"

She shook her head; catastrophe seemed to be looming, pressing its nose against the closed door to the adults' room.

"Good." Jess watched her, as though trying to assess whether Nina really believed that she did not want to be stupid. Then she asked, "Could you do astral projection to find somebody?"

So she hadn't forgotten the *Compendium*. "Like who?"

"Somebody who's missing."

"We could try together."

Jess seemed to believe that Nina had already mastered the strange arts described in the book. Her faith was thrilling. "Okay," Jess said. "Let's go back and finish our show."

3

HOLLOW

(2005)

The group met on the fourteenth floor of an office tower near the Flatiron Building, an open, featureless room with a kitchenette and humming refrigerator, a hum that became hypnotic, a sonic cocoon in which to recite their mantras.

Before Avi arrived, the group would take out the chairs from their stack against the wall and unfold them in a circle, with one placed—gingerly, by whomever put it there, as though in anticipating Avi's body the chair itself might be imbued with the power to zap them—in the center.

That evening as Nina waited, a thirtysomething man smelling a little of weed sat down beside her and skidded his sneakered feet over the linoleum floor. "First time?" he said. His presence was a bit unusual; men were outnumbered by women in the group nearly four to one.

"No," Nina said.

"It's my first time."

She nodded, let her eyelids droop. She liked to use this time to turn her mind to her body. The scooped seat of the chair cradled her, the chilled indoor air, too chilled for October, lifted the hair on her arms. Comfort and discomfort flickered like the lights of a distant city within her. The objective of this first phase of the process was to observe the sensations of one's body without attending to them, to reorient the mind again and again, gently, back to the mantra.

"I'm Winston." He extended a hand.

"Nina."

"Nina," Winston repeated. "Nina ballerina." He chuckled. His eyes were a gray so pale as to be almost colorless. "Sorry, my social skills are a little rough right now. I'm fresh off a ten-day meditation. Total silence the whole time. Vipassana. Ever heard of it?"

Nina shook her head and glanced at the clock.

"The silence wasn't even the hardest part. It was the sitting. You wouldn't believe what that much sitting does to your body. Straight up, the first night when I went back to my room, I was so sore I cried."

"Oh, wow."

"But it was worth it, Nina," he said. "Once you break through the pain, everything drops away. You're just this consciousness floating in the darkness. When it was over, me and a couple of these Australian dudes went to a convenience store to buy some drinks. We bring them up to the counter and the clerk is just standing there, staring at us like we're nuts. You know why?"

Nina shook her head.

"We forgot we had to pay," Winston said. "We literally forgot how, like, commerce works. So one of the Australians takes out his wallet and just hands it to the guy—he had no idea what anything cost. We were just standing at the counter laughing so hard we couldn't breathe. Everything had become totally fucking surreal."

She wondered what Winston would say if she told him that she had once been able—perhaps, now that Jess had returned, would be able again—to leave herself whenever she wanted. She could hover in the void, brush against boundlessness, with no effort at all.

Then Avi entered, and the whole room tremored a little.

Initially Nina had been disappointed by Avi. She had expected magnetism, sagacity, strangeness; something like a sexy alien. He turned out to be short, with thin hair that looked a little greasy, a long nose.

Unassuming. But when he greeted Nina at her first session, he had taken her hands in his and said, "Welcome," and in that moment she felt something akin to the suspension she'd known with Jess. The rest of the room fell into darkness, and she was the only living person in the world.

Now, finished with his greetings, Avi entered the circle of chairs and stood in the center, spinning gently as he spoke so that they each had a chance to lock eyes with him. Tonight he talked of his years of search-ing and false starts, how in his desperation he had, with frantic speed, tried and discarded Bikram Yoga, ultramarathons, neo-Kabbalah, psy-choanalysis.

"I even," he said, lifting his brows, "had a brief brush with Scien-tology."

The group chuckled. This was how they knew Arete was not a cult—they laughed about cults. Arete was a process, or, as Avi put it, a ladder.

"What was my mistake?" he said, but they all kept smiling in si-lence up at him, waiting. "My mistake was I kept standing there with my little plug, going 'Where do I put this? Where do I plug in?' When the truth is—what?" He paused again. "I was already plugged in. Had been all along. As are all of you. Now close your eyes."

The darkness pulsed and shrank beneath Nina's lids. "We know it when we're children," Avi said, "but then we forget. We're encouraged to forget. Set a goal for tonight of remembering what you knew back then."

When she paid the fee to begin phase one, Nina received a mantra: *flow.* At first she felt as she had upon meeting Avi: disappointed. It was a plain word, barely a word at all, a mere syllable. But it was to be her key for unlocking what Avi called the oneiric plane, from which she might pull down her dreams and make them manifest. And Nina found that, after a few minutes of squirming against her own self-consciousness, she would start to feel the expansion in her chest, the drone of the syllable filling her to the brim. And hadn't it already, after a handful of months and more hundreds of dollars than she cared to dwell upon, begun to work? She knew her reunion with Jess had not simply happened to coincide with her work at Arete, and that eventually she must move further, leaving behind entirely the constellation of customs and preoccupations she called *herself* to dissolve into the universe—to plug in.

But tonight the word *flow* wouldn't, as it usually did, shake loose its meaning and turn into a hole through which her consciousness poured. Tonight the word triggered sensations of Jess's dark hair flowing over her shoulders and down her back, of the feeling of flowing from her own body into Jess's, of that microsecond when she was in between, floating, nowhere and no one. She was thinking, instead, of Jess's invitation. She wanted Nina to come to her apartment, examine the radio herself. She remembered the first time they switched, how Jess had believed Nina had caused it to happen, that she was some sort of sorceress. But in fact Jess had always been the one to blaze the pathways into their magic. Tasting colors, entering dream rooms— Nina had only pretended to share those abilities. It was her pretending, maybe, that Jess needed again.

"I'm going to stop you here," Avi said.

Winston turned to her, teary-eyed. "That was really something."

***

It was, from all appearances, just a radio. No smell, no static, no hisses from the beyond. Nina strode toward it when Jess swung open her bedroom door, strides to override the fear that some dark shape might come whooshing out of its holes. The radio was black, rectangular, with a tape deck, a folded-over silver antenna, AM/FM dials.

Nina picked it up, shook it a little. "This thing belongs in a museum."

Jess stood in the threshold. "You don't feel anything?"

"No. Maybe it only happens at night?" She was more interested in the room around the radio. It was a windowless cube; the walls didn't meet the ceiling, so air and light could trickle in over the edges. The building had been a factory once, maybe a sweatshop, Jess explained, until a series of intrepid squatters carved out of it what passed for livable spaces. The walls were here when she moved in, but Jess and her roommate, Simone, had built the loft for her bed. It looked stable;

beneath it was a desk, a computer with a massive screen, a scattering of eight-by-ten photo prints, a chair smothered in clothes.

"I'm pretty handy these days," Jess told her. She flexed a muscle and smiled.

Maybe it was the radio, a relic disgorged from the past, that brought on the vision of Jess's childhood bedroom superimposed onto this one, the younger Jess drawing Nina in for the first time, presenting the objects that made up her life.

Jess stood beside her, watching Nina take in the room, both their eyes coming to rest again on the radio. Embarrassed, perhaps, by its ordinariness, the quiet fact of it, Jess clapped her hands together. "Hungry?" she said. Nina followed her into the kitchen, where Jess opened a container, dumped its pungent contents into a pot. "I made curry last night," she explained. She lit the burner with a match. She was like a pioneer woman, building shelter in a territory where before only the wind had lived. On her walk to Jess's from the subway, Nina had passed an assembly of warehouses but not another soul. She'd begun to wonder, even, as she passed through the neighborhood—silent, birdless, gray with industry—whether the invitation, the whole reunion, had been some sort of elaborate trick. But then there was Jess's building, just as she'd promised, and the first other human Nina had encountered, a thin, beautiful man who sat on the stoop smoking and did not so much as glance at her when she leaned over him to ring the buzzer.

Jess stirred the contents of the pot. "You haven't told me about anything that's going on with you."

Nina could see Jess's shoulder blades through her thin black T-shirt. How could she bring her up to speed on the past half-decade? It seemed she would have to begin right after their rupture, the nights she cried in bed until she was wrung out like a dishrag. All that followed had flowed from that.

"Didn't your private eye already tell you?" Nina said.

Jess looked over her shoulder. "No," she said. "I just asked him for your address. I'm not a creep." She poured the curry into bowls and brought them over to the table, sat down across from Nina. It was hard to say, with Jess's gaze holding her that way, that her career so far amounted to babysitting a toddler and stuffing envelopes in Midtown offices. That when her apartment was overrun with mice, her father called the landlord and yelled at him until he hired an exterminator.

She stuck to safer territory. "So he's your mom's new boyfriend? How is she doing?"

"Oh, you know Anita," Jess said, breezily, as though they'd analyzed her mother dozens of times. "No concept of boundaries. Whoever she's with, she's completely obsessed with." She sipped from a glass of water. "This guy's not completely aggro, at least."

Like Rob was, Nina thought. She wanted to ask what became of him after the divorce, but now Jess had that assessing look, the eyes that scanned and evaluated. "How about you?" she said. "Any guys?"

Nina hesitated, wondering how to explain Avi. It would be easier, she thought, if they switched. Then, outside herself, she could speak of her own existence the way she would of someone else, a girl she knew pretty well, whose attempts at lurching her life forward were sympathetic, rather than the signs of a marrow-deep ineptitude. "I don't know," Nina said. "What about you?"

Another private smile. "There is someone," Jess said. "A photographer at the studio." Most of them, she explained, since 9/11, were like war veterans; they had that bond and that distance from the small business of daily life, and no time at all for her.

Except for Khaled. "Let's have a look," he'd say, and lean over her shoulder at the computer as she shuffled through photos from Fashion Week, images of fair, tottering women in architecturally impossible garments. When you put something into the world that had your name on it, he told Jess, that was your emissary; you must give it the careful consideration it deserved.

It made sense he cared more about how he was represented. The other photographers weren't stopped at every airport, eyeballed on the subway. And maybe that was why he took an interest in her, who also lingered at the edge of things, a college dropout, broke. After the studio she waited tables at a steakhouse, and after that the servers would hit one or two or several dives and it seemed wrong, disloyal not to join them. So she got sleep where she could find it, which was hardly anywhere; more than once she'd passed out on the subway and woken up in Canarsie.

"Anyway, nothing's happened between us yet," Jess said.

"But there's chemistry."

"Maybe." Jess nodded toward her bowl. "You done?" It was empty; Nina saw pleasure flash through her at the sight of it, and it occurred to her what all Jess's show-and-tell was, from the food to the radio to the voodoo doll of eons ago: offerings.

Jess started washing up at the sink. "But I want to hear more about your love life."

"There's nothing to tell."

"You never liked to just put yourself out there the way I did. You wanted someone to come and find you," Jess said. She turned, shook a wooden spoon at her. "Well, I found you, didn't I?"

***

But she was wrong: Nina had sought out Avi. She first learned of him one morning in a café across the street from the apartment building where Scarlett, the two-year-old she babysat, lived with her parents. She would bring the child there when she was napping in the stroller; Nina would drink coffee and eat a carrot muffin and listen to the murmur of wealth around her. That day a woman at the table beside them was telling her companion how, for the first time since the attacks, her heart no longer jumped like a puppy at the sound of a car backfiring. How she was no longer afraid; how now, she hummed with strength. With a glance Nina found that she did look robust, firm-fleshed, and glowing despite the early hour.

"Because of your class, right?" her friend asked. "What's it called again?"

"Arete," the first woman said. She spelled it for her. Nina, pretending to read, turned the word over like a stone in her mind. "I told you about the guy, right? The teacher? How he and his wife used to work at Cantor Fitzgerald?"

"Yes. Horrible."

"He stopped to get a bagel that morning and she went on to work. He was down the block when the plane hit the first tower."

"Jesus Christ. Saved by a bagel."

The first woman laughed and slapped at her friend's arm. "Stop. It almost ruined him." She sucked from her iced coffee. "But today, you'd never know."

Ruined. Back at the apartment Nina had plopped the toddler in front of the television and looked up Arete on Scarlett's parents' computer. It led to a web page that was blank, save for an email address—avi@arete. com—in the bottom left corner. Nina clicked it; in the subject line, she wrote, *Curious about your class*, and before she could deliberate further clicked send. A minute later came a reply:

43 west 24th street
tuesday, nine p.m.

The immediacy of the response cast a chill over her shoulders. The absence of detail gnawed and pulled at her. How did a person walk away from ruin?

She'd now been to a dozen sessions and still she couldn't fathom how Avi had done it, how he'd erected a ladder out of that loss. Many nights instead of sleeping she reran the scene in her mind: Avi in his dark banker's suit going down the block, September sky stretched flawless over him, and then the plane piercing through it, exploding the blue, like a missile launched from a parallel world.

***

Nina and Jess had never been drunk together before. They clinked their wine glasses in the CEO's marble-lined kitchen and agreed that it was a good place for their first time.

Nina placed her palm against the cool glass of the window. Below, the trees of Central Park quivered in the dark.

"This," Jess said, with a sweep of her arm, "is what's known as a *classic six.*"

"What's that mean?"

"I have no idea," Jess said, and their laughter tilted them toward each other. It was the CEO's forty-fifth birthday, and he'd invited each member of the photography studio staff, even the interns, to celebrate. *Bring a friend*, his email had said, Jess insisted, when Nina expressed hesitation about going. It was too much for one day; she needed to sift through all that had already happened, and besides that, she was wearing a T-shirt and jeans. But Jess loaned her a slinky purple dress, patted the places where Nina's flesh protruded, and insisted, "You have a shape. Shapes are good."

The CEO's eyes traced over that extra flesh on her hips when they joined the gathering in the living room, and then he turned and snaked deeper into the crowd. Khaled wasn't there yet, and everyone seemed to be talking about preschool admissions, bathroom renovations. "This is an old-people party," Jess had whispered to her. "Let's go get a drink."

Now, in the kitchen, Nina said, "Let's see who's drunker."

Jess raised her eyebrows. "I bet I hold my liquor better than you."

"Twenty bucks?"

"I'm broke," Jess said, but they touched their foreheads together. For the second time that week, Nina reentered Jess's body. This time her arrival came with relief, the release of no longer having to tense her belly against the clinging fabric of the dress.

Another guest stepped into the kitchen and then, misunderstanding, immediately backed out. "Ladies," he said.

Nina saw her own lips spread, a laugh ripple out of her throat. That they'd denied themselves this, for five years—over what?—struck her suddenly as criminal. She stretched Jess's long arms over her head, looked up and saw the light catch on the silver bangles that were, for now, hers. "I definitely feel woozier," she said.

"Liar." Jess gave her chest a squeeze. "Man, I missed having bigger tits."

"Just don't forget to return them."

Jess's eyes widened and she took a step back, her attention snatched away by something passing behind Nina in the hall. A heavy hand dropped on her shoulder, and then a man, tall, with tight curls, not unlike how she'd imagined how Avi might look before she met him, was beside her.

He bent forward, pressed his cheek against hers for an air-kiss. The wine she'd drunk was like a heavy drape over her panic. Nina glanced at her friend. Jess's eyes—*her* eyes—darted between her and the man. Nina wondered if she always gave herself away so easily.

"How's it going?" Nina said.

Khaled shrugged. "Putting in an appearance."

"Us too," Nina said. "This is my friend, Nina."

"Hi," Jess said, and extended a hand. If Khaled registered the color flaring in her cheeks, he must have attributed it to his charm. The greatest miracle of all was that no one ever noticed.

"See you in there," he said.

More people were filtering into the kitchen; a thin, deerlike woman asked if either of them knew how to make a Negroni.

Jess murmured to Nina, "Follow him."

"What? Why?"

"I can't figure out how he feels about me, but maybe you can."

"Can't you just ask?" In school, if there was something Jess wanted, she chased it down and seized it, no girlish conferencing in corners, no analysis or prayer.

She shook her head. "I want him to say it first."

Nina nodded. She understood the power of withheld information.

***

Being Jess again after all these years, before she had a handle on what in her had shifted, what remained, was unnerving. And she'd never known, really, what constituted the bedrock of her friend's personality, only that in her presence—in her skin—there was always the certainty she was living more deeply. Jess woke her, alerted her to how each moment opened onto the unknown, how anything could happen. You were told, when you were young, that *the possibilities were endless*. Only with Jess had that ever seemed true.

Nina waded into the clusters gathered in the living room and felt again the difference in how people responded when they believed they were looking at Jess. They were hungrier, it seemed. Beneath Jess's boldness and spontaneity they sensed something available. And inside the smaller frame, Nina felt somehow larger, shored up against their need.

Khaled was in the center of a small group. Though he wasn't speaking, everyone's attention hovered around him, like a cloud of gnats. Ordinarily Nina would linger at the periphery, wait to be summoned inside, or determine it was hopeless and walk away. Now she entered unhesitatingly, even elbowed someone aside a little. There was, she realized, no risk in it for her.

A man, gray-haired, maybe late forties, with a small belly and the bloody stain of wine on his lips, was talking about being embedded with the troops.

"Most of them know they have no business being there," he said.

"That wasn't my impression," Khaled said. The faces turned toward him, eager, like the faces of flowers drinking in sunlight, and the man began qualifying, "Well, maybe not *most* . . ."

But Khaled shrugged off his own power as though it were nothing. "What do I know," he said. He noticed her. "Jess," he said, "I wanted to get your opinion on something."

"Of course," Nina said, and he took her hand and led her to the foyer, where he leaned his back against the front door and pulled out his phone. "This is that project I told you about. I want your thoughts," he said. "You're the only one who won't bullshit me." His regard was unflinching; where Avi's felt like warmth, Khaled's was radioactive. He handed the phone to Nina and stood beside her, leaning over her shoulder, heat coming off him in dangerous waves. There were images of people, all ages, races, but with a uniform grimness etched onto their expressions, tired eyes, lips thinned in concentration, lines like canyons in the foreheads, the hardness of their lives splashed over them. They were sitting or standing on a bus and in some shots the city smeared by through the windows, landscapes of gray ash.

"It's the bus to Rikers," Khaled said. "I've been photographing people on it for weeks now. They're getting used to me; they've stopped posing."

"This is amazing," Nina told him, truthfully. He nodded a little. What Khaled wanted, really, was not her opinion.

"It's depressing, though," he confessed. "Imagine someone you love in a hellhole like that. And you have to be brave for them."

She nodded, unsure of what to say—unsure what Jess would say.

"The last time I was called for jury duty," Khaled continued, "they dismissed me when I told them I find the American prison system so barbaric I could never, in good conscience, send somebody there. And that was before this project. Now I know it's even worse than I thought."

"Do you ever go inside?"

"No, I'm not allowed. But I don't have to. The stories I've heard."

There were limits, Nina thought, to what you could take in of the pain of others; she had reasons to suspect she might be particularly limited. But not Jess. Khaled was shaking something out of a baggie, a little white, chalky pill with the outline of a butterfly stamped on it.

"You want?" He held it out with such inevitability that Jess must have done this with him before; it crowded out any room for dissent. Nina took it and tongued it into a pocket in her cheek. Khaled looked over her head, through the apartment, the *classic six*, and into, perhaps, the bedrooms where he took enchanted women, and would soon—she was sure of it—be taking Jess.

"I better go check on Nina," Nina told him. "She doesn't know anyone here."

***

In the kitchen, Jess was helping a woman light candles stuck into the thick frosting of a tiered cake. Nina had a moment to study them from the threshold. She watched Jess, watched herself flick the flame from a lighter and touch it to the wicks. She thought, with an old amazement, *I look just like anyone else.*

"Here's Jess," Jess told the woman, as Nina approached them. "She's been interning for a few months. Jess, this is Olivia, the birthday boy's wife."

"Thank you for inviting us," Nina said. The tablet had dissolved into her cheek. She swallowed a bitter puddle of saliva and imagined the drug beginning to hum in Jess's bloodstream.

"Thank you for bringing such a helpful friend," Olivia said. She smiled and curved lines like parentheses appeared, linking the outer edges of her nostrils to her lips. There was a dizziness behind her eyes. "Everyone else seems to have forgotten why they're here tonight."

Jess touched Olivia's arm. "Let's go remind them."

Olivia lifted the flaming cake and they followed her into the living room, singing. On the second *happy birthday to you* the conversations finally dwindled and the guests joined them.

Nina leaned over and whispered. "I'm sorry," she said. "He gave me some kind of pill."

"And you took it?"

The answer was on her face. Jess laughed silently, wrapping her arms around herself, a lightness and looseness in the limbs that Nina had never felt in them; more often her body was something to drag along, to wash and maintain, to steer around the shin-threatening objects of the world.

"Are you sure you're sorry?" Jess said. Nina wasn't, not exactly. Becoming Jess had always contained a kind of permission to do what Nina wouldn't. "Enjoy," Jess said. She had indulged that, at times encouraged it. What worried Nina was what might be expected in return. The cake was set down on the lid of the grand piano, and the CEO took a knife in his hand. Nina, watching Jess amid the crowd, saw that her ass in the purple dress was a smooth half-moon. It was better than she had believed.

Khaled, standing alone by a window, caught her eyes, raised his chin in her direction.

"He likes you," she told Jess.

Jess looked away, nodding a little, her smile deepening. Nina caught a glimpse in the window, floating in the night, of her reflection—Jess's reflection—the steadiness of the gaze she could only wear for a while, a costume of strength. Nina tried to locate, in the face in the window, the reason Jess had any need for her at all.

"Let's go," Nina said, and Jess, a bit slowly, unlocked her focus from Khaled and followed her out of the apartment.

As the elevator sank, she turned to Nina. "You're feeling it, aren't you?" Nina had been buoyed above the worries scrabbling in her stomach; she felt them fall away beneath her as she rose, as they descended, to a plane of elation where it became more and more obvious that her quotidian self, that mousy, jumpy girl, was a person to be pitied.

Outside the cool night air lapped at her. Across the street, the Central Park trees, the leaves outlined with the beginnings of orange, waved in the wind. "I love October," Nina said. She needed to talk about everything she loved. "There is someone I'm interested in," she told Jess, the sidewalk rising to meet her heels, clipping beneath them. "He's my teacher."

"A teacher?" Jess echoed.

"Not a regular one." Nina tried to explain about the sessions, about the work of remembering they were all already entwined inside the great net that held everything. About what they were capable of when they realized they were plugged into the universal current. It all made sense when Avi said it, but as Nina struggled to impart the details of his teachings, the words scattered from her like a flock of birds.

Jess was shivering. She rubbed Nina's hands over Nina's pale arms. "And what exactly is he charging for these sessions?"

"It's not bad," Nina said. The sense of suspension over everything wavered a little. "Where are we going?"

"Back to my place," Jess said. Nina stopped, startled. The day was stretching on and on, as though there was something to prove, to repay, before she could be relinquished back to her life. "I need you there tonight if anything else happens with the radio," Jess said.

"Nothing will happen," Nina said. There was the lift again. They had protected each other before; really, they were the only ones who could. "Everything will be fine."

***

Back in her body, the high dissolved, Nina rolled over in the dark. The only illumination came from a digital clock on the dresser, a thin red glare, and the streetlights outside, leaking over the edges of the walls. She looked up at the ceiling beams, their outlines visible through the haze; her thoughts seemed to bob up there, colliding against one another, shoving aside sleep. "I can sleep on the floor," Jess had said, and Nina told her not to be silly. They lay side by side, nestled like birds in the loft. Had Jess ever shared such closeness with anyone else? Nina tried to imagine one of the women from the party here beside her friend on the mattress, the two of them rubbing their feet together, listening to each other's breathing. It was impossible. Those women were too sharp-edged. They'd never let someone so near she dissolved into them, and they into her.

"I know this is weird," Jess said, "but it seems right that you're here."

It was weird, and right, to be side by side again as though five years hadn't happened, as though she hadn't had to learn, wobbling like a newborn animal, to stand on her own. Exiled for so long to ordinariness that she'd begun to believe it was better, healthier this way. Nina reached over and took Jess's hand. She felt her smallness—a smallness that hid itself most of the time.

"It got lonely," Jess said, "just being myself. And boring."

They laughed together up into the ceiling. "So boring," Nina agreed.

Jess fell quiet for a few moments, and then she said, "Don't you think it's weird my dad never told anyone about me?"

By the rules of Nina's world it was certainly weird, to treat a child as something that could be returned and forgotten like an ill-fitting garment.

"If he is here," Nina said, "I'm sure he doesn't want to hurt you."

Jess withdrew her hand. "He should've thought of that when I was seven." Nina felt her turn on her side toward the wall, pull her knees up to her chest. "But then, I guess, you and I never would have met."

Were there girls who lived out their years unpaired, abilities unrealized? Nina had tried, at times, to pry out of others what might be unusual, unnatural about them. And everyone had, they would tell you, if they felt they knew you well enough to confess it, galaxies of strangeness spinning inside them, but none of them the ability to float outward from it, leave it all behind.

She couldn't sleep. She wasn't afraid of the radio. The thing to fear was what flesh-and-blood beings could do. Maybe people just vanished and reappeared, lights flickering off and on, timelines swooping away from each other and then touching again. Nina dropped into a half-doze, kept imagining she was back in Jess's body, in conversations with Khaled that seemed to loop in on themselves and go nowhere. At one point, she told him, *I'm not really Jess*, and he leaned closer, his eyes enlarging into deep black pools.

She sensed a new light in the room, a red dot on the radio, an eye peering out. Nina heard a sound like the ocean inside a shell. Within the waves a voice spoke quietly.

"Hello," it said, or maybe, "Hollow."

She sat up straight. Jess was asleep, breathing deeply. When Nina looked at the radio, the red light was gone. Flowing into the room, over the edges of the walls, were the pale sunbeams of dawn.

4

A CHILD'S COMPENDIUM
OF THE UNIVERSE
(1992)

The second episode was recorded in Nina's bedroom, the girls seated side by side on her bed. Jess began by recounting what had just transpired, her first steps inside the Glass home.

"I just met Nina's little brother, Zachary," she said. "He's so cute." Nina watched the two holes in the cassette as the tape rolled forward, imprinted now with Jess's voice. Zachary, seven years old and rarely still, had gazed up at her when she entered, quiet for once; something about this stranger subdued him. "And Nina's mom is really nice and pretty."

Nina had never thought of her mother as such and didn't care to hear more now. She wished instead to know what Jess saw in her, with her strange vision, and in her room, which she'd tried and failed to infuse with the sense of intentional chaos Jess's had.

"I want to show you something," Nina said. She had taken out the *Compendium* in anticipation of this moment and turned now to the entry on Telesthesia, "the art of remote perception." Pictured there was a drawing of an eye, from which several lines extended across the page to a sexless figure ascending a peak, and though these images were as sketchy as all the *Compendium*'s, there was the suggestion the hiker was quite distant, unseeable to the owner of the eye through any ordinary means. "You can find people who are far away," she told Jess. "Didn't you say you wanted to find someone?"

But when she extended the microphone to Jess's lips there came a change to her face, harsh and sudden, like a shutter yanked down, that made Nina quickly withdraw it.

"We don't have to," she said. "We can do something else."

For a moment Jess's dark eyes went blank, as though she had re-treated somewhere far behind them, but then she returned, snatching back the microphone.

"My dad," she said, speaking very close to it so that when Nina played back the tape later the words were thunderous.

"He's missing?" Nina said. Jess didn't answer but it seemed safe now to probe further. "Is he lost?"

"I think so. My mom won't tell me." Jess looked at Nina, that as-sessing look she had given her before. "He's a surveyor. He goes and explores places where people want to build. I think something happened to him out there."

Out there. Through the window across from the bed a square of sky was visible, the white sky of late fall. Nina imagined Jess's father lost out there in that paleness, wandering in a place without substance. Jess's life was saturated with mystery, strange presences and absences. She knew the taste of numbers; she knew what it was to look out the window and await the return of her father from another world.

"Maybe he needs us to find him," Nina said.

"Maybe." A shift again in Jess's features, sweeping away the softness that had briefly lighted there. "Hey, have you ever been to Hot Skates?"

Nina nodded, confused.

"You know how there are boys there who help you up if you fall?" Jess said. She began telling Nina—telling the unseen audience of their show—about one of them, whom she'd spotted right away, who had wavy brown hair and a green jacket and a smile for her when she went sprawling on the rink. She didn't know his name but privately she called him Evan Greenberg, for the jacket, and she wanted to go

skating together, to go and fall on purpose so Nina could see for herself what he was like.

"Okay," Nina said, "but your dad—" This conversation was far more
earthbound than she had anticipated, and she wanted to return to the
surveying, to Jess's father plumbing unknown lands.

But Jess got up then from the bed and sat on the padded arm of the
wing chair across from it, staring at Nina. "Hey," she said again. She wig-
gled her body a little against the arm. "Ever notice how this feels good?"

The light that came on during recording was like a red eye, looking
out from the tape deck, observing them.

"Yeah," Nina said in a low voice, beneath the microphone's hearing.
There were nights when, locked out of sleep by fears she was too old to
have—like the one of the woman pouring through her mirror and skating silently over the carpet to stand at the foot of her bed, irises black,
jaw unhinged—Nina could battle the terror by pressing her body into
the mattress in a certain way, moving back and forth until she sensed
the approach of something the opposite of ominous, which suddenly,
explosively bloomed inside her.

"Do you think," Jess said, "this is like the candle room?"

She meant was it another of their powers. Feeling the warmth that
often presaged the nighttime explosions, Nina nodded. It was another
power they shared, and it was one unknown to anyone else, she was
sure, for not even the *Compendium* had an entry on it.

***

The show never really ended; it was only continued, revised, reimag-
ined over the months. They took turns with the microphone, leaning
into each other, heads close together, speaking into existence a space
that was, like the candle room, only theirs. Often, they detailed their
visitations to the candle room, recounting what they'd seen there, how
it felt to sail their astral bodies through the tunnels of dreams. If they
were at Nina's, they might attempt telesthesia, for which they developed
their own methodology, the chanting in tandem of Jess's father's full

name—David Flores Garcia—until the slight echo of the mic looped back to them their own voices and the syllables thrummed through their ribs and out into the universe. They closed their eyes. Along with their incantation there sometimes came visions. Jess saw her father shackled to a cave wall, struggling against his restraints, spitting at unseen captors. Nina saw him in silhouette, in furs, traversing an arctic landscape, the snow blinding, the sky a violent blue.

Sometimes in the midst of their attempts to make contact Zachary would come barreling into the room. Rather than shriek at him, as Nina did, Jess negotiated. Zachary had fallen in love with her, and would agree to leave only once Jess let him kiss her cheek. Eventually she'd acquiesce, leaning forward for him, her face poised in a way that struck Nina as timeless, a lady waiting for the brush of a suitor's lips forever.

At Jess's, where they were less likely to be interrupted, they practiced their other power, the sensation only they could summon, taking turns pressing the *Compendium* with its heavy hardback cover against their crotches. Jess did not want to invoke her father's name there, lest Anita or Rob hear, and so she steered the show toward the terrestrial: which *90210* actors had the cutest butts, say, or what strange notions of fashion compelled their school principal to wear a bow tie every day, or whether it were possible that anyone had ever kissed Ms. Brandon. Her wit snapped like a flag in the wind, and Nina, who could not keep pace, feared disappointing her.

One day in early February Jess introduced a new game, less a game than a kind of rehearsal. Nina's tenth birthday was approaching, and the party would be held at the roller-skating rink. It was Jess's chance to finally talk to Evan Greenberg, rather than simply fling herself down before him, but she needed practice.

"Could you pretend to be him?" Jess said.

Nina herself had never registered Evan; he was one of the countless older boys who swirled past her at the rink and out in the world, faceless as trees. She'd have to approximate. She stood, deepened her voice, stiffened her back. "Hey," she said.

The ferocity Jess's expression took on sometimes in the midst of a discussion or of chanting her father's name lifted. She looked up at Nina from under her eyelashes, softened in a way Nina had never seen before. "Help me up?" she said and stretched out her hands like a baby asking to be carried. Nina pulled Jess off the bed, to her feet, and they stood face to face in the little room.

"Uh," Nina said. What did older boys know? She saw them fleetingly, in clumps, while running errands with her mother. They hung around outside the flea market or the drugstore. They loitered, smoked, cursed, kicked at each other, went stone-faced around adults. She imagined a wall of cool stone beneath her skin. "You should be more careful," she said, in a voice free of concern.

"Maybe," Jess said, "you could teach me to skate better?"

It was the moment Nina first understood the value of ignorance, helplessness, how you could use it to rouse boys to attend to you. She felt it in herself as a boy, her arms yearning to encircle the foolish girl before her, to protect her. And she knew she couldn't show it —he wouldn't. "Alright," she said in her deepened voice. "Some time, I guess."

"How about right now? Over there, by the lockers?" Jess pointed at her closet.

"Okay. Whatever."

Jess pulled open the closet door, broke character. Rummaging among shoeboxes, she said, her back to Nina, "Now we have to practice for when we kiss."

She found a plastic shopping bag and dumped out its contents. "Here," Jess said, and held the bag over her mouth. "We can do it like this, so it doesn't count," she said, the words muffled.

Nina wanted to know what older boys knew. She felt it, as Evan, that rocky confidence, and though she was only an inch taller than Jess it seemed now she was towering over her as she tilted her head and leaned in. They pressed their lips together and then quickly drew back from one another, cackling.

"That's it?" Jess said.

"That's nothing," Nina said, herself once more.

But in the weeks that followed they practiced in this way again and again. They called it the Boyfriend Game, and their characters morphed, because Jess said it was boring to keep playing herself; if she was going to pretend, she was going to *really* pretend. So they shuffled through a host of personae before settling upon Clyde and Giselle, a couple in their twenties who lived in the city. They were forever returning from some activity, stepping into the foyer of their Manhattan penthouse in the midst of rehashing an event they'd just attended: dancing, a river cruise, a party full of *90210* actors. ("Luke Perry wasn't as handsome as I thought he'd be," Jess, as Giselle, would remark, and Nina as Clyde would say, "I'm much handsomer, aren't I?") The evening fully recreated and then exhausted, they'd collapse onto Jess's twin bed (in the game, vast and canopied) and do what boyfriends and girlfriends did: roll around, moaning, grasping each other. One of them would retrieve the shopping bag and place it between their mouths; they'd mash their lips and teeth and tongues together through the protective barrier, the plastic crinkling and straining.

But Nina's craving to play the Boyfriend Game seemed to outpace Jess's. Even though Jess was the one who had devised it, she also never, except for that first time, suggested it, and now whenever Nina's mother drove her through the familiar alleys of sycamores to Jess's house, Nina tried to harden herself against the longing to once again settle into the characters of Clyde and Giselle, to instead be sated with remaining Nina and Jess, to not need to caress, manfully, Giselle's flowing auburn hair. But she almost always failed. It was not only the thrill of rehearsing for the romances of their futures, it was the sense of sturdiness and certainty that came from becoming Clyde, the influence he had over his woman and his world. And Jess's indifference to the Boyfriend Game became increasingly an implication of all that Nina required to feel complete. She imagined, under her clothes, embedded in the center of her chest, a second mouth, smacking its lips and always, revoltingly, yawning open for more.

***

On the afternoon of Nina's birthday party, Jess was dropped off early so they could get ready together. Jess knew how to French braid, and though her plaits were not as tight as the ones Nina's mother made, it was better to sit beneath Jess's fingers, to feel them, pleased, patting their finished product. They rolled Nina's melon-flavored lip gloss onto their lips and tried not to lick it off, puffed clouds of body spray into the air and twirled through them.

Jess envied Nina for being the first to leave nine behind. Ten tasted like grapefruit, she said, which you weren't always in the mood for, but was an improvement over garbage.

They crammed into the backseat with Zachary, who sat perched between them. Jess asked him which song he hoped to skate to that night, and he told her "Remember the Time" by Michael Jackson.

Jess nodded. "That's respectable."

From the front seat, Nina's father chuckled. Jess dimmed her parents' presence; they became a distant, half-attentive audience. They were bemused by the friendship, the quickness with which the girls had become close. Her father called Jess "Firecracker."

Jess leaned over Zachary, smushing him against the seat to whisper in Nina's ear, "I wonder if Evan will be there."

He was: he circled the rink drowsily as they entered, and Jess elbowed Nina hard. Alyssa and Stephanie were already there, too, and they skated over to say happy birthday after casting quick glances at Jess. Nina had once imagined a seamless integration of her new friend with her old ones, but among the others, the girl she knew in their bedrooms flickered out of existence. In their presence Jess went quiet, watching them from across a great expanse. She might tug at Nina's sleeve and murmur a comment or two, only to her, but nothing more.

But the moment Nina finished lacing up her skates, Jess said, "Now's my chance. I'm gonna talk to him." The rink was still nearly empty, Evan still tracing the perimeter alone.

For the next hour, Nina hardly saw her. She was subsumed in the increasing crush of bodies on the rink, those of her friends and strangers. Once she caught a glimpse of Jess snaking after Evan through the booths where they'd have pizza and cupcakes later, and another time, laughing at something he said by the vending machines. Then Jess was alone at the snack counter, leaning her back against it, gazing at a group of teenagers laughing around a table.

Zachary braked beside Nina and grabbed her wrist.

"I think Jess is upset," he said.

"What do you mean?"

He shrugged. "I saw her going into the bathroom."

Nina skated over, her wheels clicking against the piss-smelling black-and-white tiles. Under the doors of the last stall, she saw Jess's rented skates, beaten brown with orange wheels.

"Jess," she said. "I know that's you." She went over, leaned against the stall door, knocked. "Open up."

"No," Jess said, in a tear-blurred voice. Nina's heart thudded. They never cried in front of each other; it was one of the things that divided them from other girls. Sometimes, during the Boyfriend Game, Giselle might weep, mewling like a baby cat when Clyde neglected her in favor of combing back his thick hair or pouring himself a tumbler of Scotch; Giselle was made pitiful by her obsession with him, by her quickness to extract what she wanted with increasingly garish sobs. Giselle, though rich and beautiful, did not have what Nina and Jess had, the toughness that came from the ability to retreat to a private shared world.

"Did Evan say something mean to you?" Nina ventured.

"His real name is Danny," Jess said, her voice firmed now by annoyance.

"Oh." Abruptly their pretending had been punctured, and she didn't know what to say.

There was the sound of toilet paper being unrolled, and then the honk of a nose. "Who cares about him?" Jess said. The door opened and she rolled out, her eyes meeting Nina's with a warning to say nothing more.

***

The last time Nina belonged wholly to herself was March 7, 1993. It was her actual birthday; now she was ten.

"Double digits," her mother said. "How does it feel?"

They were in the car on the way to Jess's house, Nina dogged by the certainty she'd hurt her mother. When she'd asked what Nina wanted to do for her big day, Nina had said without hesitation that she wanted to spend it with Jess. Her mother's face had fallen for a moment. They always celebrated birthdays as a family, gathering for Nina's, which fell in the dark days of late winter, on the couch for a movie, later standing around in the kitchen digging forkfuls of ice cream cake directly from the box.

The guilt made Nina voluble. She told her mother what she'd learned about the number ten from the *Compendium*, where it had its own entry, the only number to be granted one. "Ten is at once the great apex of numbers and the beginning of limitlessness," went the entry. "It signifies completion, and a return to the source of all numbers: one. Ten forms a circle."

"Mmm," her mother said. Nina looked at her profile for the prettiness Jess had found there. She saw a sharp nose, a cloud of permed hair. The dismay at having hurt her feelings, at being able to do so, lingered on. Alive to this sudden power, Nina felt very far from her. And with each year to come, with each birthday, she thought, she'd only recede further.

Jess greeted her at the front door with a shower of confetti. "Happy grapefruit day," she shouted, and pulled Nina inside, out of the winter sun and away from her mother's car idling in the driveway, ignoring the scraps of construction paper now littering the floor.

They recorded a celebratory radio show: *Nina Glass's Greatest Hits*. Jess recounted their first meeting, and though it had transpired only a few months before, it took on in her retelling the weight of legend. She recalled the discovery of their shared number-tasting, as guilt popped like a flashbulb in Nina's chest, and Nina's takedown of Mara, and the jokes of Nina's she found funniest; she praised Nina's elucidations of the *Compendium*, and their voyages to the candle room, and—in a lowered voice—their search for her father. By the end of this hagiography Nina was dazed. She sat back on the carpet, face burning.

"What do you want to do now?" Jess reached and removed a scrap of red confetti from Nina's hair. The gesture was surprisingly tender, the gentle tidying hand of a mother.

Ordinarily Nina played coy, hoping that once they'd exhausted the radio show and *Compendium* consultations and spelunking through Anita and Rob's stuff, they'd arrive at it naturally. But always she had to bring it up, when Jess finally, mercifully, asked for suggestions; then she had to respond, "There's always the Boyfriend Game," in a voice so casual it belied nothing but a wish to pass the time. But now it was her birthday, and Jess had just stroked her hair in what felt like an invitation, so she said it straight on, what she wanted to do.

Jess smiled. Already it was Giselle's, a smile full of the knowledge of Clyde's wants and needs and how to play to them.

"Happy birthday, honey," she said—apparently Nina and Clyde shared a birthday—and reached out and skated her fingertips down Nina's, down Clyde's cheek. They hadn't gotten the plastic bag, but it seemed wrong to pause the game, so Nina brought her mouth closer to Jess's.

Before their lips met the bedroom door swung open. Nina and Jess leaped apart, in the same moment that Anita, seeing—what? Nina wasn't certain, but she knew it wasn't Clyde and Giselle—stumbled back from the threshold in surprise.

"Oops," she said. "Sorry, girls." She wasn't looking at them. "Just checking to see if you wanted a snack."

Nina turned to Jess for cues, but her friend sat there in silence until Anita excused herself. Then she stood and closed the door behind her and leaned against it. "God!" she breathed. "Sometimes I hate her."

The dismay of the morning, of disappointing her mother, deepened to heavy sickness in Nina's chest. "What if she tells?" she said. She hadn't thought so before, but now it was clear they were doing something that could be told about, punished.

Jess smiled at her again, not Giselle's smile but her own. "She won't say anything," she said. "You don't have to worry." She sank back down to the floor and leaned forward and, in a gesture of alliance, rested her forehead against Nina's.

It happened in a moment, sensation layered atop sensation; if they were laid end to end they would stretch to the horizon. There was the familiar smell of Jess's hair—apple shampoo—and the slightly damp warmth of her forehead, and the stew of gratitude and shame that brimmed over in Nina's heart whenever she went fumbling for some bolder person's reassurance and they humored her by giving it, and then there was a tug, insistent but not unpleasant, the tug of a friend who has something they want you to come and see, except it wasn't limited to her hand; it seemed to span her entire body, prickle the whole length of herself the way the sun might. And then, for the tiniest fraction of time, she was nowhere, the smells and sensations vanished, not even a ghost of them; Nina floated in a void without end, the beginning of limitlessness. Then she was somewhere again, somewhere else.

Nina was seated across from herself. She saw herself, saw Nina, her face pinched and pale, her eyes widened, huge, the green globes of her irises floating in white. She saw her own mouth open in a precursor to a scream, and without thinking, she clapped a hand over it.

After a moment, Nina removed her hand and the girl before her, the one with her face, whispered, "How did you do that?"

5

THE OCEAN OF LOVE

(2005)

Once they had tried summoning Jess's father to them, and now they were sending him back, to that place without substance. Of course, he'd never really been lost as they'd imagined, having wandered too far afield while out surveying new lands. He'd just moved to Santa Fe. But still Nina could only picture him dwelling in the beyond, the same nowhere she hung for a moment when they switched bodies, the same nowhere you went, maybe, after death.

Or should go, if your soul weren't lodged in an old radio. Nina never told Jess about the voice she'd heard, the uncanny digital voice, the night of the party. It was an omission that caused her some guilt, but it meant Jess turning to her, regularly, for affirmation. "You believe me, right?" she often asked in the early weeks of their renewed friendship.

"Of course!" Nina would say. She might give Jess's arm a reassuring squeeze.

A few days after the party, Jess called Nina and asked her to come over that evening. She didn't have a shift at the steakhouse that night, and she had an idea.

Jess met her at the subway stop and led her beneath the clamor of the elevated tracks to a botanica. There, Nina trailed her with a basket through the incense-fogged aisles as Jess pulled packets of sage and little shampoo bottles of holy water from the shelves. Dressed in black, her hair a luminous spill down her back, she looked beautiful and clandestine, not to be messed with.

"Worth a try, right?" she said, palming a black candle labeled *La Santisima Muerte.*

"Definitely." Each word of agreement was a step toward reclamation of the territory and the power they once shared.

Back at the apartment, in Jess's cube of a bedroom, they upturned their haul onto her bed. It looked a little silly now, like discarded party favors, and Jess's confidence seemed to flag.

"I guess it's worth a try," she said.

"We'll take care of it," Nina assured her, all gallantry, Clyde again.

They sat on Jess's bedroom floor, their outstretched legs forming a diamond, the radio in its center, and got to work on its exorcism. Straight-faced, they sprinkled it with the holy water, lit the sage and let its smoke settle over the device. The lights were out, and in the dim Nina grew lightheaded from the smoke. She thought she could hear echoes of their childhood rituals reaching back to them.

Once the supplies were exhausted, Nina offered to say a prayer. "It's a Jewish thing," she said.

Jess leaned back on her elbows. "Why not?"

She started to recite the mourner's kaddish, making her way over the first bulky string of syllables before her memory ran out.

Jess smiled, eyes closed. "That reminded me of your bat mitzvah." She opened her eyes and squinted. "We switched that night, didn't we?"

"Yeah." Nina was stunned, a little, that Jess didn't seem to remember. Or maybe she was only pretending not to; maybe their picking up where they'd left off relied upon certain deletions.

"Do you think it worked?" Jess said.

"I'm not sure."

Jess chewed her lower lip. "Yeah, I don't know. I didn't, like, feel anything."

"Me neither."

"Now what?"

She was at once afraid they would switch again and afraid they wouldn't. Avi often told the members of Arete that they had to dispense with their notions of themselves as distinct and finite beings. But without Jess that was what she was: finite, confined to the same slim routes through the city and—she increasingly worried—life.

They sat breathing in the dark. Finally, Jess said, "We could go get a drink?"

Nina agreed, relieved, disappointed.

***

They slid back inside each other's lives. First came the remembering, a careful kind that stepped around the worst days of their history. Their early experimentation, how they'd swapped and slapped and pinched at one another to compare how the pain landed on their respective skins, whose suffering was worse. The thrill of deceiving teachers, other students, the cocooned, confining days of school blown open by their power, while everyone else shuffled forward, one by one, alone.

They met in the NYU bars in the Village, before Jess's shifts, or in bland coffee shops on the Upper East Side, after Nina finished babysitting, rehashing, relishing their memories. Some of them.

"You're kidding," Nina's mother said on the phone, when Nina told her who she'd been spending time with lately. "Talk about ancient history."

"She was my best friend," Nina said.

"When you were children."

She was home, lying on her back in bed. Through the window, she watched the cycling of feet on the street above. "That doesn't mean it didn't matter."

"Of course not," her mother said. There was a pause. Outside, the sighs and bleats of a bus lowering itself. "What does she want?"

She'd asked herself the same question but in her mother's mouth it sounded unjust. "Isn't it enough to want to reconnect?"

"Sure, honey." Her mother's voice softened into appeasement. "I just want you to be smart. She did a number on you. I remember that."

But they'd been children, and her mother knew nothing of what her childhood had really been like. Still, her words squirmed their way inside Nina, invasive, altering her as a virus might. A part of her broke off from the remembering to stand aside, watching for warning signs.

There were new people to acquaint one another with: Nina's college friends, Jess's coworkers from the steakhouse and the studio, Jess's roommate Simone, a painter who made money by answering Craigslist ads—getting paid, for instance, to let an elderly man in a basement apartment on the Lower East Side worship her feet. (After several sessions, he agreed to let Jess photograph the two of them, his soft, spotted face, eyes shut in rapture, caressing Simone's extended foot, arched and luminous under the lamp in his living room. He looked like an infant, not unlike newborn Scarlett in the baby portraits Nina sometimes studied while the little girl napped; like an infant, the man seemed nourished by the physical contact.)

Jess came to see her once when she was watching Scarlett. The days were still warm enough to play in the park, and both Nina and Scarlett preferred the one along the East River, from which they could look across the water at Roosevelt Island and watch tiny figures cycling around the strip of land. Nina, sometimes, as she pushed the child in her stroller along the waterfront, would tell her stories about Nellie Bly's internment there—how she'd pretended to be someone she wasn't, someone mad, for the sake of a newspaper article—and Scarlett listened from her seat in what appeared like contemplative silence.

When Jess met them they were by the dog run, and Nina had boosted Scarlett on one hip to better see the glossy-coated creatures of the Upper East Side, the French bulldogs and Afghan hounds. By way of greeting, Jess raised her camera to her eye and snapped.

"She could be yours," she said, dropping it so it yanked hard on the band around her neck.

"This is my buddy," Nina told Scarlett. "Say, 'Hi, Jess.'"

Scarlett turned to look at Jess but kept her mouth closed, her round cheek with its sweet milky smell close to Nina's.

Jess saluted the child. "Nina, you're a natural."

"You figure it out quickly. Kids are usually pretty vocal about what they want."

"I wouldn't be able to do it," Jess said. She peered over the fence at the dogs skidding through the dust, snapping their jaws at each other. The words hovered in the air with a disappointment that seemed directed not at herself but at Nina, for her easy adherence, maybe, to the ordinary.

Scarlett's head was swiveling now, back and forth, between the two of them. She pointed at Jess. "Nee-Nee?" she said uncertainly.

"Jess," Nina corrected. "I'm right here, silly."

Scarlett turned back to her. Her face creased, her features drawing together, in the way that preceded tears. She extended her arms to Jess. "Nee-Nee," she said again.

"Are you playing a game, Scarlett?" Nina said. Jess took a step backward. "I'm Nee-Nee." The child was wiggling violently in her arms now. Nina bent over, put her in the stroller, tried to fasten the straps as Scarlett continued to torque her small body away from her. "Hey!" she said. "Ready for a snack?"

With that Scarlett relented, went limp, almost, and nodded her head. Nina searched through the voluminous backpack she hauled around whenever she was with the little girl. She glanced at Jess, now at an uncompanionable distance, arms crossed over her chest. "And that's all there is to it," Nina told her.

***

One night in late November Nina came home from babysitting to find her roommate, Eleanor, sitting beside Jess on the couch, deep in conversation. Eleanor looked up at Nina, her nose pink and damp, annoyance passing like a shadow over her features. Jess bit her lower lip, chewing on some secret. In the early years of their friendship, Nina had done the work of integrating Jess with others, a sort of diplomat, cajoling, negotiating. But late in high school her guardianship ended, as the rest of their class finally awakened to Jess's value. Eleanor took to Jess as so many of the students had then, with a hurried intimacy, as though there were only a tiny window of time in which to claim her.

Jess turned to Eleanor. "Can I tell her?"

Eleanor shut her eyes, nodded.

"Eleanor's been hooking up with this guy at work. *Chase*," Jess pronounced, and Eleanor smiled a little through her distress. "He made her all kinds of promises, but Chase is also a bit of a cokehead, and we know how they are about following through on things."

It was, maybe, that she seemed unsurprised by everything; she assimilated your scandals and lies with a poker face. It made you at once want to shock her and confess.

Eleanor's phone buzzed. "It's him."

"Are you going to answer?" Nina asked.

Eleanor rolled her eyes, snapped open the phone.

"Tell me later," Jess hissed at her. Then she turned to Nina. "I have some news, too."

Downstairs in Nina's room, Jess closed the door behind her. "Don't take it personally about Eleanor not telling you," she said, though Nina hadn't asked for reassurance. "Sometimes you just want someone more objective." She sat down on Nina's bed. "It finally happened."

"What?"

"Khaled."

One of their coworkers had served as cinematographer on a documentary about a brilliant but schizophrenic magician, and they'd all gone to see it at the Film Forum the night before. Happy-hour drunk, Jess and the other interns crammed into the undesirable front row, and Khaled dropped into the seat directly behind her. Jess wanted to be attentive, she said, but the shaky footage meant to mimic the magician's state of mind made her dizzy, and she was aware of Khaled leaning forward, forearms on knees, breathing in a hypnotic rhythm. Instead of the screen she saw his face, its frame of curly hair, dark liquid eyes suggestive of an unshakable sadness.

Then, Jess said, he stood and left the theater, and something in his exit seemed pointed.

"I just knew I was supposed to follow him," she told Nina.

She had found him waiting outside, in the narrow hallway. "Jess," he said. He clasped her shoulders. Her back bumped against the wall. There was nowhere to go. "You know how I feel about you."

Her heart hadn't even started racing yet. It hadn't caught up to what was happening. "No, I don't."

"Don't do that. Don't make me feel stupid."

"That's not what I'm—" she said, and he lunged forward and kissed her, pinning her body to the wall with his strong arms and chest, a pleasant crush.

Nina's bedroom was so small their faces were only inches from each other. There was nowhere else for Nina to look but back at Jess.

They'd left the theater and walked west, then north along the Hudson, beneath the bright, coughing traffic of the West Side Highway, until they reached the Christopher Street piers. They sat on a bench gazing out at the water.

"Crazy shit used to go down here, you know?" Khaled told her. "Life happened here. Before everything got so sanitized."

Jess said she knew, though of course, she admitted to Nina, in the days he spoke of she'd been only a child. They made out for a while, his hands snaking up her shirt, until a group of teenagers passed by and cheered. Then he hailed a cab and they went back to his place in Williamsburg—Khaled had his own apartment, no roommates, confirmation he had *made it*—where he proved to be more attuned to her, more intent on her pleasure, than anyone she'd ever been with before.

"That sounds incredible," Nina said. She smiled, and her face felt tight.

"Every woman deserves a Khaled," Jess said. "That's what I now realize."

Khaled was wrong about the vitality of the city having winked out, Nina thought. Life was still happening. Jess's was unfurling before her, full of momentum, as Nina had once imagined her own in New York might be. They had grown up in the same ordinary place, but none of its ordinariness clung to Jess. And men like Khaled, whom people gathered around at crowded parties, hoping he'd hand them some small token of himself, pursued her.

"What about your guy?" Jess said. "Avi."

"Nothing." Nina knew she was being thrown a bone. She folded her arms over her chest.

Dreaminess lingered in Jess's eyes; she didn't notice. "Tell me again about him?"

Nina recounted the tragic story, Avi watching as his wife, his co-workers, thousands more disintegrated into the blue September air. How he stumbled around for years before finding the ladder out of grief. How his search had led right back to where he started, a street corner in lower Manhattan where he'd stopped one morning, four years after the attacks, to buy coffee from a street vendor. The man had passed him the cup and as their fingers brushed each other's Avi saw suddenly that he, the vendor, had an ocean of love within him, limitless. In the next moment Avi understood that *he* had the same ocean within himself. And in the next, that everyone had one; it was the same ocean; it was the force that drove the universe.

"Okay," Jess said. "Well, that's reassuring to hear."

"It sounds stupid the way I'm telling it." Nina looked out the window. It had already grown dark. The year was winding down. She could see only the outlines of trash cans just beyond her room, gleaming in the light of streetlamps. There was no way to explain what it meant to learn there was an elemental force within her, an ocean out of which anything could be made manifest. "It's not really any weirder than what we can do," she told Jess.

"You have a class tonight, don't you?"

"Yeah."

"Why don't we switch so I can go and experience it for myself?" The steakhouse was closed Tuesday nights, and Jess had complained more than once that on her only evening off Nina was tied up with Arete— *your culty thing*, as she called it.

It would be the first time they'd switched since the party. "What should I do in the meantime?"

"Whatever you want."

The more they switched, the smaller the terrain that belonged exclusively to her. That had always been the trade-off. But in exchange, in Jess's body, new latitudes unrolled before her. She nodded. They leaned forward and their foreheads met, skins soft, a little oily. Nina looked at herself, saw her mouth opening, the reddish cavern of her throat dropping away into blackness, and out of it came a laugh. Inside Jess, her lungs loosened a little. Calm refilled her.

***

In college, there had been a movement for body positivity. *It's my flaws that make me beautiful,* said the posters plastered by the campus feminist group in dorm common areas and the student center. Nina could think of no one, not least herself, made lovelier by acne or eczema, but for Jess the platitude held truth. Nina stared in the mirror of the bar's bathroom, at the ghost of a worry line bisecting Jess's forehead, the smudged indentations beneath her eyes. An interesting face, one an artist would want to sketch when he saw it on the subway.

A woman came out of one of the stalls and met her glance in the mirror. Nina tossed back her hair and raised one eyebrow, and the woman blushed.

She did not ordinarily go to bars alone. She never knew what to order, where to sit, how to arrange her body so as to project the aura of having done this a hundred times, like a real person. But as Jess it was as though she'd been granted entrée to the entire world.

At the bar, she sat close to the door and ordered a tequila and soda, Jess's usual. She took a sip and then set the glass down, gripping it, watching the tendons on her hand—Jess's hand—rising, indifferent to the fact that a foreign consciousness powered them. Another memory from college drifted back, a line that lingered—the only thing that did—from a survey of Western philosophy class. *Thou art a little soul bearing up a corpse.*

A few seats away, a man was telling the bartender that the smoking ban was bullshit. Its passage, he claimed, was the exact moment New York died.

"But I get to live longer," the bartender said.

Nina laughed, and the man glanced over at her. He looked young, perhaps her age. There was a wistful downward tilt to his eyes. "You have to die somehow," he said, more to Nina than the bartender.

"But not necessarily from, like, esophageal cancer," she told him.

"Okay, Ms. Public Health. So why are you out getting drunk on a Tuesday night?"

"Why are you?" She had learned this trick from her old editor at the college newspaper: when you don't feel like answering, just volley back the question. The inquirer only asked so they could tell you.

"I'm a poet," he said, "so it's required."

Nina smiled. "I'm so sorry."

He laughed. Then he stood up and came over to where she was sitting. "May I?"

She nodded slightly, looked down into the dark waters of her glass. The man sat, leaning back a little, his eyes round and hungry. He had not been expecting her.

"Gregory," he said, extending a hand, and she took it.

"Janine," she said, and it felt not entirely like a lie; it felt like she was, now, a third person. No one could see inside you, Nina had learned from her years of switching. You decided what they would see, what you wanted to shine through.

"What do you do, Janine?"

"Nothing worth discussing."

"What *is* worth discussing?"

She raised her drink and wetted her lips with it. "Poetry?"

He laughed again.

"Why don't you recite your favorite poem for me?"

Gregory considered. "I will if I can kiss you first."

People were always negotiating for pieces of Jess. Tonight it was up to her who'd get one.

"After," Nina said. His eyes were so blue they looked chlorinated.

"Shit," he said, "I'm several deep here. Might fuck it up."

Nina leaned back, waited.

"The poem's dedicated to Jesus—actually, 'to Christ our Lord'—but I'm not a Bible-thumper or anything. To my parents' great disappointment. They're true believers. So maybe I memorized it in some roundabout way of trying to understand them, right?"

"I don't know, Gregory. I'm not a social worker."

"Wow. Okay." He lowered his lids over the blue glare of his eyes and wavered a little on the stool. She worried for a moment he might slide right off to the damp and beery floor. But instead he steadied and began, in a loud and sober voice, the words lifting and descending, collapsing back in on themselves, sucked down into a sinkhole, then pulsing outward, pressing against the walls. It was too ecstatic for the sour little room. She leaned forward and, to halt him, kissed his entranced face. He kissed back, forcefully.

The charge the pressure of his mouth sparked in her was different, in some subverbal way, from the one she felt ordinarily; it was part of the unique language of Jess's body. She thought then of Jess in session, meditating, lighting up her own boring old body like a lantern and catching Avi's regard, the way she'd caught Khaled's. She imagined him stopping her after, his hand cuffing her wrist. *Wait*, he whispered, as the others exited. The scene shifted; he boosted her onto the kitchen counter, the lights were out, the neighboring towers of the city glinted around them, he thrusted and moaned her name into her hair.

She pulled back from Gregory, in a state of disorientation so deep she briefly believed she'd never surface from it. There's an ocean of love in me, she thought. But which one am I? Then someone outside on the street leaned on their car horn and she turned and saw a blear of white headlights through the dirty bar windows.

"I've gotta go," Nina said, and grabbed her purse and fled before he could speak. Let him wonder about her. Let him wonder the rest of his life.

6
SEA-CHANGE
(1993)

Nina noticed that Jess's mouth tasted sweet: she had been chewing a wad of watermelon bubble gum. Jess was a couple of inches shorter, and from Nina's new perspective, the whole bedroom looked askew, the walls papered with collages and magazine tear-outs, the dresser laden with tubes of lip gloss and perfume bottles craning away from her at dramatic angles. Her feet, crammed inside sneakers with no socks, were clammy, and the soles squeaked against the rough insides of the shoes.

Nina turned her head, saw herself again. Her face was round and flushed; wispy hairs had come loose from her high ponytail and formed a frame around her head. Her shoulders were hunched forward, her back rounded, in a way she was sure she never ordinarily held herself.

"How did you do that?" she saw herself hiss again.

There came three quick raps on the door, and then it inched open, a slice of Rob's tanned face, his black beard, visible through the crack, before he pushed it open the rest of the way.

"Girls?" he said. "What are you up to?"

Nina looked over at Jess again and did not find the usual reassurance, only her own frozen face. It was unthinkable what sort of punishment they might receive for this.

Rob laughed, a dry little laugh, then leveled his gaze on Nina. "Come here a sec."

As she stood, feeling Jess's legs at once spindlier and stronger beneath her, there arose like a wave within her an urgency to flee the room, the body, an ill-fitting shell clasped shut around her.

In the hallway, he crossed his arms and continued to regard her. "You still mad at me, kiddo?" he said. "You still giving me the silent treatment?" There was a laugh around his mouth that didn't make it all the way up to his eyes, a woundedness there Nina had never seen in her father, who in the largeness of his authority seemed impossible to hurt.

"No," she said, and hearing Jess's voice come from her throat, wanted to hear more. She glanced into the bedroom and saw the girl with her face shaking her head, eyes wide and wild. "I'm talking to you right now, aren't I?"

Rob considered. "Glad to hear it," he said, and gave her a light punch on the shoulder. He waved at the blond girl on the bedroom floor. "How's it going, Nina?"

"Fine," she blurted, and then Nina was relinquished. Jess grabbed her then, as she stepped back into the bedroom, wrapped her arms—*her* arms, Nina's; they were very smooth and white—around her shoulders, pressed her forehead into hers. Again, there was the pull, not malicious but insistent, the microsecond of suspension over a vast nothing, and she was back inside herself.

"That wasn't me," Nina insisted, "I don't know how—" and Jess bent over and vomited onto the carpet.

***

Then began the season of experimentation, which Jess approached with scientific gravity, a level of precision she had never applied to school subjects but of which Nina had long suspected she was capable. (Jess was incisive, always, in her analyses of other *people*, deploying descriptions that left them pinned and diminished as dead insects on display under glass; Ms. Brandon was "the old witch," Mara had not only blond hair but a "blond heart.") After swaps, first brief—two minutes in the hallway as they walked from lunch to music class, say—then lengthier—for all of recess—she would interrogate Nina about the sensations, the thoughts, whether it seemed there were any physical or mental repercussions to exercising their ability. (How to verbalize the stew of relief and disappointment when she was returned to her familiar and limited self?) As Nina responded, Jess's eyes would float upward to a fixed point as she mentally scribbled her field notes in an invisible but permanent ledger.

What they were finding was that there was no transfer of inner monologue, no exchange of memory; Jess could feel, for instance, that Nina's big toe was sore, but she had to be told that it was because she'd stubbed it getting out of the bath the night before. Nina was particularly sorry that she did not get to experience Jess's number-tasting ability, though relieved that Jess would never find out that she didn't really share the talent. But they were learning what it meant to live inside each other's skins, and all claims of comparative weaknesses and strengths could be settled once and for all: Jess *was* a faster runner, but Nina was better at push-ups; Jess's hair got oilier, and Nina had more stomachaches.

At first, Nina had been barely able to register such information; she was conscious only of her terror of getting stuck permanently inside Jess's body. But with each session it became clearer that they could swap in and out with ease; there was never a sense of resistance to the transfer. The *Compendium* had an entry on Prodigies, who, the moment they set fingertips to piano keys or took paintbrush in hand or laced their feet into running shoes, felt their previously untapped gifts flood through them, realized in a moment the truth of their lives. It had started to seem that this was it for her and Jess, what they were built for.

The advantages of their power began to emerge one morning in gym class. As they sat in their places on the squeaky, fragrant floor, Jess turned to Nina with eyebrows lifted in question. Nina listed toward her and they touched their foreheads together.

Mr. Vitale told them to get to their feet; from his perch in the metal folding chair beneath the basketball hoop, he started calling out the warm-up exercises. Nina stared at his shining, bald scalp, the thick gray beard crowded around his unsmiling mouth. She thought perhaps Jess's eyesight was keener—something to report back later. He flicked through the papers on his clipboard with rapid movements, as though what he saw there disgusted him and he could scarcely stand to glance at it for long.

"Jumping jacks," he muttered, not looking up. This was easier in Jess's body; within her smallness was energy condensed, ready to burst forth.

The teacher glanced up from his clipboard. "Raymond," he said. He got to his feet; his voice boomed over the space. "What kind of jumping jack is that?" He mimicked the boy, flapping his hands like they were boneless. Some of the students stopped exercising, giggling too hard to continue. "No girly jumping jacks," Mr. Vitale pronounced. He sat back down, gestured for them to start up again. Nina resisted the urge to peek at Raymond; she figured it was the best she could do, not add to the eyes on his face.

Mr. Vitale looked up again. "Nina," he called.

She stopped.

The teacher frowned. "Jessica, you don't have to do *everything* she does." Nina turned and saw herself still amid the sea of churning arms and legs, her own damp face upturned, eyes locked on Mr. Vitale.

She heard her voice resound through the space, louder even than the teacher's, sailing over the thump of sneakers. "What's wrong with doing things like a girl?"

"Who said you could stop the exercises?" Mr. Vitale said.

"Jess is a girl. She's the fastest runner in the class," Jess continued. (It should be obvious, Nina thought, that this was Jess speaking through her; Nina had never once talked back to a teacher.)

Now everyone was watching. Mr. Vitale crossed his arms over his chest, a gesture that had come to indicate to the students he was weighing how best to berate one of their number.

But Jess, inhabiting Nina's body, her voice, went on. "Raymond," she said, turning to him. His chin seemed to wobble slightly. "You should thank Mr. Vitale for giving you such a nice compliment."

Raymond's lips parted and came together several times. Finally he settled on closing them. He looked at the floor.

"Alright, enough," Mr. Vitale said. Then, in a voice with less gravel in it, "Start jogging."

The children began running alongside the white tape that outlined the gym floor, running in a silence that reminded Nina of temple when the worshippers first filed in for service, before they had time to get restless and start shifting in their seats, hissing to their children to be still. She held herself back from running as fast as she could. Jess came up beside her; Nina thought she would never get accustomed to seeing herself appear in her peripheral vision, her own arms and legs pumping, her face stiff with concentration.

"Sorry if I got you in trouble," Jess whispered, the words jagged with effort.

Nina shook her head. Hearing herself mount a defense of Raymond, it became clear that she should have done so long before, and she could not explain why she never had.

At the end of class, Mr. Vitale summoned them to their assigned spots on the floor, and the girls took the opportunity to press their foreheads together and switch back. (The gentle pull, the single moment of non-being.) Returned to herself, her legs full of water, Nina looked up at the teacher. He scanned the room and his eyes came to rest on her, his expression inscrutable. Surely now she would receive her punishment.

"Get out of here," Mr. Vitale told them, and they got to their feet and filed out.

Waiting in the hallway for Ms. Brandon to retrieve them, a remarkable thing happened. Mara approached, chewing her lip a little.

"Nina, I think that was really nice what you did," she said.

Jess stood beside her, eyes gleaming. "It wasn't a big deal," Nina mumbled.

"Yes it was," Jess said. "It *was* a big deal. It was the right thing to do."

Mara blinked. "Anyway," she said, and returned to her friends. It

seemed to Nina that she should apologize for taking credit—but what
else could she have done?

Jess patted Nina's sweaty hair. "That was a fun one," she said.

* * *

There emerged other advantages to switching. It was a kind of high-order
game of dress-up, in which they played at being each other. Once, leaving the school building for the day, Nina in Jess's body had swung out
a hand and said to their principal, standing cross-armed at the door,
"Gimme five, Mr. Levine." She dared to heckle some of the boys who
wrestled at recess, laughing as they tumbled and strained in the dirt and
sparse grass of the soccer field, as the security guards came harrumphing
over. And the boys looked up at her, saw her, something newly pene-
trative in the eyes inside their damp red faces. In Nina's skin, Jess spoke
far more in class. In fact, the effect of her habitations seemed to extend
beyond the bounds of impression, and Jess began devoting hours each
evening to reading and homework, the better, she explained, to believ-
ably become her friend.

As Jess, Nina learned what it was to be denied a teacher's approval.
In class, rendered mute (Jess insisted that they strive for faithful imi-
tations of each other, although the fidelity she required of Nina was to
a version of herself that had already been shed, the Jess of the month
before, who purported to care nothing for learning), Nina watched
Ms. Brandon survey the children. When her gaze came to rest on her,
across her features passed an expression of repulsion. To the teacher Jess
was something better not dwelled upon, a wad of phlegm spat into the
street. Nina longed to raise Jess's hand and reveal one of her friend's insights—they were sometimes startling—to see Ms. Brandon rear back
in surprise, but Jess wouldn't let her. "There's no point," she said. "She
hates me." And Nina had to acknowledge this seemed true.

Finally, through swapping, Jess was integrated with Nina's other
friends. In Nina's body, Jess basked in their familiarity, their memories
and jokes and small caresses, earned through shared childhoods, from

the sandbox years into the presumable future. And as Jess, Nina ventured shyly closer, spoke a bit more than her friend had been previously capable, even once confessed, as they sat in a circle on the sun-warmed blacktop during recess, the repeated thwocking sound of the boys playing Suicide in the background, that moving had been hard, that she'd had to leave so many friends behind. At this, she saw her own body assume a foreign posture, a rigidity that belonged to Jess, that meant anger blooming; with this admission she perhaps had gone too far, finally said something Jess never would. But it was rewarded: Stephanie said, "We're your new friends!" and they'd all clustered around her in a hug. Later, having swapped back, Jess was quiet as they returned to the classroom, and Nina waited to be accused of a failure in representation. But Jess just glanced at her and muttered, "They're nice."

                                        ***

But the game was best when they had no audience but themselves, when on weekends they sat in the privacy of Jess's or Nina's room. Their radio show had taken on an investigative quality, the candle room, the tasting of numbers having been dispensed with in favor of outlining what they discovered over the previous week of swapping.

One Sunday in May as they slouched on Nina's carpet, Jess took up the microphone and remarked that their power seemed to cost them nothing.

"After a switch, neither of us feels sleepy or dizzy or anything," she said. Here her invisible ledger, her note-taking came into play. She had crystalline recall, a scientific rigor none of their teachers knew a thing about.

Nina agreed. The only physical toll of swaps was the black-and-blue, the paper cut each of their bodies might sustain while the other inhabited it; the body held the injury even after the one who'd clumsily inflicted it upon herself had vacated. It was remarkable there was no greater consequence than this, no psychic wound stemming from the use of their power.

"Let's look at the *Compendium* again," Nina suggested. The tome had not yet surrendered any clues as to their ability but she was always, in paging through it, stumbling upon some entry she'd never noticed before. Its brittle pages spoke of many wonders of the human mind—extrasensory perception, precognition—but nowhere could she find the capacity for it being lifted wholesale out of one person and into another. Still, whenever Nina crouched over the book and thumbed through its entries, it occurred to her that any of these things—shapeshifting, demonic possession, Satan himself—could be real, if what she and Jess were doing was real; it could all just as easily be true. Alone sometimes, particularly at night, she felt surrounded, overtaken, by this congregation of the possible.

"Wait," Jess said, "let's do it first," and they clunked their foreheads together and switched, each rubbing, with her new hands, her new skull, the tender spot where they'd collided, laughing. Now Jess, in Nina's body, thumbed through the book, and came to a stop on the entry for Hauntings.

The page was divided down the center into two categories, *Residual haunts* and *Intelligent haunts*. The former the *Compendium* defined as a "psychic impression or afterimage; the residue of the energy of a human or animal that once dwelled in a place. The living inhabitants of a home afflicted with a residual haunt, often marked by repeated, unexplained sounds and appearances of a Phantasm, are in no danger from the Apparition." The latter, by contrast, was "intentional; the Apparition deliberately seeks to interact with the living, whether out of ignorance of their own passing, unfinished business on the mortal plane, or the desire to terrorize and maim." Unusually for the *Compendium*, there was not a crude drawing here but a photograph, of white fog in the shape of a woman levitating above a dark staircase. *The Brown Lady of Raynham Hall*, the caption read, *likely an intelligent haunt, for she was reported to have grinned diabolically at the master of the house.*

They took turns reading aloud from the entry into the microphone, testing each other's voices as they did, lifting and dropping them to absurd registers, but even as they giggled Nina was chilled by the words she spoke.

At the bottom of the page, in bold text, was an additional message: "Should you require to rid your own dwelling of a Spectre, turn to the

Appendix." Nina grabbed the book and lifted a brick of pages until she found the reference point amid the dense squiggles of print.

It was a poem, of sorts.

"Should we say it?" Nina said, and Jess nodded. She held the microphone between them and they read, and these words Nina didn't understand at all, but their voices—hers now Jess's, and Jess's hers—twined together into a single, resonant thread and she felt, across the whole surface of her other, second skin, a different kind of chill:

> *Full fathom five thy father lies;*
> *Of his bones are coral made;*
> *Those are pearls that were his eyes:*
> *Nothing of him that doth fade,*
> *But doth suffer a sea-change*
> *Into something rich and strange.*
> *Sea-nymphs hourly ring his knell:*
> *Ding-dong.*
> *Hark! now I hear them—ding-dong, bell.*

***

It was about a dead man—a dead father, that much Nina could tell, and she turned to Jess to see if she could see any reaction, a fragment of Jess's true self surfacing in her own blue eyes.

But it was then Nina's mother came in, without knocking. She stood over them shaking her head. "Shut up in here on such a gorgeous day," she said, and tugged open the blinds, which went up with a rasp as spring light poured in. "Listen," she continued, "Zachary is feeling neglected."

Unknowing, she had of course addressed Jess, who looked up at her, startled; she'd never experienced Nina's mother's reprimands before.

"I know it's not your job to entertain him, but he's so happy when you girls give him just a little bit of your time," she said. She stood in the center of the room, waiting.

"You're right," Jess finally said. "We'll include him more."

Her mother smiled. "Thanks, Nee-nee."

It was not a faithful impersonation. Nina would have resisted, disagreed, told her mother they were in the middle of something.

But Jess went on, the falseness thickening around her. "We can play with him right now. Maybe basketball in the driveway?"

Nina felt lodged in the back of her throat a question, but she couldn't extract the right words to voice it. The revolt in the gym, the pronouncements in class, the serene submission to her mother's wishes: it was beginning to look like Jess was mounting a kind of mutiny against the parts of her she found most wanting, building a better Nina.

"That would be great," Nina's mother said, beaming now, and leaned quietly over Jess and stroked her hair. She murmured something in her ear, and Nina could imagine what it was, because she had been granted these beatitudes before: *Thank you for being such a wonderful big sister.* And Nina watched a smile spread across her own face, one so unconsciously blissful she was sure her features had never stretched quite this way before, as though she had never experienced such warmth and love in her entire life.

***

Their play took on new dimensions, shades of violence. They began testing their pain thresholds, switching then pinching and slapping at each other's thighs to gauge whose body registered more intense sensations. Often this exercise concluded in a dead heat, their soft legs turned piebald, red welts on pale skin. Once or twice Nina suggested a return to the old rituals, but Jess had tired of telesthesia. All their chanting to her father had yielded no results, not a phone call or a postcard, whereas in swapping the effects of their magic were instant.

They tried to outdo each other's invocations, performing their radio show as, in part, a contest of exposure. As Nina, Jess would pronounce tremulously into the microphone, "I'm afraid to sing, because then everyone might notice me," and Nina, as Jess, would counter, "I'm not

afraid of anything. Really! See?" and belt out the next song, mangling
the lyrics. One afternoon this ratcheted up until a vicious current seemed
to encircle them, each of the girls snatching the microphone from each
other and bellowing, *I'm Nina, I'm like this, I'm Jess, I do this*, until suddenly Jess dropped her voice, looked into her lap, smiled a sheepish smile.

"Jess," she said softly. "I have a question."

"What?" Neither of them was ever so gentle these days. Dread trick-
led into her chest.

"Can we play the Boyfriend Game?"

It was the ultimate revelation: all attempts to conceal her desire for
the game were proven feeble, her layers of feigned casualness peeled
away to the throbbing core, the hunger for closeness with Jess that only
Giselle and Clyde could deliver.

"Stop making fun of me," she mumbled.

"I'm not!" Jess said. "I'm not." She stood and pulled at Nina's hands,
trying to get her to her feet. "Come on," she said. Nina allowed herself
to be tugged upward, led over to the bed.

"Baby," Jess said, and now she was Clyde, Jess-as-Nina-as-Clyde.
"I'm sorry I got home so late."

Nina, still stung, shrugged.

"I was just working," Jess continued. "At the, um, office."

She cupped Nina's chin in her hand, lifted her face so their eyes
met. "I don't like being here all by myself," Nina said, in Giselle's thin,
silvery voice.

"I'm here now. I'll keep you safe." And, without bothering to get a
plastic bag, without any sort of barrier, Jess leaned forward and pressed
her lips against Nina's. This time they were not interrupted. The sensation was soft and a little damp; the heat she felt on her face sunk
downward and flared in her belly. Nina opened her eyes and saw her
own face before her, undefended. She pulled back.

"I'm a good kisser," Jess said. They stared at each other a moment
and then started laughing, hard enough that they collapsed back onto
the bed. Once they caught their breath, Jess said, "Now let's switch back
and try it again."

7

N&J IN DREAMLAND

(2005)

Jess was sitting on her stoop in the vaporous gleam of streetlights when Nina came up East Sixth Street, and she was drunk enough to mistake her, momentarily, for her own ghost, a portent. She had not forgotten the *Compendium* entry on the Psychopomp, "an Apparition that appears when death is imminent to escort the deceased out of this life; it may, as with the doppelgänger, wraith, or fetch, appear in the guise of the person about to perish." Some of the book's descriptions were as embedded in her gray matter as the hooks to now-ancient pop songs. In her mouth there was still the faint smoke of the whiskey Gregory had been drinking and she wondered, as they made the switch back, whether Jess might notice.

"Honestly?" Jess said, bending over to touch her toes, then stretching her arms in a rainbow overhead, reveling in the return to her own body. "I was bored out of my mind. I tried meditation once in college but I can't sit still for shit."

"That's all?"

"You can save a lot of money just doing it on your own, you know."

"Avi didn't notice anything?"

Jess put the heel of her palm to her forehead, swaying a little on her feet. "I guess I know what you've been up to."

"He didn't say anything to you?"

Jess squeezed her eyes shut. "No. He looks sort of like a hobbit, doesn't he?"

"I don't know." There were still, despite everything, long blue distances between them. But she should be grateful, Nina supposed, for Jess's incomprehension. Avi and Arete would remain hers alone.

***

For an additional fee, you could have a private meeting with Avi. A few unused cab fares from Scarlett's father, and Nina was ready. He asked her to meet him at an address in Queens and she considered telling Jess or Eleanor where she was going, the way you were supposed to when meeting a man you didn't know very well, but decided against it.

The address led her to a lot near the elevated train, surrounded by vacant buildings doused with color, every surface graffitied and howling for attention. There were the expected epithets about George W. Bush, the tags in bubbled, voluptuous letters, but also bright, uncanny tableaux: a woman who had removed her own face, a rubbery, peach mask grasped in one hand, a huge grin stretching the exposed red muscle. Nina turned a corner into a concrete courtyard, bordered by more of these set pieces, and found Avi sitting on a ledge, staring at his phone. The act struck her as disappointingly mundane, but still, her heart squeezed when he looked up at her.

He asked her to take a walk with him. They traced the perimeter, quietly, as the egos of the artists blared around them. The images, the onlookers gaping at them, blended into a garish smear; she was only, painfully, aware of Avi's presence beside her. He asked Nina to tell him about herself.

What was there to tell about apart from her power, the burning secret that lit her life, that she couldn't speak of? She felt Avi staring. Beyond his ordinary surface was a searchlight. When its light settled upon you, you were bathed in heat.

He tried again. "Where do you see yourself in a few years' time?"

"Um." She was reminded of the job interviews for which she had tried to haul, like a bucket of water from a well, the right answers from within herself, sparkling and pure. Instead she turned up mouthfuls of mud. "I was thinking of trying to become a writer. A journalist. In high school and college I wrote—"

"Hang on, Nina." He put a hand on her shoulder and she froze, desperate for him not to remove it. "I'm not asking how you're going to sell your labor on the market. Frankly, I couldn't care less about that. I want to know where you'd like to see your *self.*"

"I want to be where you are. I want to be plugged in." There was no effort with this answer. No silty taste of falseness in her mouth. He gave both her shoulders a squeeze but the act was utterly platonic, he a Little League coach and she a jittery player on deck. Nina glanced around at the other visitors marveling at the graffitied walls and thought she would stab any one of them, right in the throat, right then and there, if it meant Avi looking at her as Gregory had looked at Janine.

"When you reach the next level you'll become *more* receptive," he told her. "You may even find you're able to pick up on people's thoughts. But it won't be exhausting or overwhelming. You'll come back to yourself with the calm you need to take it all in."

They walked on, Avi elaborating on the enhanced state of mind she was ever closer to achieving, the clarity of it, like a mountain lake whose arctic waters hid none of the tide-smoothed rocks below. The setting sun outlined his profile, his long nose, in gold. He hated charging what he did for the sessions, these meetings, he told her, having to commodify what should have been a gift. Someday they would evolve past the need for these transactions. But, he continued, if she wanted to take the next step, attend the ceremony that meant ascending to phase two, there would be, regrettably, another fee in addition to today's, to help cover space rental and materials.

"I see," Nina said. She found they had reached the steps for the 7 train.

"Well," he said. "I'll see you Tuesday."

"Wait," she said. The vision of him lifting her to the counter flickered again in her mind's eye. She told him, "I'm ready to take the next step."

He took her hands in his, that laser-beam attention leveled upon her again. "I've been waiting for you to say that, Nina." The dark eyes, with depths that sank further than Khaled's, she was sure. The trace of an unplaceable accent in his voice, her name in his mouth lilting and new.

He told her an address, a date, a time, and Nina handed over the cab cash in an envelope; giving him the naked bills would have shattered the entire afternoon. She rode home in a dream. She wasn't sure exactly what she had paid for, but she had the sense that Avi had pulled open her jaw and dropped down her throat an ember; it glowed and illuminated her from within as the subway dove beneath the East River.

***

Jess called late, when Nina was already in bed, furled around her laptop. She was reading clips written by her old editor at the college newspaper, who worked now as a stringer for Reuters; several of the most recent were about the looming possibility of a New York City transit strike. She often thought of doing so, but had never reached out to him, to ask about an in. She was unable to imagine herself doing as he did, lingering outside city hall, calling around to police precincts in search of stories.

Over the phone Jess sounded a bit winded. "I'm coming over," she said, "I just finished my shift."

"Is everything okay?" Nina was in a comfortable sulk now, about her own uncorked potential, and the thought of getting herself together had little appeal.

"I'll tell you when I get there."

Nina pulled on jeans and brushed powder over her forehead, but she needn't have. Jess arrived gray-faced, her hair holding the odor of grease and onions.

It was about the radio. "I've been keeping it on the fire escape," she confessed over the hollering of the steam radiator in Nina's living room, "and then last night I had this dream." In it the city was silenced by deep drifts of snow that rose all the way to her windows. Jess was crossing the apartment when she heard a knock. She turned and saw a hand wiping the glass clear. On the other side of it was her father, peering in, his face purpled, pocked by blisters, fluid weeping from the cavities.

"That's what happens to your body after you die, you know," she said.

Nina hadn't. She hadn't known, either, how really to find Jess's father when they were children, or how to banish him now from the radio, from Jess's dreams. She'd only ever pretended, and that Jess believed her even still sent waves of disquiet crashing in her chest.

"Can I stay over tonight?"

"Of course," Nina said, resigning herself to a string of sleepless hours in the cramped shared bed.

"Actually," Jess said, "do you think we can switch?" She chewed the inside of her cheek. "You just look so . . . cozy."

It was laughable—when just minutes before Nina was hunched in her pajamas, loathing herself—that someone might see her as sanctuary.

Had either of them ever told the other no? Jess looked beautiful, despite her pallor. But not cozy, never that. They held onto each other's arms, drew each other in.

***

They went to a bodega to pick up a few tallboys and on the walk back up First Avenue a pair of men began trotting alongside them. "Thelma and Louise," one of them said.

He was staring at Nina—but not really. It was Jess he wanted. "Wow," she told him. "Timely reference."

"You look just like them," his partner said.

"We look nothing—" Nina began. He reached out to stroke her hair—Jess's hair—but then plunged his fingers into it. Her head snapped forward.

"We're not interested," Jess mumbled, and it wasn't clear whether this was her impression of Nina or she was genuinely frightened.

They sped up, but the men kept pace. "Where are we going?" the first asked.

They looked about the same age as Nina and Jess, unextraordinary, and the neighborhood continued to course around their group, cabs smearing by, girls tripping out of bars and down the sidewalk. Nina turned abruptly into another bodega and the men followed her through its plastic-sheathed entryway, toward its wooden shelves lined with fruit and flowers, leaving Jess outside. She looked in at Nina through the windows.

What the hell? she mouthed, eyebrows drawing together, shaking her head.

Rage crested within Nina at the sight of herself out there on the sidewalk, discarded. She turned and lunged at the second man, who was skinnier, sinking her shoulder into his sternum hard enough that he stumbled backward through the door.

"Crazy bitch," the first said, and at this the bodega owner stepped out from behind the counter and glared over at them. The man went back outside, helped his friend off the sidewalk. They moved on, barely glancing at Jess.

She was peering around the corner when Nina came out. "I don't see them." She looked at Nina. "You're insane, by the way."

It was impossible to tell whether this was performance, an invocation of what she perceived as Nina's caution, or something else. Her face, Nina's own face, was unreadable to her. The excitement of the encounter drained away into silence. She had, Nina realized as they walked the rest of the way home, used Jess's body recklessly, and not for the first time. She might have hurt her shoulder, or the men could have answered her violence with their own. What she had done was perhaps not an embodiment of Jess at all, but a discharge of a feral impulse all her own.

***

"This is Nestor," Avi said, draping an arm around the shoulders of a short, black-haired man. In the unlit gym, his irises, too, looked black. "My man from Iquitos." Nestor lifted his eyebrows slightly at the name of his hometown. "He's a *curandero*, here to help with the ceremony. He's seen probably thousands of people through their encounters with The Grandmother."

There was something about the article, the *the*, that unsettled Nina.

Just "grandmother" might have conjured images of a benevolent matriarch, but *The* Grandmother had an ominous heft, like a creature hiding inside a grandmother suit.

Perhaps the unease came only from the site for this ritual, reanimating in Nina her old fears of authority. Avi had met them on the front steps of the high school and, with one finger raised to his lips, ushered them down the hallways—lined here, too, with the institutional green tile, the sun-aged posters bearing messages of forced cheer—and into the gymnasium. Nestor crouched now in the corner near the locker room and stirred something in a clay pot. A substance with the slow ooze of molasses clung to the ladle. A potion, Nina tried to persuade herself, that might indeed be administered by a kindly grandmother of the Old World, who knew how to forage in the woods and brew curatives that soothed colds and heartache.

Avi muttered something to Nestor that no one else could hear, and the man nodded.

"It's time," Avi told them. "Come forward."

There were twelve of them—the number twelve was auspicious, Nina overheard a woman say. Twelve disciples, twelve months, twelve days of Christmas. She turned and looked. It was one of the women from the café, from whom she'd surreptitiously learned of Avi. The others waiting in line chuckled about the high school setting, wondering how and why Avi had selected this place. It was because they'd all been purer then, as adolescents, the woman replied; more themselves, idealistic, untainted by the so-called real world, and they needed to return to that. Incredibly, no one disputed this.

The blue gym mats squeaked beneath Nina's feet, sighing out generations of teenage sweat. The faces around her were pale but charged with excitement.

Winston was ahead of her in line. When he reached Nestor, who was portioning the goo into small tea bowls, he looked over his shoulder.

"Well, if it isn't Nina ballerina."

"Are we crazy?" she asked him.

He didn't seem to hear. "See you on the other side," he said, and tilted the stuff down his gullet, shuddering a little as he swallowed.

Reprieve denied, Nina approached Nestor. Avi stood beside him. He caught her drifting eyes with his own as one would a housefly.

"I'll be here," he said, "the whole journey."

Heart in mouth, she took the bowl and swallowed the liquid. It was thick as gel and the taste was evil, sweet-rotten.

Nina made for a spot by the wall, huddled against it as the stuff scoured its way down her throat. There came a feeling like freezer burn, filling her esophagus with frost.

"Yecch," said a girl in a Columbia hoodie sitting beside her. She was hugging her knees to her chest. "I seriously wanna rip my tongue off."

"Please don't say things like that," Nina said. It seemed to her that here, at the beginning, an idea might get lodged inside the thick potion and linger, poisoning all that was to follow. She lay on her back, knees steepled toward the ceiling, and tried to breathe in the smell of burning incense but not the perspiration beneath it. Inhale, count to five. Hold, count to five. Exhale, count to five. Picture a lake, a perfectly flat, silver lake. Someone started moaning, shooting ripples across the water, but with her mind she smoothed it still again. The Grandmother, they'd been promised, would take them beyond the boundaries of their bodies, directly to the truth about what they were: pure light. "We are energy that never dies. This life is only the current and brief manifestation of energy that will go on forever," Avi had told them.

Nina tried not to acknowledge what was happening, which was that her nausea had grown so intense it was practically a presence beside her. She rolled over onto her stomach and stared at a poster on the wall of laughing, multiethnic children playing on a jungle gym. The moaner was now retching at an almost comedic volume; it sounded as though she was expelling demons. No exorcisms, Nina reminded herself. The children were helping: they were trying to bury her stomach pain in the playground's sandbox. Scarlett was their leader, speaking in full, grammatical sentences. "Nina needs our help," she was saying. "Let's dig a deep, dark hole." The sound of her plastic shovel plunging into sand sent chills down Nina's thighs. Scarlett shouldn't see her like this. She rolled over, turned her face from the children.

A complaining came from someone's guts. Nina sought out the of-fender but then, with the next viscous gurgle, she sensed that the source of churning was within her.

"Is that me?" she asked. No one responded. The noise was too loud to be normal; she was harboring some creature readying to burst forth. She stood and made her way to the bathroom, but three women were tangled on the mats before the door, giggling, limbs interlaced.

"If you want to go in, first you have to get past the three witches," Winston told her. He stood over them, leaning against the wall.

They were witches, Nina understood. She shrank back, stumbled through the doors to the parking lot behind the gym. The blankness of the night sky disoriented her. She'd been expecting, for some reason, to see stars, but there were none, only telephone wires and the trestles of the elevated train laced over blackness. She sucked down cold air to still the scrambling in her stomach. Why did the ceremony have to be held at a high school? For what purpose was The Grandmother pulling her with tidal force back along her own timeline, to the blazing point she least wanted to feel the scorch of again?

Among the empty coffee cups and napkins and beer bottles tossed around the lot by wind were other things skittering around—children, she thought, perhaps the ones from the poster. She saw the whip of a blond ponytail here, a sneaker with its laces dragging there. The sneaker she recognized—they were the kind that lit up when you ran, which Jess had had; she remembered her fleet feet shooting starbursts off the blacktop as she circled its perimeter at recess.

It was them, little Jess and little Nina, and the nausea was receding in the cold January air, in their presence. The girls were hiding behind a dumpster, and Nina began moving toward it. She squatted, extended a hand for them to nuzzle. She had to warn them.

"Listen to me very carefully," she whispered, and the small faces peered up at her expectantly in the dark.

The door slammed behind her, and she saw Avi and Nestor step out of the gym. Avi struck a match to light a cigarette, illuminating stub-ble on his cheeks.

"The other day you told me forty percent," she heard Nestor say, in an accent that was pure Brooklyn. "I could lose my fucking job for letting you in here." She stumbled back from her crouch and the men looked over at her.

Avi cursed. The girls fled, disappearing behind the dumpster again as she got to her feet. Nina felt somehow that she ought to apologize, that she was the one who had been deceitful.

Avi crushed the cigarette beneath his heel and approached her, gingerly, as though she might startle. He hugged himself in the cold. "What are you doing out here all by yourself?"

"I didn't know you smoked." There were questions waiting behind her teeth, but no language available with which to voice them.

"You know that isolating is not the way to go here," Avi said. "It's absolutely the wrong direction."

Behind him the door slammed again as Nestor went back inside. He was right: Nina was receding into the distance where her nausea had gone. Under her eyelids there formed the bleak image of a shoreline, a gray thundering ocean, gray sky, gray sand. The Grandmother had exiled her there. She felt the lip of the dumpster press into her back from across a great expanse.

Avi cupped a palm under her chin. "What's the matter, Nina?" Her eyes fluttered open as his face drew nearer, lips parting before the tunnel of his throat. Another face materialized atop Avi's, its features fired with anticipation, too bright, the thrilled look that preceded a plunge inside her. She knew who it belonged to, and that he'd come back for more, which meant that she must be in Jess's body, but she couldn't remember having switched. The tip of his tongue slithered forth, testing the air, and her nausea returned, rising to meet it. She buckled over and vomited what seemed an improbable volume.

"Jesus. Fuck," Avi said. He backed up, tried to shake some of it off his feet. "Well, that's—" He shook his head, turned, and walked back toward the gym.

The girls were gone; pacing the parking lot, Nina found only more trash. The effect of the drug, too, was already waning. She searched herself for some residue of wisdom left behind, like debris cast onto the sand when a wave pulls back, but found nothing.

She left the lot, walked through the crosshatched side streets until she reached Northern Boulevard. She hailed a cab; she'd already blown the month's budget on the ceremony, so what did it matter? She rolled down the window to diffuse the smell of vomit on her shoes, and the car sailed over the Queensboro Bridge, the lights of the city blurring past her half-closed eyes into something that looked like a sneer.

***

After a few thin hours of sleep Nina had awakened with the certainty of the sinister presence of the drug still within her, wriggling its way through her nervous system, and fled through the dawn for home. There she told her mother she had food poisoning, which was in a sense the truth, and that she preferred to recuperate in her old room.

"Of course," her mother had said, and delivered to her bottles of Gatorade, packets of Pepto-Bismol.

On another of her visits to the bedroom, her mother placed a cool hand on her forehead, feeling for fever.

"It's nice to have you here, even under these circumstances," she said. She sat for a moment. "You were such a secretive kid. It scared me, to think of what you might be hiding." The late-afternoon light filtering through the blinds filled the cracks around her eyes.

"It was just stupid teenage stuff," Nina said. Her mother looked down at her and nodded, smiled, lifted her hand away.

Now an intestinal twist ejected her from the cave beneath her comforter and into the bathroom. She'd been so certain during the ceremony that she had a message for their younger selves, a warning. She had known every word she needed to tell them. But it had all been emptied from her.

When she emerged, her mother was standing in the hallway holding the cordless phone.

"It's Jess." She cupped her hand over the mouthpiece and whispered, "So weird to talk to her after all this time! She sounds so grown up."

Nina took the phone. "Hey."

"Hey yourself," Jess said. "Jesus, you're hard to reach."

"I turned my cellphone off."

"I know. I tried that like ten times. I still have your home phone memorized," Jess said. "Your mom sounds good."

"She's pretty much the same."

"So. Are you planning to tell me what the fuck's going on?"

It was the first time she'd felt it since their reunion, Jess's bite, the teeth within her conversations.

Nina closed her bedroom door. "I went to this ceremony thing Avi does. It was just, like, not a great experience."

"Not a great experience? What does that mean?"

"It just wasn't what I was hoping it'd be."

"There's something I need to tell you," Jess said. "You have to promise you won't be mad at me, though."

Nina crawled back under the comforter, pulled it over her head, sealed herself in. "Just tell me."

"I had George look up Avi," Jess confessed. "He's a total con man, Nina. He did time for tax fraud."

At a shrine outside Tokyo, Nina had noticed the statue of something that looked like a demon, eyebrows slashing downward across the bronze face, one eye squinting with dangerous skepticism, fangs jutting, a sword in one hand, a rope in the other. This was Fudo Myo-o, explained a classmate—one of the many boys perpetually waiting, it seemed, for opportunities like this one to unleash their knowledge of Japanese culture—a Buddhist deity whose name meant *immovable*. The rope was in fact a noose, which Fudo Myo-o slung around the necks of the wicked to drag them through their delusions until their sight was cleared. Nina understood the value and pain of this service: it was what Jess had done, more than once, to her.

"Probably goes without saying," Jess continued, "but he never worked for Cantor Fitzgerald. He made up all that shit about the dead wife."

Under the blanket she couldn't see a thing. Jess had been dying to tell her, Nina knew; that was why she'd tried calling a dozen times.

"His whole tragic story was a lie. Pretty dark, huh?"

"I guess," Nina said.

"Oh, come on," Jess said, but she wasn't ruffled in the least. "Are you mad at me? I was just trying to look out for you."

"It's not you I'm mad at."

"If you want, we can switch," Jess offered, "and I'll tell him I'm out, that I can see through all his manipulative bullshit."

"No." Nina sat up and the room rushed at her again. "I can handle it."

A sigh on the other end, a little disappointed. Jess was the one who made the voodoo dolls, pushed the needles in.

***

Avi had been trying to reach her, too; already in her short residency back home on Long Island the messages had accumulated. *Missed you in class last night*, he texted Wednesday morning. *What gives?* The following day came an email from avi@arete.com warning of cancellation fees if she skipped more sessions. *I would hate for that to happen. You've been making such good progress. Students like you don't come along very often.* A day after that a brief voice mail, the orchestrations of a city street blaring behind his own nasal voice: "Nina, you need to call me back right away. I don't take well to being ignored."

He had her address; she'd included it on a form she'd had to sign before attending the ceremony. She lay awake that night in twisted sheets, imagining him showing up at the apartment where Eleanor now slept, alone.

Nina went looking for old reassurances. Hadn't the *Compendium* contained a vast appendix of charms, chants, spells to ward off malign influence? The book had lived once on her shelves, but before she'd left for college she'd shoved all the most important detritus of her childhood into boxes stacked now in her closet. These she pulled down and began sifting through, and thought again of the little girls, their little selves, that had appeared to her, crouched like raccoons behind the dumpster. What had she wanted to warn them of?

The *Compendium* was nowhere. She lifted the lid from another box, ready for her fingers to brush its familiar cracked leather cover, but found instead stacks of cassette tapes. On the underside of the lid was written in big, childish letters, *THE N-AND-J RADIO SHOW, DEC 92–JUN 93.* Inside the dash was the discovery of their power. It must have been audible, the change, in their voices. Nina took the tape to her boombox—a gift upon elementary school graduation, still chugging along—put it in the tape deck, and pressed play.

There came Jess's voice, impossibly young, impossible to believe the child it belonged to had seemed so enormous. "Look, it says if you have a ghost in your house, you should read this poem. Should we say it?"

"Yes!" It was her own voice, high and faint, almost fragile. "Let's do it together."

"Okay, on three," Jess said, and she was sitting across from Nina on the soft carpet of the long-ago bedroom. "One, two, three."

"Full fathom five thy father lies . . ." They both pronounced fathom incorrectly, in the same way: *fay-thom.* But it was there, their magic. Nina grabbed her phone. On the tape, there came the sound of Nina's mother interrupting them, telling them to get outside. She typed out a message to Jess: *I think I know how to fix your radio.*

***

Nina had contacted Jess only once during the long years of their separation, late in the night on September 11, after the phone lines and internet started working again. Over the course of an hour she typed in the glow of her computer screen, one of thousands of bluish lights brightening rooms across campus. Her roommate was asleep somehow, and although she had no idea that Jess existed, a spark of the illicit ran through Nina's hands at doing the unthinkable, severing the long silence, right beside her. The odor of cigarette smoke hung in the room, because they had decided that morning, staring at the news on the little RCA atop their dresser, that if ever there was a time to light up indoors this was it.

In the message that was never sent, she told Jess how the first person she thought of, when she understood what was happening, was not her mother nor Zachary nor even her own self—there were rumors this was only the beginning of a series of strikes that would pepper the United States, from east to west, with smoldering craters, that soon the black rain would fall—but her, Jess, the best friend she'd ever had, in fact more than friend, more than family, and didn't times like these, if there was any meaning to be derived from them at all, serve to remind you what mattered most? She read it over, so tired that the words doubled in her vision, looked doubly mortifying, and then deleted the entire thing, replacing it instead with *Just wanted to make sure you are safe.* She never received a reply.

She thought of this, bundled in her coat on the steamy L train as it shuddered across Brooklyn. She thought of Avi's lie about that morning, how it had left her lying awake aching for him, how it made her believe in reinvention in the wake of disaster. In certain lights it became difficult to loathe him. Who didn't wish for an event powerful enough to annihilate even their mistakes?

In her living room, Jess hauled open the window and leaned out to retrieve the radio from the fire escape. Nina asked, lightly, aiming and missing again, just as she had always missed when she would ask about playing the Boyfriend Game, if Jess had ever gotten her email.

"Umm," Jess said to the outdoors. She pulled in the radio, placed it on her desk, wiped her hands on her jeans. "Yeah, I did. But I figured you would hear from someone else that I was fine. And I was still pretty mad at you then."

Wind blew in through the open window. Mad enough that the anger wasn't overwhelmed by the worst disaster of their lives? For all the nights of the year that followed 9/11, Nina found the path to sleep obstructed by a new law: she had to concentrate on everyone she loved, their faces, their forms, beaming wellness to them across the miles, or they would die. Her mother, her father, Zachary, their grandparents, aunts and uncles, cousins, people from high school, even the ones she hardly spoke to anymore, and of course, Jess, each figure stepping forward from the wings to be spotlit in her nighttime mind, bathed in her goodwill, and therefore spared.

Jess shoved shut the window. "So," she said, "what's your big idea?"

Nina pulled one of the tapes from her bag. "Play this."

Jess looked at the label on the cassette, on which was written in fourth-grade scrawl, *N&J IN DREAMLAND*. "Where did you find this?"

"At home. Long Island."

Jess slid it into the tape deck. "I'm kind of embarrassed to hear what nerds we were," she said, but pressed play. Jess's voice of thirteen years ago fuzzed out from the ancient speakers, reading about hauntings. *"It says there are resid—residual and intelligent haunts."*

"What's that mean?" Nina heard herself say.

Jess shook her head slightly. She brought a finger to her mouth, chewed on it a little. "That's not you, you know," she told Nina. "That's me. We were switched for this."

On the tape their girlish voices went on. Nina hadn't remembered; she had fooled even herself. She had grown to resent, in her childhood, the people in her life who never recognized when they were not themselves. She resented especially her mother, for not seeing even once that the girl she had carried inside her body was now in the body of another.

"Should we say it?" came Jess's voice, and again Nina heard the recitation of the poem. When it finished Jess reached over and pressed stop, the last words of it echoing, the childish seriousness of them like something astringent in the air, making Nina's eyes water. If she closed them she could see the outlines of what had been their fantasy kingdom. Jess exhaled a long streamer of breath from between her lips.

"Did you feel that?" she said.

Nina opened her eyes.

"There was this weird vibration," Jess said. "Like when you're standing on the street and a subway goes by beneath you."

"I'm not sure," Nina said, but then it came, a sensation like all her organs thrumming, like glasses in a cabinet chiming together during an earthquake, there and gone. Was that it, the ejection of her father's spirit, or whatever piece of him had managed to linger on this level of existence long after the rest was gone? There had never been a whisper, not a stir, when they touched their foreheads together, when the exchange took place; what flowed out of each girl and into the other had no weight at all. Had she truly felt, then, his departure from within the radio to—*out there*? It was not unlike the candle room, an idea Jess pulled from the ether and molded into something real, something Nina, too, might inhabit.

Jess picked up the radio and weighed it in her hands, put it back down and ejected the tape. "Here," she said, returning it to Nina. "I don't want to hear this ever again."

***

By Christmas Eve the messages from Avi were coming daily. Once he tricked her into answering by calling from a different number.

"What did you tell the other students?" he said when she picked up.

She was minding Scarlett, the child asleep and nestled warmly in her stroller as Nina pushed it up Ninety-First Street. The anger in his voice struck a note of such discord she was frozen by it. "Who is this?"

"I know you told them something to make them stop coming," Avi said. "You think you're hurting me, but you're only hurting yourself. And them. It's just astonishingly selfish, how you're determined to drag everyone else down with you."

She was tempted to hurl the phone down into the cellar of a restaurant as she passed, but instead snapped it shut and tucked it into her back pocket. She reasserted her hold on the stroller, squeezing to stop her hands from shaking.

***

Nina had declined her parents' offer to come home for Christmas; they didn't celebrate it anyway, and she'd thought she might relish the sense of the city emptied out. But now Eleanor was gone, and Jess was spending the holiday with Anita and George, and she was alone in the apartment with the air of Avi's ferocity all around her.

She could call Jess, hop on a train and stay over at Anita's with her, but then she'd have to admit why she was so afraid: that she hadn't, as she'd claimed she would, handled the situation with Avi at all.

Instead she went out. Walking the blocks frozen into silence felt safer than hanging around the apartment. Eventually she found she had reached the same bar she'd gone into the night they switched and Jess went to Avi's class. Through the windows she could see it was decorated flamboyantly for the holidays, which only made it all the more divey, cheer plastered over the grime of decades. A few figures sat at the bar, shoulders hunched around their drinks. She went in.

Nina saw immediately that one of them was Gregory. Though of course he would not recognize her, his familiarity was a beacon, and she slid onto the stool beside him and ordered a tequila and soda again.

"Merry Christmas," she said, and he returned the greeting, but cursorily, no gleam of interest in his eyes this time.

"I'm Nina."

"Gregory."

"So why are you spending Christmas Eve here?"

Was that a small sigh of resignation she detected? "Just couldn't swing the flight home." He snapped his fingers in mock disappointment. "You?"

"Jew," Nina said, and this at least got a small chuckle. She sucked down the drink. Fear, and tequila, made her giddy. "I thought it might be nice, staying here, like having the whole city to myself, but now I'm not so sure."

He nodded, shared a brief but meaningful glance with the bartender. All her magic was gone. Outside of Jess, as her plain old self, she was nobody. Still, it was the safest she'd felt in days, and she pressed on.

"I'm sorry if I'm bothering you. I just didn't want to be alone tonight."

"It's fine." He'd decided, perhaps, that this would be his act of Christmas charity.

"So what do you do?"

"I'm a poet," he said, "unfortunately."

She nodded and forced herself to fall silent for a few moments. Then she said, "I don't know a lot about poetry, but there's this one in particular I've always loved."

"Oh?"

"You'd probably think it's lame, though."

"Try me," Gregory said, and signaled the bartender for another.

Nina had looked them up, of course, those burning words he'd recited at her. "It's called 'The Windhover,' by Gerard—"

The change was immediate and complete. He clamped a hand around her wrist. "You're kidding."

"No?" she said, and infused the syllable with nervous uncertainty.

"That is," Gregory said, "my all-time favorite fucking poem."

"Seriously?" Nina said, and stared back into his pool-blue eyes, and let their waters envelop her.

8
SLEEPOVER
(1993)

One afternoon in May, the end of the school year finally looming, Jess asked Nina if she wanted to have a sleepover. Nina assumed she meant that weekend, and was ready to suggest hosting it at her own house; when she stayed over at Jess's, the gateway to sleep retreated further from her than usual. The house's creaks and sighs were of a foreign vernacular, its rituals awry. Rob did not greet Sunday with a morning walk and a return home carrying a brown sack of bagels, as her father did; instead he often sat on the back porch in a spot of sun, sipping from a mug of coffee in hostile silence.

But, Jess clarified, she meant sleep over at each other's houses. She meant switch for the longest stretch of time they had yet. And she meant right now.

The bell rang. Nina scrambled for a reason not to—an obligation, something Jess could not convincingly navigate—and found none. They both, somewhat dismayingly, had everyone convinced. Nina nodded. They pressed their foreheads together and it was done.

"Have fun!" Jess told her, and stepped into the hall, into the swirl of students heading for the front door.

"Wait," Nina said. She jogged after her. "What if we can't switch back?" she said, when she caught up. They were outside now, Jess striding toward Nina's school bus.

"Why wouldn't we?"

"We've never gone this long before."

"Nina," Jess said, quietly, so no one else could hear. "It's our superpower. We can do whatever we want." Then, brushing a strand of blond hair out of her eyes, she smiled. "This isn't your bus."

***

In Jess's driveway, Rob was shooting hoops; the clatter of the basketball against the board sounded down the street. The dark hair on his arms was damp with sweat.

"Care to join me?" he said.

Nina shook her head. She rarely saw Jess interact with him, had nothing to go on. Silence, distance was the best approach.

Rob hurled the ball upward again, this time sinking it. "Suit yourself."

Inside the house there was no trace of Anita, and Nina wondered if she had a long shift today. Jess's mother, an OR nurse, worked for twelve-hour stretches, from which she returned either barely verbal or wired from some horror, like a reeking, infected leg stump post-amputation or a patient vomiting cascades of blood. Nina was alone with Rob.

She went up the stairs to Jess's room, sat down at her desk, and found that she, with no premeditation, she'd later persuade herself, was rifling through its drawers. Like muscle memory, like she'd let go the wheel of Jess's body and let it steer itself. In the second drawer, hardly hidden, was a thick, square book with a marbled cover, which could be nothing but a diary.

Had Jess not wanted her to see this, Nina reasoned, she would have stashed it away somewhere more obscure. Perhaps this whole sleepover had been engineered specifically so that her friend could share with her the things she wasn't able to say aloud.

She opened the book and thumbed through its pages as she might shuffle a deck of cards; wherever she landed, Nina decided, she would read, and nothing more, leaving the delivery of the unspeakable up to fate.

The book flapped open, absolutely of its own accord, to February 24. *Dear Katie*, that day's entry began, and a spear of jealousy flew through her before she realized that Katie was Jess's name for the diary, rather than that of some unmentioned friend.

School was boring, the entry continued. *The ground is still all slushy from the blizzared so we couldn't go out for recess. They made us play dodgeball in the gym, I don't like it but I'm pretty good at it.* (This was true; Nina recalled that Jess had nailed Mara squarely in the face on that afternoon.) *Anyway, Rob is taking us to the Pasta Grill tonight so I gotta go. See ya!*

This was so unextraordinary that surely, she should give the shuffling game another try. This time the book fell open to a page midentry.

Asked my mom yesterday and she said he isn't missing he just moved to Santa Fay. I said then where can I buy a Santa Fay phone book to look up all the Garcias? and she said no idea but if I were you I wouldn't bother he isn't interested. I hate to tell you kiddo she said but you deserve to know the truth. I don't believe her. I think she wants me to forget him and pretend Rob is my Dad and always has been but my real Dad is still out there. So he doesn't even know we moved to Long Island and he probably doesn't know me and Nina have been looking for him. What if he's looking for me too? Anita and rob are UGLY. LIARS.

These final two words had been dug with black pen into the lined paper so that their imprint echoed across the subsequent pages. *Out there.* She thought again of David Flores Garcia lost in a horizonless gray void. But the vision was being wiped away by Anita's words; they landed in Nina's heart with the dull thud of fact. Didn't their experiments with telesthesia—which she knew, deep down, was just another game—make her the liar?

She realized that she had read two entries prior to their discovery. What had Jess written about their power? This warranted one more glance, and Nina flipped through the pages again, looking for March 7 and the days after. There was one final written entry, in Jess's slanted letters: *SOMETHING HAPPENED TO NINA AND ME* pressed hard again into the paper, followed by a series of sketches, as though language itself had failed her. Many, it occurred to Nina, studying them, were portraits of Jess herself. Not self-portraits, she thought, but Jess's renderings of her face, the back of her head, the angles of her shoulders, the motion of her feet across the linoleum floors of the school, as seen from the outside, from the vantage she gained while inhabiting Nina. It was a sort of self-surveillance, and Nina felt a plummeting disappointment when she saw that her own likeness was nowhere to be found. The closest Jess came was in her representations of Nina's bedroom, the star and moon stickers pasted onto her ceiling, the sunlight slanting in through her windows as seen from the bed when you woke up in the morning. The drawings were very good, entirely in pencil but so clear that her mind easily did the work of splashing them with the right colors. But Jess had never found this talent worth noting. She had so many, perhaps, that it didn't even rate. Which meant, Nina realized, that she likely had even more hidden abilities, and there might be *another* diary in which there were inscribed still deeper secrets, secrets even underneath the ones they shared together.

And what would Jess discover, if she was doing the same thing right now in Nina's bedroom? Nina thought, envy rising again, that she had no secrets, that Jess already knew everything, that nothing she might read in Nina's diary would arouse any surprise at all.

***

The rest of the evening passed smoothly. Rob boiled hot dogs and they sat eating them on the couch, watching *Roseanne* reruns and trying not to drip mustard onto their shirts. It was easy: Rob made a crack about something the characters had said or done, and then Nina responded with her own, first trying to cultivate particularly withering jokes until she saw that Rob would laugh or give at least an appreciative grunt in response to anything she said. He wasn't so different, she thought, from her own dad, or the boys she and Jess would sometimes tease together, during recess; all they wanted was for you to make it easy for them, to fall into their ebb and flow, and they were so relieved, even grateful, when you did.

Rob was younger than Nina's own father, and trimmer; he had heavy dark eyebrows like Jess's, and could have feasibly been her real dad. She had once overheard Anita tell her mother that they'd met when Rob came to her house in Arizona to repair a leak under the sink. Lying on his back, reaching with a wrench, his shirt had crept up to reveal a set of washboard abs, Anita had said, and *that* attracted her attention. Anita and her mother had laughed then, and Nina lingered by the front door where they stood, baffled, imagining *washboard abs* to be some other kind of tool, and thought one day when she was a woman she might understand their allure.

The living room was growing dimmer. She looked over at Rob again, imagined him slinking out from under the sink, his stubbled face reemerging; as he climbed to his feet and stood tall before Anita, she grabbed his sandpaper cheeks and kissed his mouth.

The credits on a third episode rolled, and Rob said, "Do your homework?"

She had really become Jess, not just impersonated her; she had forgotten it completely, had turned into someone who didn't care.

Rob raised his eyebrows and turned back to the TV. "Your mom's gonna come home cranky as it is. All I'm saying."

"I'll go do it now," Nina said, and he nodded without looking at her. He was a nice guy, she thought, as she ascended the stairs; there had been nothing to worry about.

He didn't come to check on her the rest of the evening, for which Nina was grateful; she wasn't sure how Jess's interactions with Rob were supposed to go without the buffer of *Roseanne*. The house was still as she brushed her teeth and washed her face, as she pulled on Jess's pajamas, smelling of an unfamiliar detergent (but first she had stood, staring in the mirror at her friend's naked form, had started to drift one hand downward just to see, for a moment, if the sensations were the same in this body, when she'd heard the creak of the floor in the hallway as Rob headed to his own room, and jerked into action, dressed herself quickly). The stillness had seeped into her by the time she settled under the comforter, heavier than her own, whose heaviness must also have been like reassurance, because she felt close to sleep already. As she started to drift, Nina thought of the different types of loneliness there were, the loneliness of being among people who couldn't imagine what you were thinking, the loneliness of sleeping on one side of a drafty house with another person on the opposite side, the light coming from your windows' two beams that never crossed, the loneliness of having a dad in a distant city whose name you can't even spell.

***

Anita, eyelids drooping like a sleepy iguana's, warned her to be quick if she wanted to make it to school on time. But Jess wouldn't want to make it to school on time, Nina thought, standing under the shower spray, skidding her soapy hands down her friend's belly (slight protuberance, less than her own), coaxing the apple shampoo into her hair (longer, coarser; it took some doing to untangle). Nina seldom thought much about her own body but now she saw, by comparison, how particular it was.

Now that the end of the sleepover was approaching and she was nearly released from her pantomime, Nina wondered for the first time what Jess was doing. Had she managed to be Nina-like, or hadn't she bothered, trampling over her small kingdom, upending its order?

Anita knocked on the bathroom door. "Jess," she said. "Get a move on."

Hair dripping, Nina returned to the bedroom, in a rush selected an outfit Jess would surely disdain. At the front door, Anita pressed a granola bar into her hand, patted her wet head. "That's a look," she said, surveying her clothes. Nina fled to the bus stop in shame.

***

There was always, would always be, the shock of seeing herself; in some lower compartment of her mind, Nina never grasped that she had ceased, for the world, to be Nina. When she got to the classroom, Jess, in her, was already seated at her desk, smiling slightly into the distance, a knowing smile.

"Hey," she said, as Nina approached, and stood up. They touched their foreheads together, returned to their rightful places. The smile traveled with Jess. She ran her hands through her damp hair.

"Everything was fine," she said. "Your mom made spaghetti and meatballs."

"Rob made hot dogs."

"I'm glad I missed that."

"Did anyone notice anything weird?"

Jess shook her head. "I was just like you! I even finished my homework before dinner." She smiled again. "Zach and I watched MTV. I wish I had cable."

"I was just like you, too," Nina said. "I did my homework late."

Jess laughed. "Bad girl," she said, shaking her index finger.

***

What Nina learned then—and what she'd learn again, in a few years—was that once you granted a person access to something, they assumed it was perpetual, for good. Once you kissed a boy, or let him suck your nipples, or slide fingers inside you, you could not then say you no longer felt like doing these things, that a door had creaked briefly open but was now closed. A forever had emerged, a forever of tolerance, of teeth-clenching and waiting for it to end.

So it was with sleepovers. A once-a-week swap, Jess argued, wasn't much; in fact, it was barely anything. They knew now that they wouldn't get stuck, wouldn't be caught, so why not embrace the variety, the freedom, even, of stepping out of their homes, their lives? They had been gifted this power (by whom, Nina wondered), and it was wasteful not to use it.

She resisted only weakly, because within her resistance was the implication that would only strengthen Jess's argument: that Nina's house was better, her family better, so much so that she preferred tedium and routine to adventure, exploration. Were this the case, then it was Nina's duty to share, just a little.

But over the weekly swaps, the losses quickly began mounting. What Nina missed: An outing to see *Jurassic Park*, which everyone at school, too, had seen, and which she then had to feign knowledge of when Zachary did an impression of a velociraptor, hopping around the dinner table snapping his jaws as their parents laughed; staying up late with her dad to watch the Canadiens beat the Kings in the Stanley Cup ("I have no horse in this race," Jess reported Nina's father saying, which confused her); a night her mother made lasagna, Nina's favorite; the development of an elaborate code of knocks on the wall that divided her room from Zachary's, so they could communicate after they were supposed to be asleep.

At Jess's, it wasn't bad, exactly, but it was more solitary, which Nina supposed she didn't mind: there were open expanses of time to read, to daydream. One night, Anita gave her a gift, an incense burner with fuzzy, fragrant sticks, and showed her how to use a hot pink lighter to ignite them. Nina liked to lie on her back on the floor and watch how the smoke curled toward the ceiling, to manipulate it by slowly trailing the sticks through the air. And she got to know Rob better, even went so far as to shoot hoops with him. After teaching her how to play Horse one afternoon, he'd briefly thrown an arm around her shoulders and said, "I'm glad we're finally getting along." (The next morning in class when she informed Jess of this, that she was becoming friends with her stepfather, Jess had frowned and refused to reveal what she had done at Nina's house the night before.)

Nina was vigilant for evidence of Rob's supposed villainy, and found none until one Wednesday in late June, the final week of school. Anita, he told her that evening, was having a Girls' Night with her friends. To honor Jess's resistance to friendship with her stepfather, Nina retreated to her bedroom when she got home, inventing an end-of-the-year project to work on. Then another dinner in front of the television, during which Nina joked less, and Rob cast frequent glances her way, and she went back upstairs. Lying on her back in Jess's bed, Nina wondered, bitterness pooling in her chest, what she could be doing instead of pretending to dislike this man, perhaps even wounding him. The sour feeling expanded as she thought of how her own parents never noticed anything, neither the swap nor the return; they saw in Nina only perfect continuity. All their claims to knowledge of her, to having borne witness to her particular, special self bobbing to the surface like a lily pad on a lake, from babyhood to today, were invalidated. What did they know, if they didn't have an inkling when she wasn't there at all?

That night, suffused with abandonment, she couldn't sleep. It was past midnight when she heard the front door open and Anita's heels clack across the floor. Then voices, initially just below discerning, then lifting until Nina, now sitting up and straining, could catch several distinct words. She heard Rob say *slut*. It was Nina's first encounter with the slur; it certainly wasn't in the *Compendium*. But she gleaned in it something nastier even than the taste of the number nine.

Anita's reaction confirmed this. "You son of a bitch," Nina heard her say. Her heels clacked again, then something scraped across the floor, something fell with a thud.

"Shit," Rob said. "Anita." There came a moan that sounded inhuman. Her parents' own arguments had never ended in such a noise. The moan pitched upward and became a wail. She could call her mother, Nina thought (she was now at the bedroom door, her right ear pressed against it), and confess everything—surrender, be released from this house and this power.

There was a knock on the door. Nina lurched back to bed. She was trying to arrange herself under the covers when Rob came in.

"Jess," he said. "Your mom had an accident. We gotta take her to the ER."

Nina sat up in bed.

"Get dressed."

He left, closing the door behind him. Nina got to her feet in the dark. Her legs disappeared beneath her; she stood on columns of air. She pulled on Jess's pair of Converse, the pink ones with paint splatters that Anita found on a trip to the city, that everyone in Ms. Brandon's class, no matter how they felt about Jess, admired.

Downstairs, Anita sat curled over the kitchen table, her face puckered, outlined from eyes to chin in mascara trails. She cradled her right arm against her, glanced up at Nina and then away. Nina thought of the words carved into the journal. Ugly liars.

"Ready?" Rob said to Nina. He helped Anita to her feet, her wince deepening as she moved. Outside, all the other houses were asleep. A haze of gnats glowed under a streetlamp. Anita yelped once as she got into the car, then leaned her face, eyes shut, against the window, breathing hard. Nina slid into the backseat behind her, and as Rob pulled out of the driveway she watched Anita's silhouette, rigid and unreachable, flicker against the dim scenery through the windshield.

Over the course of the short journey Rob delivered a fractured monologue to his wife. "I swear to God," he said. "You were coming at me. What was I supposed to do? I think it's dislocated. You're gonna be fine. Once they pop it back in you'll feel so much better. Happened to me once when I was ten or eleven. Tomorrow it'll be a million times better."

"Jesus Christ," she hissed through her teeth.

"Fucking kills, right?" Rob patted Anita's uninjured arm gingerly. They passed the 7-Eleven, the only place in town that appeared to be open, glowing with icy light. Nina wished she could be there instead, with the lone clerk, mopping, barricaded by bright aisles.

***

Rob said they were lucky they didn't have to wait long, that they were probably taken back so soon because the nurses saw what a quick fix Anita's arm was. It might have been even sooner, he added, had they gone to the hospital where she worked, but in the car Anita insisted they drive on to the next town. They were brought to a kind of holding pen, curtained in hospital green.

Anita patted her bed for Nina to sit down, and spoke to her for the first time. "Honey," she said. "I'm sorry you have to see this."

"Jess, there's nothing to worry about," Rob said. "Your mom's gonna be fine."

The curtain drew back and a nurse with thick black hair, glossy as sealskin, came in. "Ms. Garcia," she said. "So you're thinking dislocated shoulder?"

"I'm almost positive," Rob said.

The nurse smiled at Nina, perched on the edge of the hospital bed. "And how did this happen?" she said.

"I slipped on the kitchen floor," Anita said.

The nurse's smile thinned. "I need to take off your mom's shirt to examine her," she said to Nina. "Do you guys mind giving us a little privacy?"

She followed Rob back to the waiting room. A clock on the wall said it was 3:15 a.m. Her brain had turned to water, her thoughts sloshing in circles, slippery as fish. She saw Jess in her bed, sleeping, spared; her parents upstairs, her father snoring, her mother dreaming, cradled in the certainty that their children were under their guard, were safe.

"She came at me swinging," Rob said. "I just grabbed her to make her stop."

He was staring ahead as usual, speaking to the wall rather than to her.

Nina stared at his profile as she had many nights, outlined in the glow from the television screen, and then the venom came bubbling up, brushing her lips. "My real dad would never do this," Nina said.

A vibration passed under his stubbled chin. Rob leaned forward a little and put a hand over his eyes. "I swear to God," he said again. "I love your mom to death."

He made a weird honking sound, and Nina realized he was crying. She had never seen her own dad cry, seen any grown man's solidity dissolve. The other people in the waiting room didn't react; they sat stonelike in their plastic chairs, hunched against their pains.

Unnerved, she stood up. "I have to pee," she said.

In the bathroom mirror, Jess looked back at her, brown eyes wide. "That isn't me," Nina said, of the girl reflected there, but neither was the voice that declared this.

***

The sun was coming up when they left, Anita's face unpuckered, her arm folded in a white sling. In the car, she became talkative, recounting how before the nurse reset her arm, which had indeed been dislocated, she'd given her a drug that transported her to outer space.

"I was floating and there was all this broken glass around me," Anita said. "And I could see your face, Jess, between the shards of glass, but I couldn't reach you."

Rob chuckled.

"Can you believe people do that for fun?" Anita said. She turned in her seat. "Jess, promise me you'll never take that shit."

Nina thought of the skunky green marijuana in Rob's dresser. "I promise," she said. She was so close now to returning to herself, separated from school by only an hour or two. All she had to do was stay awake enough not to slip, not to say something Jess would never say.

"You can stay home today, hon," Anita said. "You must be exhausted."

"School year's almost over, anyway," Rob said, as though there was no reason this conversation might be anything but ordinary.

Tears rose, flooding her throat. "No, I need to go. I need to see Nina."

In the front seat, Anita and Rob glanced at each other.

"Okay," Anita said slowly. "Of course, baby. Just, maybe you don't need to tell her all the gory details about what happened." She looked at Nina in the rearview mirror and lifted her wounded arm a little. "I'm all better now, see?"

Nina blinked away the blurring in her eyes.

"My sweet girl," Anita said. "You like to pretend that you're not, but I know."

***

Nine was to blame, Jess argued, foul number nine; the whole year was poisoned. It was recess and they were sitting at one of the picnic tables, its plastic latticework scarred by cigarette burns.

Jess had responded to the news of the night before with a strange animation, sitting up taller at her desk, shaking her head. "I knew it," she said. "I knew something like this would happen before I turned ten."

Nina, back in her body, had been too tired to respond. The exhaustion traveled with her. The bell rang, and Jess turned to face the front of the classroom, still shaking her head as you might at a dog that had made a mess.

"It'll be better soon," Jess told her now. "My birthday is only three months away." She began to tell Nina about her plans for the party, which she wanted to have at Adventureland; she knew Nina didn't like roller coasters, but maybe if she switched and tried one in Jess's body, it would feel different, she would experience not her usual nausea but a soaring, a detaching from the Earth.

Having a September birthday was one lucky thing, Jess continued; it being the beginning of the school year, the students all shuffled into new rooms, there was no expectation that she invite her whole class. She could pick and choose. She wanted Zachary to come, Jess said, since he was starting to feel like her brother, too. She hoped that she and Nina ended up together again, which would be easier for their switching, of course.

The trees leaned over them, creaking under their green burdens. Nina's tiredness was a fog she couldn't see to the end of.

"I don't want to switch for a while," Nina said. "I want—a break."

She braced for an argument, jeers about her timidity, but Jess just blinked.

"Oh," she said. "For how long?"

Nina shrugged. Jess looked down, started trailing her fingers over the picnic tabletop.

"Can't we go back to some of the old games?" Nina said. "Like the candle room? We haven't gone there in forever."

Farther down the blacktop, a group of boys had wrestled themselves into a churning heap, and the adults, one afternoon from release to summer break, just let them.

"There's some stuff you need to know," Jess said after a while. "Zachary and I added some new knocks to our knock code. And your dad started teaching me some hockey moves, so act like you remember if he asks you to play."

"Okay," Nina said. An urge washed over her to retract what she'd said, but then she thought of Anita hunched in the kitchen, Rob crying in the waiting room. She and Jess fell silent, not one of the warm silences that sometimes enveloped them like a quilt. They'd each settled deep within themselves, into private pockets, out of reach. Then one of the adults blew the whistle that meant they all had to go back in.

9
DEEP DOWN
(2006)

Gregory had a flaw in his left eye, a spot of brown embedded in the blue. When he was hired to teach composition at a private Catholic college in Brooklyn, Nina imagined his female students crowding into the front row of the lecture hall to better see it, to track over the ninety minutes the movement of that dark speck, praying to Jesus it might come to rest on them. He assured her no one found him nearly as entrancing as she, and the thrall was mutual. Perched on his mattress, midkiss, he'd pull back, smooth her hair and frame her face in his hands, with the delicacy with which a surgeon might cradle a donor organ. Then he'd shake his head a little and turn away. Nina knew her beauty was not blinding. She didn't know what he was seeing that was too much to look at for long. He had found something in her even Jess could not find.

Now she understood what Jess had felt that last year of high school, what must have seemed to her the violence with which Nina destroyed it. Now she saw again Jess waiting in the hallways for him to pass, the agonizing thrill when he noticed her and smiled, the charge of meaning through her days.

Nina lost ten pounds. As she was pushing Scarlett's stroller through slush one morning to the Natural History Museum, her jeans slid down her hips and a motorist honked his approval.

Jess said she felt the difference when they switched, a new insubstantiality in Nina's core. She asked if Nina was starving herself for this new boyfriend. The truth was she was too electrified much of the time to eat. A few bites and then her stomach seemed to shrivel around the food. She lived on something else. She wanted to tell Jess what was happening with Gregory, how the fulfillment of lying beside him in bed flipped over into gnawing as soon as they parted. And terror, too, that this might be punctured by her failure, say, to understand one of the poems he sent her, his own and those of others that, presumably, communicated something essential about the two of them but remained to her hieroglyphic.

Nina delayed their meeting for as long as possible, until finally over the phone one evening Jess asked, "Who is it you're embarrassed by—me or him?"

A blush overtook her. "It's not that," she insisted. She couldn't confess, of course, to her dread that Gregory would remember Jess and realize she was the one he'd sparked with first, immediately and naturally. That it was her he was looking for when he held Nina's face in his hands and peered into it.

But when they met, very late at a bar after Jess finished at the steakhouse, there was no recognition in his eyes. He'd been drinking for a while—had been drinking for a while, as well, the night Nina kissed him with Jess's mouth—and perhaps his memory of the encounter had been scoured away by alcohol. They quickly fell into conversation about their work, Gregory's poetry and Jess's photography, the frustration of trying to steal time for it between shifts and lesson-planning, the indignity of having to commodify the uncommodifiable. Nina watched, eyes flicking back and forth to catch the charge of attraction the moment it flared between them, but it never came. He'd been drawn to *her*, she reminded herself, to the Nina inside Jess, not Jess alone. But maybe that was the problem. Maybe now he was hunting for the Jess inside Nina, and each of them had irrevocably left her residue within the other, and neither could any longer stand on her own.

***

And maybe that was the unsaid *thing* inside their arguments. It was always the same argument, unfolding in varying shades of severity.

"I'm a failure," Gregory told her. "A nobody." They sat in plastic weather-stained chairs on the shitty rear patio of his apartment building, legs tucked under themselves to avoid the rodents that started scurrying after dusk fell. They drank wine and filled the ashtray balanced on Gregory's lap. There was always an air of humid dissipation to their time back here, to their conversations that opened a wormhole from the drab yard into the infinite.

"You're too young to be a failure!" Nina said. She tried to keep her voice light. "You haven't been at it nearly long enough to make that kind of declaration."

"I keep submitting and getting rejected. That's the definition of failure. Literally, I'm failing repeatedly at my goals."

She knew he saw himself this way, for the reams of unpublished work, the time wasted grading freshman papers, pen poised over them like a syringe, for barely a minimum wage, each red mark pushing him further from recognition. But she wondered whether his sense of defeat sprang in fact from another source, from an unspoken inkling there was something absent from their relationship. If *she* were not the ghost, the nobody.

"Maybe," Nina said, "it's just a matter of changing your metrics for success."

He lit another cigarette and squinted at her through the smoke. "You don't know what it's like to bang your head against the wall, year after year."

"There have been plenty of times I didn't get what I wanted."

"This isn't like a *pizza*, Nina," he said. "It's not like, oh, man, I could really go for a slice, but the *pizzeria* is closed."

It was in these moments the truth came hurtling into her, that their relationship proceeded from false premises. "Is that what you think," she said, "that my desires are so fucking basic? Like I'm a simpleton compared to you?"

"Where did I say that? Please, tell me where I said that."

Their arguments traced wild trajectories. First, the spiral into minutiae: each deconstructing the other's previous, loathsome statement, then the other disputing the analysis, the initial conflict abandoned, receding hopelessly to the horizon. Then, the explosion into macro: none of it mattered, the nitpicked phrasings, the injured feelings; they'd be dust soon, Gregory argued, the nonexistence to come rendered all hurt absurd. And finally the meta: Then why do anything at all? Nina asked. Well, Gregory would say, you gotta do something.

This was the point at which she might leave, the implication that partnering with her was only maybe better than nothing. She stormed out more than once, but always went back. The farther she walked, the more the anger that had borne her outward shriveled to a gnaw in her chest, returning the only method of relief. He'd be waiting at the door to enfold her in his arms. She might cry, then, at the sense of rightness returning to her body. There would be a dissolve into laughter, into bed. They'd joke later, the bloom of self-awareness returning, about what they had said, perversely delighted by their own ridiculousness. By the time she left his place, or he hers, all that acrimony was only a dream, and she would stand on the stoop and watch him disappear down the block and be seized by something like grief.

***

"Are you sure you're eating?" Jess asked a few days later. They were drinking margaritas in Nina's overheated living room. The window was open and the curtains pushed back, and passersby on the sidewalk kept glancing in.

"I'm telling you, it's not like a deliberate thing," Nina said. "You have nothing to worry about." She felt compelled, still, to keep concealed much of what was underway between her and Gregory. It seemed she should hover over it, sheltering it with her body. Once, walking with Jess, stopped in her steps by the flush that came with one of his messages—*You are my girl*, he had written—Jess snapped the phone away from her and read what was on the screen and then shook her head, handing it back, saying, "I can't believe this."

But now Jess was distracted. She smiled at Nina as she spoke but behind the smile she was far away. She kept looking at her phone. Finally, she confessed, "It's been thirty-six hours."

"What was the last message you left?"

Jess cocked her head to the side, reassuming a mantle of outrage. "I told him he was a fucking asshole."

"So maybe that's why you haven't heard back?"

She looked out the window, her jaw thrust forward. "But it's true. He only wants me around when it's convenient for him. And then I'm supposed to just drop everything?"

"So don't. Don't go running to him."

"I don't 'go running,' Nina." She turned back to her with an expression of such disgust that Nina flinched, for a moment sure Jess would throw her drink in her face. Instead she exhaled, set the glass down on the floor. "Where's Eleanor?" As though, Nina thought, her roommate might have something better to offer in the way of understanding, of sympathy.

Nina tried to swallow her unease. "She's out somewhere with Chase. She's never around these days."

"You know she's picked up his habit," Jess said. She pressed a thumb against her right nostril and sniffed.

Nina had not known. She congratulated herself on having the wisdom to avoid a Khaled, a Chase, the self-worth to fall for someone who had also fallen for her.

"What do you think she sees in Chase?" Jess asked.

"Maybe he seems glamorous to her."

"If she thinks that's glamorous, that's fucking depressing."

"Maybe he's good in bed." She was pulled in easily, always, to the nasty thrill of gossip, the way it walled off its targets. A border rebuilt itself around her and Jess.

Jess snorted. "No way. He probably has coke-dick. You know that's a thing, right?"

"I thought it made you always ready to go."

Jess shook her head. "Who do you think is the best in bed, out of all our boyfriends?"

"Well, I guess Chase is immediately ruled out. Because of the coke-dick." Nina pronounced it slowly, to make Jess laugh, to make her proud of opening Nina's eyes to the world yet again.

Jess picked up her drink and took a long swallow, watching Nina through the bright liquid at the bottom of the glass. "What if we switched to find out for sure?"

A coldness enclosed Nina. "What do you mean?"

The corners of Jess's lips curled upward. She watched Nina's reaction coolly, as a scientist might observe a specimen.

"Wouldn't that be—" Nina began. She saw Jess enter Gregory's sparse bedroom, sail past the sagging bookshelves, approach the bed. Swing one lean leg over Gregory to straddle him. Then, she thought, then— he would remember. There was a scrambling in her head. "Wouldn't that be like rape?"

Jess squinted at her. The line between her eyebrows deepened, the line that appeared when she was denied something. "I wasn't being serious, Nina," she said. "Jesus. What kind of person do you think I am?"

"I'm sorry," Nina said. "I didn't think you really meant it."

"I have no interest in fucking your boyfriend." Jess lifted her glass again and drank from it. "You know I don't like short guys."

Nina forced a laugh. "I never cared about height," she said. "I don't even really notice it." She felt an urgency to move forward in the conversation, like the urgency to step away from the source of a foul odor; like the urgency to see Gregory, look again for the brown spot in his eye, when they had to be apart.

"Obviously." Jess seemed to relax, soothed by her own barbs. She let her head fall back against the couch. "So," she said. "Do you ever hear from that cult guy?"

She knew his name was Avi, though she would never say it. His pursuit of Nina was flagging, although not entirely; in occasional emails that sent her heart plunging he claimed she still owed him several hundred dollars in drop-out fees, demanded to know how it felt to have surrendered to the sick tug of ego. *Why*, he asked in his most recent message, *are you so determined to drag everyone else down with you?* But she couldn't unburden herself to Jess about Avi any more than she could about Gregory. At last she had her own trove of secrets.

"You know," Jess said, "whatever that guy told you about finding your true self or whatever. Just because we invent our personalities doesn't mean they're not real."

"I know that." It was imperative she make clear she was free of his grip. "But what about what we really are, deep down?"

"No such thing," Jess said. "There's only what you do, and what you don't."

***

A distance formed between them. They were swirled into the vortices of their new relationships; Nina had little time for anything beyond Gregory and her feelings for Gregory, ballooning inside her, pushing against her borders. One day at work, Jess snooped on Khaled's computer and found a flirtatious email from someone named Celeste. She pursued him, shouting, into the darkroom, upturning pans of developer, and was fired. After they made up he promised to keep mentoring her privately, help her get a start freelancing.

Nina, for the first time, had a passion, an aliveness that matched Jess's. Her love for Gregory ate at her, a pleasant erosion, as she rode the subway, as she played with Scarlett on the living room floor. Was Jess having the same experience? When she fought with Khaled in the darkroom, had she felt, as Nina did during fights with Gregory, that she had stepped outside her body and stood watching in bewilderment? It nagged at her, the separation that had materialized the afternoon they sat drinking on Nina's couch, how it seemed to hold things unspoken, not just from the past few months of their reunion but their entire history, and was, with each passing moment, swelling to an expanse too wide to be breached.

"There's no place here for people like us," Gregory said, gesturing toward a cluster of silver high-rises. They had met for a drink in

Williamsburg after one of his comp classes and now were walking along the East River. Gregory was sitting at the bar when she arrived and wouldn't say for how long. Now there was a waver in his step. The waterfront was punctuated by cranes, bent over dust-choked construction sites in a manner that looked almost motherly. "Look at this," he continued. "Who do you think is going to live in these buildings?"

"Bankers?" Nina guessed.

"If you're not great at making money, if that isn't your whole purpose, then get the fuck out," he said, speaking, she assumed, as the city itself. Nina thought of saying there was more to New York than that, but she wasn't sure what, exactly, and Gregory seemed to have an outsider's clarity on it all. He'd been an Air Force brat, his father's assignments bouncing the family from Texas to Florida to New Jersey and even to Aomori—that's in Japan, he'd told Nina, and she said she knew, she had lived there once, to prove she was no provincial either.

"Let's get something to eat," Nina suggested, hoping it might elevate his mood. When Gregory was walled off from her by his own black thoughts, she grew more keenly aware of the fact that she had manufactured their relationship, that its genesis relied on trickery.

But when was that not the case? What didn't begin in concealment—and then, slowly, the obscuring layers peeled back . . .

Up on Bedford, her train of thought was halted by what she saw through the streaked window of an anonymous pizza place. It was Avi, alone in a booth at the front, lifting a steaming slice to his mouth.

It was like a bad dream, Nina frozen across the street; if he looked up he'd see her. He'd do so any minute now, and then his face would change, and he would make his way toward her with impossible slowness, the slowness of wading through hip-deep waters, and there would be nothing she could do, locked to the concrete as she was, but wait. He had promised he would not be ignored. Her throat felt coated, again, with the thick potion she had drunk. She could taste its rot on the back of her tongue.

They were standing in front of a boutique. "Come on," Nina said, and pulled Gregory inside. The shop seemed to have no theme other than uselessness. Under soft lights were tables piled with porcelain coasters, scented, shell-shaped soaps, thick glass tumblers. Gregory picked up one of these, turned it over to read the price, frowned.

"You want something from here?" he asked. He was trying to arrange his face into an expression of neutrality, but she could see that he was worried she might ask for a present.

"No, no," Nina said, watching the pizzeria. "I'm not into stuff like this. I just have to find a birthday present for my mom."

Gregory relaxed. "Does your mom like . . ." He lifted a piece of fabric. "Thirty-dollar tea towels? What even is a tea towel?"

Nina said, "Something for the bankers." She hoped she was hiding her distraction. Avi emerged onto the street and she noticed for the first time he slouched a little, rounded his shoulders forward in a defensive posture. His long nose looked red at the tip—spring allergies, perhaps; the trees were yawning open, exhaling pollen into the air—and he raised one hand to wipe pizza grease from his lips.

He was just a man from this vantage, neither prophetic nor particularly threatening. Her heartbeat settled down. There was no reason, probably, why she couldn't tell Gregory everything about him. He wouldn't judge her. He might even find her more interesting for her messy muddling-through. He had deep reservoirs of empathy for the most surprising figures: the far-right senator, for instance, who'd been caught trying to pick up a young man in an airport bathroom. Everyone else—Jess, Scarlett's mother, Nina herself—had torn into him, his hypocrisy, with gusto, but when she brought up his name to Gregory, he flinched a little at the contempt in her voice. "Imagine the shame he must have been living with," he said. Sometimes, Gregory told her, when a person stirred in him feelings of disgust, irritation, he would try to remind himself that they were somebody's child. Try to see them as a child.

Now, when she could remember to, Nina attempted the same, to see the senator, Avi, Jess as new to the world, chubby and unblemished, lifting their arms to the people who stood over them, expecting nothing but protection.

Beside Gregory she felt enlightened, literally, a glow starting up inside her. In the boutique she looked at him and smiled.

"Let's get out of here," Nina said.

Back on the street she asked him what he meant when he said there was no place here for people like them—who *were* people like them?

Sometimes there were long silences before Gregory responded. He really *considered*—he took the time. "People who aren't scrambling to figure it all out," he said, "because they know the *it* isn't actually it."

"There is no it," Nina said.

"Doesn't seem to be."

His steps were steadier now, and they walked faster, storefronts streaming past. She thought again of Fudo Myo-o with his noose, dragging his victims to lucidity.

"What if we left?" Nina said.

"You mean New York?"

"And maybe even the country." The statue of the deity had distracted her, at first, from the shrine itself, its swooping roof, a bell hanging like a uvula in the center, as it had for centuries. She wanted to steal him away, somewhere remote, somewhere her life was only hers, only for him.

"Nina," Gregory said. He turned to her, and she found herself staring again into the brown spot in his eye. "I would go anywhere with you."

10
A GUIDE FOR THE PERPLEXED
(1995)

Middle school was when girls began their slash-and-burn campaigns, hacking into themselves in the hopes that something tender and green would sprout from the damage. Many days after lunch Nina would step into the bathroom just as another girl fled it, the acidic fog of vomit suspended in the air. How terrible it was to be confined to one's body, pocked with its bumps and blemishes, emitting its odors and gurgles. The impulse to destroy it, to shove open its heavy doors to the light and set the self free, was to Nina perfectly logical. Her awareness of the flaws in her own form was keen, and she scanned for them constantly, her mind's eye lighting first upon her pillowy breasts, then her oily face, then her translucent skin, the networks of thick blue veins beneath its surface.

Still, she never cut or threw up or starved like the other girls, because that would mean hurting not just herself. Though they had stopped using their power at her behest, a part of Nina wanted to keep her body safe for Jess.

In the meantime she cloaked it as best she could in baggy clothing. But she couldn't escape everyone's notice. After Nina returned from sleepaway camp in late August, Jess took one look at her and noted, "You got boobs."

Nina looked down, and there they were, as though they'd just materialized in that moment, twin bulges beneath her T-shirt.

A boy in homeroom clocked them as well. One morning, sailing past her desk to his friends clustered in the classroom's back corner, he said to her in a voice low and wet-mouthed, "Gimme some of that."

At first Nina thought he meant the granola bar she was gnawing on. She watched in confusion as he joined his group of stenchy boys and began cackling into their faces. Then a girl sitting beside her nudged Nina and told her she was lucky.

"He thinks you're hot," the girl said.

After that initial ingress, each morning brought a new remark from the boy. His name was Jordan Applebaum and he had a face round as an orange, punctuated by red hair.

Another day Jordan stopped before her, planted his palms on his desk, and asked, "Want a Jolly Rancher?"

Thinking this was perhaps a peace offering, Nina nodded.

"Go fuck a farmer," he told her, before erupting in laughter again.

The comments were less come-ons than spasms of hostility. She tried to stay still, silent, sensing that any acknowledgment would only rouse extremer outbursts, like looking a mad dog in the eyes. Sometimes he addressed not her but his friends, spouting vulgarities in a continuous hiss aimed at her back. These boys leered when she entered, when she left. One morning after the first bell she fled the classroom before Jordan could speak to her, telling the homeroom teacher, an old man sunk in near-retirement oblivion, that she needed to use the bathroom. She spent nearly the whole fifteen minutes there, sitting clothed on the toilet seat, watching slivers of girls come and go through the gap in the stall door. Why had she been targeted? And would it be worse if there were some reason for it beyond her discerning, or none at all?

She returned to retrieve her backpack before the second bell and one of Jordan's friends asked loudly where she had been.

"Nina Glass," Jordan answered, "was taking a big old shit." A few faces of distaste from the girls, but laughter from most, even an unsuppressed chuckle from the senescent teacher. That was the one she'd remember best.

A few days later Nina and Jordan entered the classroom at the same time, his arm brushing against her breasts as they passed through the doorway.

"Oops," Nina said.

He turned around. "Oops," he mimicked, slackening his jaw until he looked brainless, until he looked, presumably, like her. "Oops."

His regard was decidedly unlucky, a missile newly launched her way each morning. But probably, eventually, he'd lose interest, she told Jess in the hallway before homeroom.

Jess's nostrils widened and the corners of her mouth sank downward, as though she'd smelled a big old shit.

"It's only going to get worse," she said.

They were a mere three weeks into September. Nina thought of the school calendar, its confederation of days, with despair.

"You have to fight back," Jess said.

But how could she rouse her body, drowning as it was in fabric, to do that?

Jess crossed her arms over her chest. She, Nina knew, was developing her own loathing, of her breasts' smallness, of her thighs, too thick and muscled, of her eyebrows that she claimed were wiry and unruly, which she overplucked into wispy lines.

She said, "Let me help you."

"How?"

"You know how."

Nina had doubts, actually, that they could still do it, especially here, in a place so devoid of magic.

Jess watched someone pass behind Nina. "That's him, right?" she asked. Nina turned and saw the back of Jordan's red head. It was stuffed with plans for her—for the whole year. "It's just fifteen minutes," Jess said. The bell rang. "Come on," she said. "What's the point of having it and not using it?"

Why had Nina cut them off, the two of them, from their gift? There were reasons, she was sure, a reclamation of certain inner territories. But none of it seemed so important now. She closed her eyes and leaned in, right into the old sensation, there waiting for her; she surrendered her self, whatever that was, to its seductive tugging force.

***

She would never know precisely what Jess had done to the boy; she was frustratingly inexact whenever Nina asked. "I told him off," was all she revealed. But the shift was clear the next morning when Nina returned to the classroom. Neither Jordan, nor his friends, would meet her eyes. All around her, in fact, as she lowered herself into the seat, there was a stiffening of bodies, a coming to attention.

She spent the short period soaked in unease. She had been braced for anonymity, punctuated by Jordan's taunts, not this chilly command of her peers. She remembered, now, how after the thrill of uncovering their powers there was always the matter of what they would do with them. A door once closed had reopened.

When she stood to leave, a new boy approached her with an odd formality, one hand extended.

"Nina, right?" he said. "I'm Leo."

She shook his hand in silence, waiting to see whether this might be the prelude to a more unfriendly verdict.

"It was cool," he said, "what you said to Jordan. That guy's such a dirtbag."

"What did I say? I don't remember."

Leo laughed. "Right." He trailed her to the hallway, where Jess was waiting. There was more hand-shaking; Jess looked over at Nina with an unreadable expression as his fingers slid between hers.

Once he parted from them for his next class, Jess clutched at her violently. *He's cute*, she mouthed. Nina looked back at Leo and saw: dark lashes and eyes, the sweeping planes of his face. But she'd had to be alerted to it. Jess had a way of seeing, an eye wide open to the desirable, while Nina was still asleep.

The girls met again at the end of the day, as was becoming their ritual, in the parking lot outside the gym. "What are we going to do?" Jess said.

"What do you mean?"

"To keep Leo interested." Her gaze floated upward, as it had when they were first testing the boundaries of their talent. Something inside Nina nagged like a strained muscle, hesitated. But only for a moment.

Across the street, a man stopped mowing his lawn to stand and eye them with suspicion. Nina remembered the Halloween house by the elementary school, where the owners had only sugar and smiles for children who passed by. Now they'd all gone sour, and the faces of grown-ups, puckered and wary, reflected to them their turning.

When they switched now it was for brief, focused intervals, homerooms in which Nina sat in Jess's classroom, Jess's body, huddled around the knowledge of their new project, aflame with it. As Jess, still flat-chested, she managed to go mostly unremarked upon. There were advantages to this. She could study the other students, hunting for the presence or absence of whatever it was Jess had spotted in Leo, crouching just behind their faces as she crouched within Jess, everyone hiding, little burrowing animals. But no one was hiding a gift like theirs. When they switched, Jess made Nina into someone bolder. She shook down Nina's hair from its ponytail, teased Leo, reported back to Nina on his delighted reactions. She seemed to understand instinctively how to direct Leo's eyes where she wanted, as though this knowledge was written into her genetic code and activated with the onset of middle school.

When they didn't switch, when Nina was herself, she retreated from him. He had to coax her out, which he did mostly through monologuing: about the Smashing Pumpkins' new album, the MTV show *120 Minutes*, the vacuity of the aesthetic preferences of their peers. Afternoons, the girls compared notes in the parking lot. They squatted over the blacktop and recounted their exchanges with Leo, what he seemed to respond to, what he didn't. He disdained conformity. He thought Nina's earrings, which resembled little bunches of grapes, were weird, but he liked her camouflage T-shirt. He painted his fingernails black;

he playfully punched her shoulder when she told him it looked gay. He
was starting a band but needed a bassist.

"You volunteered," Jess told Nina.

"You mean *you* volunteered."

Jess plucked at a weed sprouting through the concrete.

"We don't know how to play bass."

"He's going to teach us, dummy."

Of course, he didn't know there was an *us*; he thought his dealings
were solely with Nina. The aim of this work, of sharing her body to capture Leo's regard, was unspoken; so too was what they'd do once the work
was completed. But better than his heed of her was the high of deceiving him. It used to disturb her that their switching went unnoticed, but
now she felt large with the secret of it, so superior to the secrets of the
other students, like the ones who shared the lot with them, standing in
a clump and passing around a stolen cigarette, their shoulders hunched
over its illicit little flame as if it were something worthy of concealment.

***

They were invited—Nina was invited—to Leo's house for band practice, and she brought along Jess, who skillfully feigned total ignorance
of him. They were ushered past the living room where Leo's father sat
watching television behind a screen of cigarette smoke, up the stairs and
into the bedroom. There they met the other band members, Lars and
Anthony, the first a pale noodle of a boy, the second dark and squat.

"You can practice on this," Leo told Nina, gesturing at a guitar leaning against the wall. "For now we're just doing covers, but eventually
we're going to write our own songs." He spoke to her but was watching
Jess, who leaned, arms folded, against the closed bedroom door.

"What are you?" she said. She looked at him as though for the first time.

Nina was confused, but Leo knew exactly what she meant. "My
dad's from Peru."

Excitement straightened Jess's spine. "Mine's Mexican."

Telesthesia had been dropped, along with many of their other old adventures, somewhere along the path from childhood to here. Now they rarely spoke of Jess's father. For Nina, he had simply stopped existing. For her finding him had only ever been a game, and she glimpsed now the unfinished task to which she had abandoned her friend. Leo nodded and said something to Jess in Spanish.

But Jess had the same amount of Spanish as the rest of them taking the seventh-grade intro course. "This is America, you know," she told him.

"No shit," Leo said. "That's where we are?" The other boys started laughing and Nina saw a flush race along the white line of scalp where Jess's hair was parted. That was how it was with Jess and Leo, from then on: an endless trading of barbs, a simmering just beneath enmity. The boys nicknamed her Psycho Killer, after the song, but she was never barred from the house. Leo knew what he had and it made him magnanimous: not just his own bedroom but his own bathroom, and inattentive parents who let him lock all the doors.

He had, too, a roof you could easily clamber onto, a hot tub on the back patio, stacks of CDs, a guitar, a bass guitar, a ukulele, a tambourine, many pairs of drumsticks, a typewritten copy of *The Anarchist's Cookbook*, and a drawerful of M-80 firecrackers. Band practice was always held at his house, and more often than not it turned out to be more like hanging out in Leo's room, where he introduced them—mostly Nina, because Jess pulled faces of disdain to nearly everything he shared—to different artists: the Velvet Underground, the Dead Kennedys, the Butthole Surfers, Kool Keith, Liz Phair.

"Why don't you listen to anything you can move more than your head to?" Jess asked him. When he spidered his limbs around Nina's, to show her something on the bass guitar, Jess observed with a look like a shove, eyes narrowed to dark gashes and lips slanted to a sneer. Other times she would leave entirely, crawl out onto the roof and perch there until she sunburned. Nina never knew in these moments what had stirred Jess's disgust, Leo or herself or the slow progress of their project, itself undefined; the unknowns accumulated in great drifts around her.

But when they were alone Jess became familiar again. They conferred in Leo's bathroom, lights out, sitting in the tub with their legs steepled, feet against feet. They told the boys they needed space for Girl Talk, and it was where they plotted and also where they switched, pouring themselves back and forth into one another, the bathtub their version of Superman's phone booth. They could linger a long time and not be bothered. The boys kept a respectful distance. Good boys. Or maybe they were busy constructing fantasies of what went on in there, against the cracked shower tile.

"Did you see?" Jess asked Nina one afternoon in October, after engaging Leo in a wrestling match. "He had a boner."

Through the walls came the fuzz of an amp turned on and then guitar blaring through it. "But it's you he'd rather wrestle with, you know," Jess continued. She rapped her index fingers in rhythm against the edge of the tub. "Do you think he thinks about you when he jerks off?"

"How should I know?" And what exactly, Nina wondered, would he be thinking of? What little showed of her body through her voluminous T-shirts and jeans was decidedly unerotic, calves and wrists, dirty sneakers.

Jess said, "He wants you to—" and poked her tongue against the inside of her cheek, the side of her face turned tumorous, bulging outward, then smooth again. "Let's switch now," she said. "My turn to be you."

She closed her eyes and let Jess come to her, let herself be sucked down the funnel out of her body, passing through her troubling flesh and into Jess's. They stood in the tub and looked into their own faces.

"He's going to kiss us soon," Jess whispered, in Nina's voice.

Back in the room, Jess assumed Nina's spot on the floor beside Leo, picked up the guitar. Nina flopped backward onto his bed, stretching out her arms and legs, reaching into the alien length of them.

"Jess," he told her. "Get your nasty shoes off my bed."

Nina sat up. To be Jess here was to be a spoiler, at war with Leo, exiled from his graces. No wonder she handed over her body like an afterthought. This was the pulled-muscle feeling that dogged Nina: that their switching was no longer a sliding into each other's lives, a pushing against the bounds of their respective realms as it once had been when they were children, but only a route to closeness with Leo.

Still, there was relief in being released from his attention. Now it lasered into Jess, tucked away inside Nina's body, and she met his gaze with a dopey expression that Nina found unfaithful.

"Wanna go on the roof?" Anthony asked her, and she nodded. They climbed out Leo's bedroom window and onto the asphalt shingles peeling up at the edges. Anthony pulled a handful of something from the cavernous black pocket of his jeans and showed it to her.

"What is that?"

"Creamers," he said. "Like for your coffee. I stole them from Burger King."

She laughed at him. She didn't know to what extent this mean streak was an invocation of Jess or something all her own. It filled her chest with a feeling like sunlight.

Undeterred, Anthony said, "Watch this," and hurled one of the containers at an SUV passing on the street below. It sailed through the branches of an oak and burst white against the car's sun roof. "Holy shit," Nina said, and laughed again. He looked quickly at her and smiled. The late autumn air bit at them and Nina watched the skin along Jess's arms pucker into goosebumps. "Anthony," she said, "do you ever think of me when you jerk off?"

He reared back, startled. Maybe she'd gone too far, even by Jess's standards. But then Anthony nodded a little. "Yeah," he said, and a blush swam to the surface of his face. She had done that. She had called that up.

He handed her a creamer. "Okay, Psycho Killer. Now you try."

There was a hectic joy in becoming the exile, beholden to no one. She pulled back her arm and threw as hard as she could.

***

The final months of 1995 were filled with chanting. Nina met weekly with Cantor Nussbaum in his office on the second floor of the temple, in the same wing where Hebrew school was taught by ill-tempered retirees and full-time teachers in need of an extra buck. The cantor passed many patient hours with twelve-year-olds who pumped out nervous sweat over pages of Hebrew, at having to lilt their voices along its backward

alphabet. Nina's bat mitzvah, at least, would coincide with an interesting Torah portion—woe to those forced to interpret Mosaic law. Her
verses concerned the golden calf, melted into its bovine form from the
rings and bracelets of the Israelites, who got bored of waiting for Moses
while he wandered the mountaintop amassing commandments. God
caught wind of their worship—He caught wind of everything—and
told Moses, "Now therefore let me alone, that my wrath may burn hot
against them and I may consume them." God with His gaping maw
and infinitely long throat.

"I don't blame the Israelites," Nina told Cantor Nussbaum. The
golden calf, warm and buttery under the desert sun, was clearly prefer-
able to the Lord.

"They're only human," he agreed. "Moses makes mistakes, too. He
throws the first set of tablets on the ground and has to go back and ask
God to write the Ten Commandments again. God made them that way, so
why does He act surprised?" It was hard to muster up much reverence for
Him, here in this office where the smell of old books was a stronger presence to Nina than that of the one who had supposedly made everything.

Cantor Nussbaum leaned back, his head nearly brushing the bookcase,
its shelves sagging beneath loads of must and authority. "Maimonides wrote
in *The Guide for the Perplexed* that God is perfect and therefore unchange-
able. You can't actually change his mind on anything. You can't negotiate.
So why might He lead Moses to believe that he could?"

The cantor liked asking questions that weren't really questions; he
liked sending them, the boys and the girls, into states of puzzlement here
in his book-lined domain, which, it would not occur to them until much
later, was tiny. He watched Nina mulling, satisfaction at how he'd awed
her seeming to pull up the corners of his mouth. (The book they read in
temple during the High Holy Days had, embossed in gold on its cover,
The Days of Awe.) But she wasn't thinking about God's head games with
Moses. She was thinking of her own power. Didn't it suggest that in fact
anything was feasible, the laws of physics merely suggestions, applying
only to those who lacked imagination? If there was body-swapping, why
not telepathy, telesthesia, astral projection, demons, angels, God? And

if He were really there, why had He given this talent to them—as far as she knew, to them alone—and what did He expect them to do with it?

The cantor had a system for teaching her the correct way to pitch her chanting along each line of Hebrew. He highlighted the lines in different colors according to how she was to modulate her voice, and it struck her as a shortcut, a cheat, hot pink or blue dashed with unholy casualness over the ancient letters. All she had to do, really, was remember what each color signified, not the meaning of the words or why they were to be chanted a particular way, which was hardly an accomplishment, hardly made her worthy of being deemed now a woman.

Nina stopped in the bathroom beside the cantor's office on the second floor and sat on the toilet. It was that dead stretch of days between Hanukkah and the new year, and there were no Hebrew School classes in session, no services scheduled for that evening. When she peed the sound thundered in the empty room. Then she looked down and saw: a spattering of rust-colored spots in her underwear that could have been shit but weren't. She wiped. Bright blood, the purest red smeared on paper.

She imagined God peering at her over the lip of the neighboring stall, leering like Jordan. The blood seemed to rise and flood her face, but what leaked from it was water and snot. Nina wiped it away with a starchy nest of toilet paper, then stuffed more into her underwear.

She could hear it rustling as she descended to the ground floor and pushed open the great wooden doors to the sanctuary. There was the musty bookish odor again, and the sweet smell of recent vacuuming; the carpet stretched away to the altar where she stared, eyes blurred by boredom, Friday after Friday. She waited there in the threshold, shifting from foot to foot, for something to come rocketing down from the domed ceiling overhead and strike her. But apart from the noise of paper crunching against her body, blotting up her blood, there was silence.

***

On the drive home Nina realized she had been waiting, foolishly, for her mother to notice the change in her. Instead she spoke of plans for the bat mitzvah celebration, who they could expect to decline the invitations, which had gone out earlier that week; great-aunt Sylvia was unlikely to make the trip up from Florida, she suspected. Nina watched her mother's lips move as she talked. Then her profile hazed over in Nina's vision and the scenery rolling by through the window beyond her came into focus. They turned onto the main road. It was ugly and treeless, dotted with strip malls, and ahead in the gray distance the swelling of the town dump was visible.

She could tell her. She could tell her right now, and her mother would be so happy; she might even pull over and park the car and gather her into an embrace, squeezing her, her daughter, who was growing up. How could she expect her mother to sense it, such a small thing, really, when she had never perceived the times Nina was vanished from her own body, replaced by an impostor?

But no. She would handle it herself. She would tell them she was taking a walk, go to CVS and get what she needed. Do what women did.

11

A GOOD PLACE

(2007)

What was the stuff of a week in Japan? A child biked straight into a telephone pole because he was staring at Nina as she walked to the train station. Heading home late after drinks with Gregory and Charles, she watched a businessman in a gray tailored suit lean over the railing and vomit into the Naka River. With time to kill before her evening Japanese lesson, Nina wandered around the massive stationery store over Tenjin station, contemplated the variety of calligraphy brushes and ink stones, and purchased several sheets of stickers of the official mascots from each prefecture to give her students as encouragement, whenever they dared to raise their hands and answer questions in English class. Fukuoka's was a little girl with a hydrocephalic look and massive, cheerful eyes. As Nina took the elevator back to the street level, a singsong recording called her an honorable customer and thanked her repeatedly.

Then there were the roaches. Nina and Gregory guessed that they were coming up through the drain in her shower room floor. Nina tried covering the opening with the copy of *War and Peace* she'd spent her winter evenings reading, lying on the futon, wrapped in the thick gray quilt that the Canadian who lived in the apartment before her had left

behind. He left, too, a rice cooker, a small vacuum, and a combination
air conditioner/heater with a remote control whose Japanese she'd spent
the first cold night deciphering, trying to switch the functionality to
warm as her breath slowly grew visible, until finally she'd relented and
texted her supervisor. Kimizuka-sensei responded that Nina must press
the button that read 暖房.

At least there were no roaches during Japanese winters. But now,
mid-August, rainy season over, they were somehow managing to squirm
past *War and Peace* and into the apartment from whatever dank drain-
pipe they'd been living in; they were beginning to seem like a curse.
Gregory rarely had any, and Charles swore he had none, despite living
directly beneath her and in much greater squalor. The roaches were the
size of a fat man's thumb, glossy, black, and multitudinous. That night,
upon finding one on the lip of the sink where she intended to wash up,
she sprayed it with poison, which only provoked three of its comrades
to come scuttling forth. Nina held down the nozzle and let loose with
a panicked fusillade before slamming the shower room door and running to the balcony, where she sat smoking a cigarette and crying a little.

Nina called Gregory to ask if he'd come over now. He had told her
he'd be by later, once he finished that evening's writing session, and
though she'd agreed to give him his space, to not put him in the position of resenting her by slicing away at his dedicated work time, the
horror of an infestation seemed a fair reason to renege.

Gregory sighed harshly into the phone. This had been his phobia
first. His family's stint in Florida had thrust the trauma of palmetto bugs
upon him; once, as a teenager, while he was daydreaming on the toilet,
a particularly enormous specimen had plummeted from some unseen
perch onto his bare thigh. He'd written a poem about it. Nina admitted
there was much she pilfered from her boyfriend, out of admiration or
simple osmosis, but she thought developing a parallel terror of roaches
wasn't hard to understand. It had become very much her own thing.

Gregory knocked on the door and she opened it. He entered carrying a grapefruit *chu-hai* and frowning. He didn't bother leaving his
brown loafers in the *genkan*. "*Non serviam,*" he liked to say when Nina

attempted to abide by Japanese etiquette, when she cringed at the sight of his outdoor shoes on her tatami mats.

"Do I really have to do this?" he asked her, standing in the narrow hallway. "I don't like them any more than you do."

"Please," Nina said.

Gregory sighed again and opened the shower room door, flicked the lights on, and scanned the space before stepping in. Nina hung back in the kitchen.

"Looks like you got 'em all," he called. "Paper?"

She handed him a roll of paper towels across the threshold. "There should be four."

"Yup, four."

Nina heard him walk to the toilet room and flush. "Can you get my toothbrush and toothpaste and then close the door again?" she asked.

He brought them into the kitchen. "Are you just never going to go into the shower room now?"

"Not at night," she said. "That's when they come out."

"That seems inconvenient."

"Everything here is inconvenient," Nina said.

Gregory laughed. "Cig?" he said, and she followed him back onto the balcony, into the humid, buzzing night. They sat and let their smoke drift upward into her work blouses hanging damply from the clothesline over their heads. Across the street, the lights of the Kawashoku supermarket switched off one by one. Gregory swigged from his *chu-hai*. Nina wondered what number he was on but didn't ask.

***

Friday night, the school week over, they drank beer in the tiny ramen shop across the street from their apartment building. The proprietor and his wife sat in one corner watching television as they smoked. They were watching a game show in which contestants were challenged to see who could keep the straightest face while riding a roller coaster. The people on the TV squashed their lips together, trying to bite back screams or nausea. Eyes bulged and chins quivered; veins pulsed forth on foreheads. A little box appeared in the corner of the screen, showing the reaction of the host, who had collapsed with laughter.

Gregory told Nina this was the perfect metaphor for life. "We are the contestants and the host is God."

"That's brilliant," Nina said. "I wish I'd thought of it." But it made her nervous, because sometimes when Gregory drank, one dark assertion would beget another, until it was like he'd exhaled a toxic black cloud that settled upon them, though he never seemed to feel any better for ridding himself of it.

She decided to divert the conversation before it could begin its hurtle toward nihilism, and brought up Jess's impending visit. Gregory said he was looking forward to it, because the girls would entertain each other and he could spend the week holed up in his place, writing.

"You're not going to hang out with us?" Nina asked.

"The two of you together—it's a little much," he said. "A person could start to forget they exist at all."

He envied their friendship's long history, something his peripatetic childhood had kept him from sharing with anyone else, but their closeness seemed to unnerve him. "You've really never slept with her?" he asked more than once.

It was true that when the three of them spent time together Nina often elbowed him out of conversations, fearing the moment he'd finally snag on some utterance or gesture of Jess's and recall her as the mystery woman from the bar, the one who received his recitation. And so Jess had not been able to get a handle on him at all, nor on Nina's reasons for expatriating. Before they left she had taken to reminding her, every time they met, that Nina could still back out of this whole Japan thing, that there'd be no real trouble for her or Gregory if they decided to void the yearlong teaching contracts they had signed.

"But I *want* to go," Nina kept telling her. "And I want you to come visit."

"I will," Jess said, "but for the rest of the time, I'm just going to pretend you're dead. It's less stressful that way."

"Me being dead is less stressful?"

Jess had shrugged, glanced away, perhaps already banishing Nina to a distant corner of her mind.

***

But the truth was she couldn't wait to share it with Jess, all of it, starting with the moment she stepped out of her apartment and into the summer heat, thundering with cicadas, into the air that since the end of rainy season had thickened until it felt almost sentient, as though they were living inside the mouth of an enormous animal.

She would explain about the woman that she and Gregory saw on their walk to the train station each morning, whom they'd dubbed Hunchy for the way she leaned over the handlebars of her pink bicycle, which she peddled with stilettoed feet. The woman—tiny, manicured, teetering—looked like a professional pixie, but steered the bike grimly, right into their private language, becoming one of the characters that gave Nina the sense they were building a small world together, standing shoulder to shoulder and peering through its windows, protected and separated from chaos.

That morning, she whirred by just as they were passing the community garden, where a grandmother in an apron bent to yank something from the soil, and Nina said, "In some ways, we are all Hunchy."

"You more so than I," Gregory said.

"I don't know. You're pretty determined."

"But I never forget how absurd it is."

"I forget sometimes," Nina said.

"I like that," Gregory said. They were nearing the station. "It's cute."

They kissed goodbye at the top of the stairs. Nina felt a flare of pleasure, inextricable from relief at getting such a clean start. Today, she could release her mind from his welfare, *their* welfare.

Boarding the train, she thought again of Jess, who would have to depend upon her entirely. Were this Tokyo or Osaka, a monolingual American could navigate okay enough. But Fukuoka was far off the international tourist track; few in the city spoke English, and they were in a suburb where they still elicited almost daily alarm, despite having lived there a whole year. In an entirely new way, Jess would need her.

On the train she tried to see everything anew. She remembered how, in the early days, the landscape through the window had seemed to pulse with her own discomfort; the flooded rice fields alive with insects, the houses humped together on the hills and glowing from their windows like a many-eyed creature. The crows had perched on telephone wire and shrieked at her. She had been rocketed back to infancy. Now, at last emerging from dependence on her few bilingual colleagues, Nina had convinced Gregory to stay on a second year. The first twelve months had been a panicked, fumbling adjustment; now they could actually enjoy it.

How lucky that Jess had seen none of that, that Nina could let her friend think that she had always moved through the days with the fluidity she now possessed.

Nina got off at her stop and walked the blocks to school slowly. Already there was the prickle of perspiration at her scalp and down her back. She passed the soba restaurant and reminded herself to find out why owners put out little piles of salt at the entrances to their shops, in case Jess asked. Inside the school's *genkan* she opened her locker and swapped her outdoor shoes for the indoor ones. During her first week she had come to school in flip flops, and when Kimizuka-sensei saw her changing out of them she cautioned, "You had better not wear those again." Why did her outdoor shoes, which none of the students would see, have to be professional? No matter: this was the way. (Gregory called all of Japanese etiquette, mockingly, Way. "We must follow Way," he'd say to her, when they saw the electrical workers doing morning exercises in unison, in the front yard of the plant, or heard the thwacking sounds of old ladies on balconies beating the dust out of their futons on Sundays.)

You could live inside the absurdity, like Hunchy, or outside it; Nina knew which one was easier. As she ascended the stairs, a group of tenth-grade girls stopped her in the hallway.

"Nina-sensei," they called. "Good morning."

She returned the greeting. They began conferring with each other in rapid Japanese and she waited, aware that her blouse was pasted to her back with sweat. Finally, they reached a decision and pushed one of the girls forward.

"Do you know," she said slowly, blushing, "head, shoulders . . ."

"Knees," another girl offered.

"And toes?" Nina finished. "The song?"

They all nodded.

"Will you sing with us?" the first girl asked.

Nina had used to wonder if such requests were elaborate jokes at her expense, if the students were experimenting with extremes of humiliation to which they could bring their foreigner. But no, the students who dared speak with her appeared thrilled with themselves for their outreach. All her life she had passed beneath notice, her secret locked so securely inside she looked from the outside like no one, like anyone. Here at last she was somebody. So she opened her mouth and began to sing, and the girls joined her, grinning, touching the corresponding body part, and some of them stumbled on eyes and ears and mouth and nose but they soldiered through. It was one of the moments that Nina felt herself pass through the flushed and sticky surface of her skin and hover, watching, looking down on her own life in utter disbelief.

***

These dissociative flashes, these moments of awe and disorientation, she was confident, were not in evidence when she picked up Jess at the Fukuoka airport and herded them into a taxi. "Do you know Murasaki Station?" she said in Japanese to the driver, who gave a little nod. "Oh my God," Jess said as they slid into the backseat. "Who are you?"

"That was nothing," Nina said, but she glowed with pleasure. "Are you completely jet-lagged? Wanna just go back to my place and crash?"

"Hell no," Jess said. In fact, there was not a trace of sleepiness in her face. She swiveled from one window to the next as they drove down the freeway, looking at the mountains huddled together in darkness.

"I've been studying Japanese super hard," Nina explained. "I have to. Like, to survive. The first thing I taught myself were the characters for different foods, so I could identify things in the grocery store."

Jess laughed. She tapped a nail against the window. "What's that?"

"Driving range," Nina said. There were dozens scattered along every Japanese highway, as far as she could tell. There was so much to disclose. Nina knew she had to dole out information in small parcels or risk overwhelming her friend into a glazed half-attention. She told Jess about the *yatai*, which each evening lined up along the river, indistinguishable to her eyes, though some had long lines while others languished, their plastic curtains breezing open now and again to reveal a lone diner. She and Gregory visited one early in their stay—she had read that they were what Fukuoka was known for. (She had researched and researched, scanned guidebooks and message boards.) Inside, clouds of steam hung over broth bubbling in massive vats. The proprietor ladled it into bowls, then swirled in nests of noodles. Nina had gulped back her fear and dared: she pointed and said in her guidebook Japanese, "What is this?" She smiled widely to counteract any brusqueness.

"We've had to accept that we're children again," Nina said to Jess, in the taxi. They were pulling off the freeway. "At first we didn't know how to do anything. It was pretty humbling."

"That's lucky," Jess said. "It's lucky to get a second childhood."

But it was nothing like her first. In her first childhood, there were times she was the opposite of helpless, huge with their power.

"How long has it been?" she asked.

"Fourteen months," Jess said. It seemed they both waited for the other to say she had missed it. Nina thought that switching with Jess was like ducking into a *yatai*, the bright, noisy confrontation with a foreign and self-contained world. It had its rules, its shape, but inside of it you were still you. Jess said, "I'm hungry."

Jess didn't want to stop at the *jutaku* first, so Nina brought her into the yakitori place by the train station, dragging her suitcases behind them. "*Irasshaimase*," the men called as they entered. The men stood behind a long glass counter displaying the options, orderly arrays of meat on sticks; behind it they existed in a chaos of smoke and shouting.

They were roughened versions of the typical young Japanese men Nina encountered, who had coiffed, complicated hair on their heads but nowhere else; these men had shaved heads and stubble, thick arms and solid chests beneath stained T-shirts.

"Let's sit at the counter," Nina suggested, and Jess said, "Obviously."

The one who liked to practice his English came over, smiling a little at the opportunity, and Nina explained, slowly, "This is my friend from America."

"Oh," he said, and nodded. "Why you . . . come Japan?"

"To see her," Jess said.

The man nodded again. "And where is boyfriend?"

"Boyfriend is home," Nina said. She felt Jess's eyes on her face. "He's very tired tonight." She turned to Jess and began explaining the different items aligned in the glass case, crowding out the man's questions in a flurry of ordering. Jess's energy seemed now a bit dimmed by the alien tumult of the place, the team of salarymen sitting on the floor in the corner and bellowing laughter, the ancient man at the end of the bar smoking steadily.

But after a few minutes she picked up the line of inquiry again. "How's everything with Gregory?"

"You know, there's been a lot to adapt to here. But it's never boring. I think we were starting to feel a little stagnant back home."

"Uh-huh."

The old man watched as though he could follow the conversation. When Nina turned to him, he ground out his cigarette in an ashtray and glanced away.

"You can smoke basically everywhere in Japan," Nina said to Jess. "It's a time warp. I kind of love it."

"Since when do you smoke?" Jess said.

***

Gregory's light was on in his apartment, but Nina couldn't make out any movement as they walked up the gravel driveway, tugging Jess's bags. She explained loudly, thinking he might hear and come out to the balcony to call down a neighborly welcome, that they'd been placed in the same building but not the same apartment because of their host schools' old-fashioned reluctance to house unmarried couples together.

"So most of the time we stay at my place," Nina said. "His is like the office."

They headed up the damp, cement stairway. "Don't expect much," Nina said. "It's basically glorified camping." Inside the apartment she explained about the *genkan*, the removal of shoes, adding that they didn't *have* to follow the Japanese rules.

Jess kicked off her sandals. "I want to follow them." She took in the blond tatami mats, scuffed by generations of foreigners, the sliding shoji doors, their paper peeling, the toilet room with its cracked tile, the drooping plants placed hopefully by the windows, the concrete balcony and its view of the supermarket, the hills, the telephone wires, and blinking radio towers.

"I need a shower," Jess said.

"I should warn you . . ." Nina told her about the cockroaches swarming up from the drain, their nightly visitations. But when Jess opened the door and stepped into the shower room there was nothing. It was pristine.

She looked at the deep tub and detached showerhead and back to Nina.

"So, the Japanese are super into baths," Nina said. "They shower outside the tub and then soak in it." She'd been excited to teach, to share, but now she was beginning to feel like a tour guide buzzing over the shoulder of a visitor who took in everything with cool detachment. But Jess said, "That makes a lot more sense than the way we do it," and asked for a towel.

Once she heard the water running, Nina went onto the balcony to smoke and text Gregory. *Jess is here*, she wrote. *She seems a little overwhelmed. It's hard to learn Way!* After a few minutes, Gregory responded. *Haha. I'm making it a point not to learn it.*

"Nina," Jess called, and she felt an icy stab to her stomach: had she seen a roach after all? But when she looked into the shower room she saw, through the steam, Jess immersed to her shoulders in the tub. "Come in with me," she said.

Nina peeled off her clothes, dropped them on the sweating green tile, and climbed in. "The Japanese would be disgusted," she said.

"Yeah, we're basically soaking in your dirt." Jess looked at Nina. "I get why people like this. It's more than just getting clean. You undo the day." She tilted her head back and let her dark hair stream over the side and Nina remembered the days they sat together in Leo's bathtub, in the dark, and it was like the tub was a ship and the boys' voices, on the other side of the wall, washed up against its sides and then slid back into the night.

"You know what?" Jess said. "You have a great rack. I've always been jealous of it."

Nina glanced down at them, floating white pillows coning to pale pink. They struck her as somehow childish. "I've always been jealous of your body," she confessed. "There's nothing extra."

Jess laughed. "That isn't true." She cupped her hands into the warm water and splashed it over her face. Then she stared at Nina again. "Are you doing okay here?"

An answer bobbed to the surface of Nina's mind: *I've never been so lonely in my life.* But was that true? When was the last time she hadn't been lonely? She cast a searchlight over the field of memory: when they were children who had stumbled on a secret, in Jess's childhood bedroom.

"I'm on an adventure," Nina said.

***

The Nishitetsu super express shuddered south, its percussive motion cradled in the green palm of the valley. Nina leaned back against the thrumming windowpane and glanced over at Jess. She was watching the rice fields hurtle by. Charles wavered overhead, holding onto a strap, swinging toward them and then away. If he falls, we're done, Nina thought. They had bumped into him on their way to the train and he took an immediate, obvious interest in Jess. When they told him their plans to see the fireworks by the Chikugo River that night, Charles had invited himself along. From his color, it was clear he had started drink- - ing early in the day.

"I think he might just look like that permanently now," Gregory had murmured to her earlier, as Charles lurched out of earshot on his way to buy a ticket at the station. He looked raw, like his entire body had been abraded. Two girls in *yukata* sitting across from them kept darting their eyes over to the group, and Nina had the ungenerous urge to physically distance herself from Charles and sever the association.

Nina had been surprised when Gregory selected Charles out of all the other foreigners in Fukuoka as a friend; the night they first met, at the yakitori place, Charles was boisterous and bragging. He spoke at length of his friends back in Honolulu who, despite his being a white boy with parents from California—interlopers, non-locals, a grave sin, so it seemed, in the Aloha State—had accepted him as one of their own, their mascot. He spoke of their exploits with women in a way that most men knew to reserve for their own company, and Nina had expected Gregory to be revolted, but he'd only nodded. Perhaps he was seeing Charles as a baby then, as pristine, once, before he was clobbered by circumstance into this incarnation. Gregory, too, had spent his boyhood mostly as an outsider, a perpetual newcomer, had desperately wanted, never had enough time to make his way in. His friends, Charles then admitted, encouraged by Gregory's attention, had in fact sometimes used him as bait, sending him bumbling ahead, exposed, when they were out wandering the streets of Waikiki; they left him wriggling at the end of the line, waiting for some other group to bite, to sneer, "Fucking *haole*," and then they would spring to the front to strike.

He wasn't as big then as he was today, Charles had said, but still, he was good in a fight. He gave the play-by-play of several such scraps.

By then Charles was quite drunk. They would learn that Charles was almost always quite drunk, and wonder how it was that his supervisors at school had not yet noticed themselves. There were weekend mornings when Nina woke up and took her coffee to the balcony to see Charles heading back from Kawashoku, six-packs already in hand. And she worried, increasingly, that Gregory's generosity toward Charles stemmed from his seeing him as a portent, the kind of drunkard he might become.

The train came to a stop, and a recorded announcement singsonged that they had reached Kurume, their destination. The town was what Fukuoka people called the *inaka*, the sticks.

Nina had only just recovered from the walk to the train station in Chikushino, her face tight with the salt of dried perspiration, and now they had to venture back into the steaming dark mouth of the night. They followed the river of people, girls wrapped like presents in their *yukata*, boyfriends draping their arms atop the huge bows tied in the back.

"I wonder if we'll run into anyone from our schools," Nina said.

Gregory made a startled face. "I hope not."

The path to the riverfront took them through a narrow alley between walled-off houses. An old man peered over one of the walls at the moving mass.

They emerged at the top of a hill, a pouting lip over a drop to food stands selling *okonomiyaki, yakisoba,* and, oddly, something called *hotto doggu*. Groups of people poured over the green expanse. Gregory identified a spot halfway down to spread their blanket.

"You guys stay here," he told Nina and Jess. "What do you want?"

"Whatever looks good," Jess said. "But how are you going to find us?"

"You're the only white people," Charles said. The men started down the hill, freeing them from navigating the crowds, but also, Nina knew, freeing themselves to quickly down a few. Before Jess could remark on either of them, Nina asked her about Khaled.

It was a good distraction, bypassing whatever Jess might have been readying to say about Charles and Gregory. Khaled was working as DP—director of photography, she explained—on a documentary crew, and was at this moment at work on a short about Mongolian nomads. He was living with them in their yurts, eating yak cheese and drinking their burning liquor. Because he traveled so often for work now, they'd both agreed that monogamy was not feasible.

"So, are you seeing anyone else?" Nina said.

"No," Jess said. She scanned the crowd, all the gift-wrapped girls shrieking at each other. One of her hands stroked the grass beneath them. "But I *could*, whenever I feel like it."

So she was not alone in loving a sometimes-difficult man. Khaled's difficulty seemed worse, actually, Nina thought, little sparks of satisfaction popping within her.

Jess straightened up, face wiped free of worry. "We'll have to break up eventually. But not yet."

"You should wait at least until you get to go with him to the Oscars."

Jess looked at her for a moment, her expression inscrutable, but then she said, "Yeah, I really should."

Nina thought it might be better to be with someone before they achieved, to establish the sort of foundation upon which the changes that came from success could be weathered, from which straying would be unthinkable. She could see, from time to time, the ghostly images from her future with Gregory, long after he'd been published: settled in some college town, the glimmering outlines of the library in their home, its teeming, floor-to-ceiling bookshelves, their two children, just swirling, laughing shadows now, waiting to be called forth.

Her heart still picked up speed whenever he approached, and when they were in a good place, Nina found herself suffused with a beneficence that seemed to radiate outward, beaming goodwill at everyone, even the old science teacher at school who liked to keep her abreast of facts about the specialness of his people, for instance that Americans did not appreciate the sounds of nature as much as Japanese did.

The men returned, flushed, and settled in on the blanket, Gregory to the right of Jess, and Charles to the left of Nina, and she felt a prickle of resentment that she was made responsible for conversing with him. She leaned toward Jess; Gregory was asking about her work.

She had landed her first significant client, Jess was explaining. It was funny to say the word, which felt like it belonged to someone else. A Brooklyn-based paper sent her out to photograph their bigger stories, and some of them were interesting enough. She'd tagged along, for instance, on an investigative piece about the state of the city's Section 8 housing, and had captured the image of an immense rat circling an infant's crib. That one made the cover. But then there were the interminable press conferences, standing in the sun snapping away at councilmen and comptrollers, and that reminded her of waiting tables, being on her feet all day and treated like she was invisible.

Nina dared to glance over at Charles, risk having to talk to him, and saw he was lifting forkfuls of *yakisoba* to his mouth and staring vacantly at the river.

"What I actually care about is the stuff I do for me," Jess said. Then, after a pause, she added, "I was in a show."

Gregory asked to see some of these photos and Jess took out her phone and began clicking through them. Nina had seen the images already, on the gallery's website—it was a tiny gallery, in East Williamsburg, which was apparently, now, a neighborhood. She reacted to each in real time while on the phone with Jess, noon in New York and one in the morning in Japan, the hours stretched between them like a beaded necklace. They were mostly self-portraits, of a kind, that must have been taken by setting a timer and positioning the camera just so and then leaping away; in several there was Jess in black and white, on a sidewalk begrimed with ancient smudges of chewing gum, looking over her shoulder, hair flared out as though she had heard something looming behind her and snapped her head around to see. The effect was that you felt you were the one stalking her through the city, stealing her image. It was a "self-surveillance," the text on the website read, "but one which implicates the viewer." On the phone Nina had almost blurted that the portraits were just like the ones she'd seen sketched out in Jess's diary, on the night of their first sleepover, but pulled herself back in time.

Gregory was looking over Jess's shoulder, making affirming noises. And Nina was bracing, always, for him to stare up at her face and be hit with recognition. They had more in common, after all, that mystical capacity to disappear into their work, into a state of flow, while Nina, when she had tried to write in college, labored over each line, words emerging only after hours of constipated strain.

"So why aren't you taking any shots now?" Gregory asked her.

Jess said, "I want to experience things directly for once."

Gregory mentioned the Sontag quote about how photography removes from the individual taking the pictures the obligation to participate in reality. Jess said she'd never heard that before but that it was a great way of putting it.

Gregory went silent. Nina could see he was astounded that a professional photographer had never read *On Photography*. She felt again that queasy satisfaction. Then, to her relief, the fireworks began.

***

They noticed a pattern: the explosions were grouped into rounds, and between each one a row of characters would appear in red and gold lights across the river.

"What does that say?" Gregory asked Charles, who had studied the language in high school and somehow retained it all this time later, unblurred by years of boozing.

"Kawasaki Heavy Industries."

"What? Why?"

The fireworks resumed.

Charles leaned over and said something in Japanese to a man sitting on a blanket beside them. The man leaned slightly away from Charles, shaking his head.

"No English."

"That's why he asked you in Japanese," Gregory said.

Charles laughed.

"Gregory, don't be a dick," Nina said.

"But what's his problem?"

"He can't believe a guy like me knows Japanese." Charles was red-faced and gleaming now to the point of incandescence.

Gregory swigged from his beer. "He actually thinks we're animals."

The man returned his attention to the sky but held the tensed and distracted posture of someone aware he was being spoken about.

"Well, I think those are sponsors," Nina said, after another series of characters appeared. "I guess they have to pay for them somehow."

"Jesus Christ," Gregory said. "It's just like America. You fly halfway around the world," he said, "expecting to find something new, but it's the same: *consume, consume.*"

A firework sizzled away, leaving fleetingly behind a silvery powder.

"I don't get what's so terrible about it," Jess murmured, just to Nina. The light of another explosion caught the suggestion of a smile around her lips. In her peripheral vision Nina saw Gregory watching them and kept her eyes skyward. He liked Jess, he had told her; he couldn't imagine sharing with someone a history so deep—but maybe *we* will, one day, he had said, back in Brooklyn, on that shitty rear patio. His prophecy could still come true, Nina believed, though where Jess might exist in this future was murkier to her than the dream of the library, the college town, the children.

No one spoke, and a smattering of fireworks rushed in to fill the space.

"I dunno," Jess said. "These are definitely better than the ones at home. I think it's worth the sponsorship."

There was a rustling in her hair, and Nina turned. The older Japanese man had swatted at it. "Shut up," he said, thickly accented, so that it sounded like *Shah ttup*, and Jess snorted. Yes, it was funny; couldn't it all be funny? Nina had often felt, during fights with Gregory, that she was flickering between laughter and rage, a door swinging open and shut.

Gregory was on his feet immediately, unsteadily. "Are you kidding me?" he said to the old man. "Did you just fucking touch her?"

"Gregory, I don't care," Nina told him, and Jess's eyes floated to her, to Gregory, to Charles, seeking confirmation of something. Gregory waved a dismissive hand at her, still looming over the man. Behind his unfocused eyes was the contained violence of something undetonated. The other groups gathered on the grass watched them, faces orange and pink in the light of explosions.

Charles got up too. "Alright," he said. He dropped a heavy arm around Gregory. "Time to get out of the *inaka*."

***

Earlier that week, Nina had prepared dinner for herself and Gregory. The manager at the grocery store helped her find everything she needed; she'd told him she wanted to make *mizutaki*, and he'd led her around, dropping mushrooms, leeks, and chrysanthemum greens into her basket. These moments, of strangers' generosity, previously unfathomable, weighed more, ultimately, than the ones of scolding and shame, Nina thought, and was eager to tell Gregory about it. He arrived at her apartment just as she finished cooking, and they stretched out on the tatami in the living room under her low table.

He leaned back against a pillow. "I just need to close my eyes for a sec," he said.

"It'll get cold."

"That's okay. It'll still be delicious."

He shut his eyes; after a few moments he snored. At first, she ate silently, watching him. Then her bitterness began to rise, and she pulled her laptop in front of her to block out his rattling, slumped form and finished her dinner while clicking unseeingly through articles about the president striking down stem cell legislation. The next morning, she asked Gregory how much he'd had to drink before coming over and he apologized, eyes watering a little. He said he knew he had ruined another night for them. Nina reassured him that *ruined* was extreme. There would always be other nights.

He was far from tears now. He laughed at something Charles said and socked his shoulder. Nina and Jess walked side by side in silence as she tried to figure out what she owed her—an apology, an explanation—when Jess said, as they rounded the last corner, "You guys go ahead. We'll catch the next train. "

"Why, what are you doing now?"

"I want to check out this town."

Gregory shrugged. "Not much to see."

As they walked off, Charles called out, "*Ki o tsukete*"—take care.

Once they were out of earshot, Jess said, "I thought you could use a break."

What was there to say? It was terrible, sometimes, to be seen. Jess pointed at a *konbini* across the street. "Can we buy beer there?"

She nodded. "Great," Jess said. But when Nina took a step toward the store Jess grabbed her wrist and pulled her close. She draped her hands over Nina's shoulders

"Shall we?" Jess said.

"And then what?"

"Just be someone else for a while."

They switched. If Gregory and Charles were to turn and look back, they'd only see them holding each other with that weird intimacy, that slightly unsavory blend of the familial and the sexual that women friends often seemed to have. They wouldn't understand it, the men, nor would they trouble themselves to try. It was one of those mysteries you could comfortably live with, like the strange languages shared by twins, or the knowledge that powered migratory birds to return to nest in the same place year after year.

***

The train car churned with light and sound as though trying to digest them, but as they drank the roiling eased. Jess invented a game for the ride: When we catch someone staring at us, drink; when a passenger dares to sit beside us, drink; when we pass a rice field, drink. As they neared Chikushino, a young woman sitting across from them tugged at her bracelet until it snapped, sending a rain shower of beads down the floor of the car. Every man, woman, and child, who until then had been seated quietly, leaped from their seats and then sank to their knees, gathering the fallen pieces. "*Gomennasai*," the woman called repeatedly. Within moments, all the missing pieces were retrieved and returned to her waiting palms. She bowed to every passenger.

Jess and Nina watched the ritual in a stupor. Jess said, "I will never see anything like this again in my life."

"Now we have to finish," Nina said, and they chugged from the cans, laughing and gurgling. The stress of the evening had been pushed aside. Nina could feel it pacing at the back of her mind, far enough away for now.

Back at the apartment, Jess, unthinking, pushed open the shower room door. "Wait!" Nina said.

From inside, Jess said, "Nina. There's nothing in here."

She was unconvinced. She washed up over the kitchen sink. As she straightened, rubbing her face with a towel, she felt Jess behind her. She turned and saw her own face was wan and oily but for now it didn't really matter; it was not her responsibility. Inside Jess she felt less drunk and still distant from her own problems. Outside them.

Inside Nina's body, Jess yawned, swaying. "Let's go to bed."

They lay down on the futon. Nina smelled the beer on her breath. She curled Jess's knees up, pushed her long hair off her neck, comforted, somehow, by the sense of taking up less space than usual. Darkness enclosed them, and she fell asleep with her own face looming before her. She woke up the next morning to the trilling of cicadas, and Jess wasn't there.

12
DAYS OF AWE
(1996)

On New Year's Eve came the cramps. An organ she'd never known before lit up with pain, announcing itself.

"I have to tell you something," Nina said to Jess. They were at Leo's for the holiday, her parents, as usual, under the impression there would be supervision. Why wouldn't they believe so? Nina always came home by curfew, as far as they could see uninjured, so there was nothing to question. Questions led to knowledge, and then there might be things you could never un-know.

They slipped into the bathroom and locked the door. With the lights off, Nina shared her news. Jess whisper-squealed, a high-pitched *eeeee* sound.

"Can I slap you?" she said. "It's tradition."

"What?" Nina said. "Why?" Months later she would find, on a bored afternoon paging through *The Jewish Book of Why*, pulled from her parents' bookshelves, the answer: The strike awakens the girl from her childhood slumber. Perhaps Jess had learned it herself there, during one of their sleepovers; perhaps Nina's mother had told Jess about it, believing she spoke to her daughter, to ready Nina for the strike to come. "You can do it soft."

Jess reared back theatrically, but then brought her hand forward as though raking it through water, and brushed her fingers softly down Nina's cheek.

"I want to know what it feels like," Jess said.

It was so naked an admission from Jess, who never said aloud what she wanted, only dropped a trail of clues for Nina to follow to her desire, that she leaned forward and touched her forehead to Jess's immediately. It was a relief at first to be released to a body unvisited as yet by that particular pain. Jess, inside her, lay hands over pelvis, tilted head down.

"Wow," she said.

It occurred to Nina that nothing was only hers anymore, not even her organs.

***

Without the pretense of band practice tonight everyone was looser, all waiting for the old year to flip over into the new one. And Lars had a vision: He'd constructed a kind of explosive Frisbee by hole-punching a paper plate around its edges and looping through the wicks of the M-80s, which he would light in quick succession before hurling the disc into the night, the moment it became 1996.

While Lars undertook this project, Leo was at work on his own. They stood on the slippery back deck, arms crossed over their chests, scant flurries feathering their cheeks as he pulled the sheath off the hot tub. Nina watched herself crouch beside him as he twisted a thermostat dial. She could hear him orating about music again, listing off the best singles of the year, Jess from her squat staring at the movement of his mouth as it spoke. So much of their time at this house passed in states of suspended animation while they observed the boys playing guitar, playing video games, passing back and forth their exegesis of this album or that movie. "'Wonderwall,'" Leo declared, was number one as far as he was concerned, sure to have staying power, and he gazed into the Jacuzzi as if the future were written across its murky water. It began to bubble to life.

Lars emerged from the house then, bearing his Frisbee and a brown bottle. He nodded at the tub. "'Til it warms up," he said, and took a swallow. He passed it to Nina first and the rest all turned to watch. For them there was no question that Jess would drink. And as Jess, there was no time for Nina to consider; she was loosed from her careful weighing of things. She tipped the bottle back and opened her throat. The bourbon lit a trail of flame past her jaws and coiled in her stomach.

They passed it around, Jess taking quick, timid little nips in a manner that seemed to Nina like mockery. The house next door was alight, and she could see adult-sized shapes moving within, people perching on the arms of sofas or hovering by punch bowls, talking about whatever it was the old talked about, their lawns, their taxes, the Clintons.

"It's ready," Leo said. Swaying, he stripped down to his boxers, stepped over the edge of the tub, and plunged in. He came up, tendrils of steam rising from his hair. "It's like soup," he told them.

They followed, Lars resting his explosive delicately on the ground before undressing to reveal his form: long, pale, hairless as a worm but graceful as he lowered himself in. Anthony followed; Nina saw he was hairier, his back speckled with acne. Jess and Nina kept their eyes on each other as they removed sneakers, clothes, until they stood in bras and panties, looking at their uncovered bodies not as in a mirror but from the vantage of lovers. In they went, and humming warm water closed around them.

"Nina," Leo said, arms spread across the rim of the tub, head lolling, "I dare you to flash us."

"Oh," Jess said, "are we playing Truth or Dare?" She looked around the tub, eyes flitting too quickly for Nina to catch her attention. "I will if you guys do, too."

"Huh," Leo said, crossing his arms.

"You don't want to?"

"No," he said quickly, "I'm just surprised." As he should be. This was a Jess suggestion, not a Nina one; it was Jess who knew how to toss grenades of real risk, exposing whatever they were playing at for the game it was.

Their rule of striving, during swaps, for fidelity to each other, was unspoken but long-established, and she tore it down as though it had ceased to be enough for her to be Nina for a while, as though she needed now to be Nina *and* Jess, leaving Nina with nothing.

"So?" Jess said.

"Of course," Leo said. "It's only fair."

Jess lowered herself beneath the water and reached behind her back, undid the clasp on Nina's bra and slid it off her shoulders, scanned them again to ensure she had their full attention. She sank lower, gathering energy, then sprang upward, breaching like a whale beneath the buzzing lights of the back patio. Nina saw her own body, shining, curved, breasts pointing at the sky, a shower of water droplets arcing over the tub and onto the deck as her wet hair snapped back in the air. She saw not herself but a woman. Everyone cheered.

Jess shrugged the bra back on. "Your turn," she told the boys.

They looked at each other; Lars was chewing his lips. "One, two, three," Leo said, and as one they lowered their shorts and pulled out their cocks, which flashed whitish and floppy beneath the water like sea cucumbers, resolutely unfrightening, Nina thought, with a trace of disappointment. She tried to imagine how it might feel to put one of those pallid floating things in her mouth, as she had heard of certain girls at school doing. These girls were smeared as sluts, but it seemed to her it was the boys who committed a terrible relinquishing, surrendering the tenderest part of themselves to the sharpness of female mouths. It was hard to remember now, though it had been only months before, why she had been so certain, when Jordan tormented her, that he was the one who had the upper hand.

"What about Jess?" Anthony said, looking at Nina as he tucked his away.

"Jess doesn't have to," Jess said, lips curved slightly. "She only has mosquito bites, anyway."

Nina had never heard the phrase before; she'd never have uttered anything so contemptuous of her friend in front of the boys. Who was this contempt for? Leo looked over at Jess, grinning, and his smile pained Nina, like a full body cramp. Jess looked back at him and laughed. Then she turned to face Leo and they leaned toward each other. They looked as if they were about to swap. Nina watched her own pale face, luminous in the night, her own pink lips brush against Leo's.

Nina climbed out of the tub and stood, dripping, over them. She climbed down from the patio and walked over the frozen grass, snapping beneath her bare feet, through the back gate and to Lars's driveway. She stood looking into the street, still inured against the cold, steaming.

Then Anthony was beside her, holding out a towel and a Parliament. "Want one?"

Nina nodded. Jess despised smoking, because Anita and Rob did it. Anita at least kept it to the yard, but Rob filled up the den, the car, with his exhalations, and they stuck to Jess's clothes like foul kisses. She wrapped the towel around her shoulders and used Anthony's lighter to breathe ruin deep into Jess's lungs.

"You're prettier than Nina," he said.

Nina knew it was true.

They sat down on the lawn, the frigid grass stabbing the undersides of her thighs, and tried to blow smoke rings for a while until Lars came running over with his Frisbee, announcing that it was time.

***

Leo and Jess kissed again as Lars's device boomed and fizzled, a half-success. Anthony and Lars kissed too, sarcastically. Nina watched. She saw how Jess arched her torso against Leo's. "Happy New Year," everyone said to each other.

Jess and Nina finished drying off in Leo's bathroom, tugging on their clothes over damp underwear.

"I'm getting tired of these cramps," Jess said. Nina leaned forward, unspeaking. After they switched she shoved Jess a little, more an abrupt loosing of her grip on her shoulders, enough to notice, too feeble to comment on.

"Now I'm not so excited to get my period," Jess continued, "now that I know."

The ache was still there.

"You're not gonna talk?" Jess said.

"You stole from me. You stole my first kiss."

Jess stopped. Her face was not what Nina had expected, trapped, defiant; she looked wounded. "*I* was your first kiss."

The Boyfriend Game. But that was a game. "That doesn't count," Nina said.

For a microsecond she saw the wound deepen. Then the tectonic plates under Jess's skin shifted, sweeping it away. "You should be thanking me," she said. "I moved things along for us with Leo, since you were too scared to do it yourself."

***

Her parents tapped on the horn outside Leo's house and Nina could feel him looking at her as he followed her down the stairs, a needling between her shoulder blades. At the door his eyes were wide and hungry. He stood in the foyer, swollen with waiting. She kept her eyes open when he kissed her. Up close his lashes were thick as tropical grass, his mouth smoky from bourbon, and her cramps dropped away behind a curtain of softer sensation.

In the car when her parents asked how her New Year's was, Nina made a neutral sound in her throat. They coasted down the dark blocks lined with identical houses, septuplets, octuplets, nonuplets. Was there an end to that kind of word? It was all drenched in unreality, the bright windows and black trees, the backs of her parents' uncomprehending heads. Having watched how Jess puppeted her body all night, using it to fool the boys, pull a little pleasure from them, just a means to an end, Nina felt now that she too was an alien entity within it, steering it around. Perhaps there existed a world in which she could tell her mother what had happened with Jess, with Leo, ask her advice on how to manage the situation, but it wasn't this world. There were too many layers of explanation required, spread atop one another so that they formed an impenetrable crust.

At home, the teenage babysitter was curled up on the couch, watching *Alternative Nation*. "He really tried to stay up," she told them. "He almost made it."

As her parents paid, Nina crept upstairs, cracked open Zachary's door. In the line of light she could see him, arms and legs splayed as wide as his twin bed would allow, face turned toward her, serene in sleep, all his tenderest spots exposed as though nothing would ever dream of striking him there.

***

Leo had a succession of gifts for her, first notes passed in homeroom, then more elaborate letters. One day when she opened her locker dozens of rose petals came streaming out. There were mixtapes he made with laboratory precision, and a necklace that spelled out in charms *Leo ♥ Nina*. You had to pay per charm at the flea market, and Nina was relieved their names were short. After his presentation of each of these items he faced her expectantly. Her role was to allow him to enfold her, to melt her posture into his, part her lips against his. She had the sense again of being shrunken down, a tiny pilot maneuvering a huge carcass. She watched him from inside. He looked ensnared.

Jess called his offerings *our presents*. If Nina was herself for their bestowals, Jess would then take them, claiming she needed to study each note and song so that she could embody Nina with verisimilitude. She was always forgetting to return them. Nina was left only with the necklace, which of course Jess could not wear, and when Leo wasn't near she tucked it under her shirt and felt the cool press of each letter against her chest.

In gym class, jogging a mile through snowmelt around the track, they disclosed new advances in the relationship so that either girl could continue with Leo what the other had begun, maintaining the depth of kisses or conversations. One afternoon Nina had an invitation to share: Leo had asked her to go with him to a Smashing Pumpkins concert at the Coliseum. Anthony would go, too, and his older brother would drive.

Jess let loose a cry of victory, leaped a hurdle where there was none.

"I told him I wasn't sure," Nina said.

"What? Why? Tell him we want to go."

"He only invited Nina."

"So I'll be Nina. I'll go." Each word was split in two by Jess's footfalls.

"I don't know."

Jess slowed. She took Nina by the arm and pulled her onto the damp thatch of grass at the center of the track. "This is our chance," she said.

"For what?"

Jess puffed out breath-clouds. "The next step?"

Overhead the naked branches of the trees spindled and waved. There was a sorrowful feeling in her chest, an ache for the old games. She had reached the beginning of nostalgia: she had grown old enough to turn back and look at their former selves, see them standing still in the past.

The sting of it made her stubborn. "I don't know," she repeated.

Phlegm rattled in Jess's throat. "You go along with everything, except for when I need something."

"What do you mean?"

"You know." She stood with hands on hips, ominous angles against the white sky. They had pretended, until now, that the project of Leo was one in which they were equally invested. It unified them, the problem of pinning down his heart. But finally he mattered to Jess more, just as her father had, and Nina had abandoned her to that longing, to her whole life. She had nestled back inside her own home, whose cozy boredom was, in its way, wonderful. To hoard it to herself, to leave Jess out there—that was a sin, wasn't it, but to share would be what the cantor called a mitzvah.

"Fine," Nina said, "you can be me. We can make it a sleepover, like the old days." The light that came into Jess's face—she had put it there. That was her power. She tugged Jess onto the track and they were taken back into the crowd of runners, the warm press of their bodies and chatter surrounding them. Of course no one ever remarked on the peculiar closeness of Jess and Nina. Girls in middle school seemed increasingly to bleed into one another, as though their boundaries, like the boundaries of towns and countries, were imaginary. They shared clothing and private dialects; there was an osmosis at work, an absorption of habits and phrases and fragrances, until it was impossible to tell who had originated what.

***

She let herself into Jess's house, the afternoon of the concert. Anita would be working late and Rob was who cared where, Jess had told her, and when she stepped into its familiar odor she felt its quiet press down into her. In the intervening years since their last sleepover Jess's bedroom had been swept of its totems, the voodoo dolls and collages with their tints of violence. "I was such a little psycho," she said of her younger self, and Nina was confused by the suggestion that Jess was no longer that person, that she'd cast her off like an old carapace. That her sense of awe had diminished. Now the walls were papered with heartthrobs, floppy-haired and bumpy with muscle. Near the ceiling was one who had blue eyes with a sad slant to them, and a full girlish mouth. She looked up into the black holes of his nostrils but he was staring elsewhere, dreaming, and the wish surged inside Nina that it was of her. He reminded her of someone. The answer hovered, nipped at her.

The silence of the house seeped deeper; it was like the silence of the synagogue. The cantor had said in Nina's last lesson that it was clear she wasn't practicing. He had asked if what she desired most was to appear foolish and lazy before everyone she knew, on the day she was to become a woman. Nina closed her eyes against the walls covered in boys and began with the V'ahavta, which every child had to chant, before moving into her assigned Torah verses, the squeaks and quavers of her voice— Jess's voice—bouncing off their glossy cheekbones and abs. Then the voice firmed up and took on a surety that did not dwell within Nina's own throat and the room filled with God's threats, pouring from Jess's mouth. Nina was a mouse without her.

***

She was awakened from her doze on Jess's bed by the sound of a door slamming and then the voices of men, in the rooms below. One of the voices, one strange to her, called Jess by name. Nina stood quickly, smoothing her clothes, bracing herself to become another.

Downstairs she found the one who had called out, a man who wasn't Rob sitting on the living room couch, long legs stretched before him. He was skinny and blondish, wearing a V-neck shirt that the pelt of hair on his chest pushed through.

He took her in, took his time doing so. "Jesus, look at you," he said. Nina chewed the inside of her cheek.

"Last time I saw you, you were a little peanut," the man said. "Remember me? I'm your dad's friend Fred."

He's not my dad, Nina tried to find the nerve to say. He beckoned her closer. Another man, this one heavyset and dark-haired, was stationed in front of the TV, the screen glow flickering over him, faces light, then dark.

"Hey," Rob said as he entered the room, beer in hand. "How was school?"

"Good."

"She comes home to an empty house?" the heavy man asked.

"She's almost all grown up," Rob told him.

"That's what I'm saying. That's exactly what you should be worried about."

What did they suppose Jess could be up to? Was there more she was keeping from Nina? "I was doing my math homework," Nina said, and tried to put an edge in her voice, because Jess would not allow anyone to speak about her as if she was not there.

"Easy," Rob said, and Fred chuckled and sank farther into the couch. On the television, in a boxing ring, a fair-skinned boxer gleamed with oil and growled threats at his opponent into a microphone. The beads of perspiration on the men's cans of beer echoed the ones on the fighter's skin, transposed from the distant, unreal world of the screen into reality.

Fred noticed her staring. "What?" he said. "You want one?"

"No," Nina said quickly.

"Don't lie," he said. "You're how old? I'm sure you've tried by now."

Besides the stinging sips of bourbon on New Year's Eve, she hadn't. She looked over at Rob, who shrugged. "You can have a little," he said. "That way it won't be such a big deal."

Fred extended his can to her, which she leaned over to retrieve without wanting to, because Jess would. Jess would tilt her head back and take a big swig, so Nina did, and tried not to sputter at the assaultive, sour flavor and the film of bubbles that swarmed her nose. She passed it back, eyes watering with suppressed coughs.

Rob smiled knowingly at her. "Looks like you've done that before." Nina shook her head again, unable to speak. Her throat burned. "I won't narc to your mother, don't worry," he said.

"I was just saying," Fred said to Rob, "I remember when this one was just a little peanut."

"Not so little anymore."

"Still only has mosquito bites, though," said Fred, and the heavy man laughed. Rob laughed. The phrase speared into her, and the confusion. It spread, a febrile heat.

Nina turned from them and retreated back up the stairs, dimming the bedroom lights, dropping again into the bed. She looked up at the blue-eyed boy near the ceiling and wondered what Jess was doing right now with her body, with Leo. She felt her hand roving downward, slipping under the waist of Jess's jeans, when she realized that the boy on the wall looked, around the eyes and the mouth, a lot like Jordan.

***

The next morning she found Leo waiting at the threshold of the classroom.

"Hey," she said, "how was the concert?"

He glanced at her, eyes unfocused. "Good."

"Did they play 'X.Y.U.'?" But he was looking down the hall. In the shade beyond Leo's notice, it was very cold. She could say anything.

"I'm not actually Jess, you know," Nina told him. Her heart lifted into her throat at the utterance of it but Leo showed no reaction. Then he spotted her, what he thought was Nina, though as she approached them she configured her body into postures Nina was sure it never ordinarily held, looser ones; Jess wore her form more comfortably than she did. Leo brushed past Nina as though she was inanimate. And she felt the fevered heat return to her skin, a rage on Jess's behalf that he thought so little of her—that so many of them thought so little, Rob and Fred, Leo and the boys, the unknowing populations of her world. Nina loved Jess better than anyone.

She was wearing the necklace, its letters shining against the black of one of Nina's T-shirts, and Nina watched as they embraced each other, as Jess tilted up her face at Leo and their lips met, their eyes closed; they were Clyde and Giselle yanked from the domain of dreams and delivered here to this odorous hallway. When they withdrew a silver runner of saliva connected their mouths for a long moment. That look Jess was wearing, on Nina's face—had Nina ever known the level of bliss that produced it?

Leo tugged at her hand. "I'll be right there," she told him. She turned to Nina. "Can I keep being you," she said, in a velvet murmur, "a little longer?"

There was a plug of something in Nina's throat. She shrugged and turned away. No, *this* was the sin, what she was allowing to happen. Her other misdeeds, snapping at her mother, maiming with her tongue, waned in comparison to this sin of inaction, allowing Leo to be deceived, Jess to use her body as a vessel. Nina's God, in her hopes, was not angry, would not think to devour her. He only understood. He forgave you for the thing you did before you even did it, because He was the one who had made you the kind of person who would do it.

But the heaviness in her chest said she knew such a God was too good to be true. He would not forgive, nor would He intervene if Jess slipped deeper into Nina's life, took it from her, ran away with it for good.

***

In the lobby of the synagogue was a carving of the tree of life whose branches stretched across an entire wall, and dangling from one of the branches was a gold leaf engraved ambiguously with the words, "Nina Glass, March 10, 1996," which, it seemed to her, could have been the date, too, of her birth or death. But it was the day of her bat mitzvah; it was today, it was still before her. She was posed in front of the carving with relatives, in twos and threes, Nina and Zachary, Nina and Aunt Lydia, Nina and her grandfather. Nina's parents had hired a neighbor's son to document the bat mitzvah, and his photographs all came out too dark. But still they would be enshrined in two large, ivory albums, the five-by-sevens of all their pale faces swimming out of the glossy gloom.

When she first got to her feet from her chair on the bimah and came to face the congregation, everyone she knew and everyone she should know but didn't remember, the great-uncles and cousins-once-removed and alleged family friends, the one clear thought that pierced her fear was that maybe this was also what she would see on her last day on Earth, an assembly of every person she'd brushed against in life sitting together in judgment. The rabbi and cantor hovered at her back like executioners.

But there was little now to judge. She had practiced; she wouldn't fumble. And as soon as she began she left herself, first amazed that it was finally happening, that she was chanting in a foreign tongue to what looked like hundreds of people filling the pews, all the way to the back of the sanctuary, the Torah unsheathed from its ark and unscrolled before her. Then the amazement passed and as her voice ably traced its way down the verses, she traveled among all the bodies, the squirming ones of the children, the soft and sunken ones of the old people, the ones of her parents and brother, rigid with pride.

Then time for her interpretation. The Golden Calf, she told them, was something far easier to understand than God, a solid and present being to run one's hands against after scorching weeks in the desert. God never intended to devour the Israelites in revenge; He understood their reasons, knew they were going to create the false idol before they did. He only led Moses to believe that He would destroy them, because He wanted to hear in Moses's own words that he, too, understood and forgave.

In closing, Nina dedicated her bat mitzvah to a stranger, a little boy named Samuel, her grandfather's cousin, killed in Dachau. She heard now a sound like a sob from the pew where her grandfather sat. When she was very young Nina had believed that all the food she ate would remain inside her body, slowly accumulating from the toes up, and she thought now maybe pain, maybe experience was like that: the older you got, the more was stacked upon itself inside you, until the terrible knowledge reached all the way to your throat and spilled out your mouth.

***

After, as the congregants crowded into the lobby, Nina went upstairs to the bathroom to put on her party dress. She felt a little ashamed to be changing costumes, like a pop star, Aunt Lydia waiting outside the stall to take the first dress, long-sleeved black velvet, and swap it for the second, spaghetti straps, sparkling, deep blue with a flared skirt. Her mother had insisted. "The girls have done this at every bat mitzvah I've been to so far," she said.

It was the same bathroom, the same stall in which she'd gotten her first period. There had been more since then, and pads filled with her dark blood, which she folded into tissue and placed in the small waste-basket beneath the sink in the bathroom she shared with her mother and Zachary. Her mother had never noticed them there, never asked. Nina felt sometimes she was a ghost haunting her own home.

Nina stepped out of the stall and Lydia fawned. "Gorgeous."

"I'll be right down," Nina told her. Once Lydia left, she looked at herself in the mirror. Her skin was very white against the dress, her breasts pressing against its sweetheart neckline. If Jordan could see her now.

From the top of the stairs she saw her father and Rob huddled by the tree of life, the crowns of their heads glowing under the fluorescent lights.

"Man," her father was saying to Rob, "What are you doing?"

"I know, I know." Rob's voice floated upward, bobbed against the ceiling. "But I can't stop thinking about her. I'm telling you. It's like she put a spell on me."

Nina's father said, "You have a good thing and you're going to ruin it."

She had not realized the two were friends, and there came another lurch of shame at the thought of her father trading intimacies with this man, who chuckled when his friends insulted Jess, who struck, at least once, Anita. Could they really have anything in common, could they share, as she and Jess shared, the hidden corners of their lives? Until this moment she had not allowed for the possibility her parents might have as many secrets as she did. From the party room, her mother and Zachary emerged, bringing with them a swirl of lights and thumping music.

Her mother looked up and spotted Nina. "It's time for our big entrance."

Rob started a little but recovered as Nina descended the stairs. "Look at you," he said. "All grown up." He elbowed her father. "Maybe I should make Jess do a bat mitzvah. She has some growing up to do."

Nina thought of him weeping in the emergency room and turned away. Her father pulled open the doors and the DJ's voice poured forth, entreating the guests to welcome the Glass family; here were Mom and Dad, here was Baby Brother, and here was the one they were all waiting for, the one they had come to see. They were pulled one by one onto the dance floor, a forest of hands reaching, faces grinning, frozen in grins, the music thudding in her stomach, the strobe lights flickering around her. Then the music shifted, the way scenes shift in a dream, turned jaunty, and Nina was pushed into a chair and lifted upward. Rob was one of the men lifting, grimacing up at her, and with each thrust into the air she caught a glimpse of Leo, Lars, and Anthony, clustered in a corner away from the celebration, arms folded, and then her old elementary-school girlfriends, shimmying at the front of the crowd, and finally Jess, right beneath her in a snug red dress, arms bare, hands outstretched to touch her.

***

It was strange, so much praise. It already felt as though it had been someone else, chanting and sermonizing up there on the bimah, some iteration of herself summoned for that moment and then disposed of. She tried to evade the adults, allowed classmates to pull her from one end of the room to another.

Leo trailed her, his face shining, his hair slicked back and hardened into a helmet. His dress shirt was too large, and wrinkled. His parents had not helped him, but he had tried to present himself as best he could for the occasion. It was a terrible knowing she withheld from him. He could never imagine how they had shared, Nina and Jess, the smell of his breath, or his confession of the times in his childhood that his mother, drunk, fed up, pinched hard at his thighs and hissed that he had ruined her. That when Nina stroked his hand and listened it was not Nina but an outsider. Or that even when it was Nina she was only pretending to be the Nina he thought he knew. It was a violation, she saw, observing him now from the other side of the day's ritual. Committing it was what made her a woman.

"I can't go out with you anymore," Nina told him.

His face at first didn't register the blow. "Why not?"

"I just don't want to."

"Wait," he said, a throb inside the syllable. She turned her back on it and wandered, numbed, back onto the dance floor. Her mother intercepted her. "Great party, huh?"

Nina shrugged.

Her smile sagged. "Really, Nina? You're gonna cop an attitude now?"

The glory she had felt in the sanctuary disintegrated. Nothing remained hers for long.

***

From the perimeter of the party, she watched the beginning of the candle-lighting ceremony. At some point, after they swapped, Jess must have righted things with her mother, for now they stood before the flickering lights beaming at each other. It seemed right that Jess should be up there, immersed in her life. Nina could see from across this expanse that she was loved so potently it might burn her alive were she to stand inside it. But Jess could withstand it.

There was a brush of fingers against her arm. She turned and saw Leo, glaring at her, and she looked down. The dress hugged Jess's small breasts— her *mosquito bites*—the soft tops of them visible above the neckline.

Leo pointed to Jess where she stood now in Nina's body, beside her parents and Zachary. "You know what she is?"

A bolt of fear. He was sensitive. If someone were to figure it out, it made sense that it would be Leo.

"What?" Nina said.

His eyes traced up and down her form, recognizing it, perhaps, for the shell that it was. His lips curled downward in a sneer.

"A slut," he said.

***

Outside the temple it was frigid, the damp March cold that slips under the skin. Nina shivered in Jess's dress, goosebumps sheathing her bare arms and legs. She tottered over the pavement in Jess's heels. They were still playing dress-up, she thought. She had run—actually run—from Leo as if he might strike her, but you could not outrun, she saw, what they wanted from you, Leo and Jordan and Fred and all the others.

She reached the parking lot and stopped. Where was she going? Nina turned back to face the building. She heard singing from inside the temple. They were singing "Happy Birthday."

13
FUDO MYO-O
(2007)

It was not the first time Jess had vanished. Once, when they were eleven, Jess had slept over—a real sleepover—and Nina had awoken in much the same way, expecting to open her eyes to the form of her friend beside her, Jess's hair curtained over the edges and planes of her face, but found her side of the bed empty. She went to the kitchen, still quiet save for the hum of the refrigerator, the prisms of sunlight sliding along the counters. In that moment she was the only person on the planet. Left to herself, Nina sometimes felt her outline fading. Without Jess's life force refracting off her surface she became nobody. Just then the front door swung open. Jess and her mother appeared: they'd gone to pick up bagels. They came bounding in carrying paper bags wafting a garlicky smell. They looked like mother and daughter. They said, "Oh, you weren't worried, were you?"

Nina wished Jess had not gone exploring in her body. She might run into someone she was supposed to know, someone who expected her to understand a little Japanese. Hopefully, there would be no one: it was Obon, the Japanese festival of the dead, and most people had returned to their hometowns, or taken the opportunity to go on vacation.

With the apartment filled with sunlight, it was safe to go in the shower. Nina lingered under the spray, probing to see whether anything about Jess's body had changed. It was the same, though no less interesting, the coarser hair and smaller, higher breasts, the skin stretched taut across her firm stomach, the pockets of fat that she tried to conceal on her inner thighs. The moles and freckles and blemishes were nearly as familiar to Nina as her own, though she found around one nipple a rosy ring of broken capillaries. From Khaled?

She walked dripping into the living room to check her phone, but it too was gone. At this a warning light flashed once in her mind. Maybe Jess had expected her to sleep much longer; maybe she saw this as an opportunity to take a walk and snoop. Permission, then, to look through Jess's things. Nina squatted by her duffel bag and reached in, feeling around the puddles of clothing, and unearthed a crammed makeup bag, a camera lens—she had brought it after all, so why hadn't she said as much to Gregory? More lights began flickering. It dawned on her that Jess might have taken Nina's body over to his apartment to extract what she would believe was a well-deserved apology for his rudeness the night before. What damage could she do, stepping into a relationship whose landscape and governance she knew nothing of, and unleashing herself upon it?

Nina pulled on a pair of shorts and a T-shirt, slid her feet into Jess's sandals, ran down the stairs. She pounded on Gregory's door.

Rumpled, squinting, half-awake, he opened the door. "Uh," he said.

"Hey," she said, trying to slow her breathing. She hadn't had time to think of what to say. "Is Nina here?"

"I thought you guys went home together last night," he said. He was looking at her the way he looked at most people, aloof, uneasy. Braced for something at best unpleasant.

"We did," she said. "I woke up and she wasn't in the apartment, so I thought she might have come over here."

"Well, she didn't." He leaned against the door frame. "Tell her to text me when she gets back?"

"Sure," Nina said. She would go home, and she would call Jess, tell her to get the hell back. As she walked the steaming path to her own building, considering what level of anger was called for, she saw Charles standing by the entrance with bags from Kawashoku.

"Hey," he said to her. "Recovered from last night?"

"Fine," she said.

He lifted one of the bags. "It's a holiday weekend so I figured no reason not to start up again."

She felt a surge of pity.

"What did you girls get up to after we left?"

"Just some train drinking."

He grinned. "Me and Gregory kept it going over here."

She had smelled it in his apartment, the sweet and sour stink of trapped vapors.

"Hey," he said. "Is Nina pissed at us?"

"Not you."

Charles peered at her with bloodshot eyes. In the old days she might have felt her guts contract with the fear of being discovered, but she had long since discovered no one ever figured it out, too enmeshed with themselves to see that she was an impostor.

He seemed to decide to forge ahead. "Gregory felt really bad," Charles said. He explained that he'd spent much of the rest of the night trying to reassure Gregory that he was, deep down, a good guy, that he, too, could get a little belligerent when he was drinking, that he and Nina clearly had the kind of bond that would see them through these bumps in the road. "I mean, do they know how lucky they are to have that?" Charles asked.

***

As the morning passed she was flooded with blacker thoughts. Jess struck by a train, skull smashed, organs flattened to a paste, or Jess bored with waiting for Khaled, bored with her money struggles, dissolved into the huge world, stepping out of herself, the final exchange complete. This latter possibility was in fact more upsetting, the contempt of it, Nina's life stripped from her like an old piece of clothing: *Oh, you didn't want this anymore, did you?* The sun rose; the apartment grew more stifling. She abandoned all pretense at calm and began leaving voicemails from Jess's phone on her own, hearing again and again her voice mail recording and then demanding, as though of herself, "Seriously. What are you trying to pull? Come back." And then, "This isn't fucking funny."

She went into the shower room and looked in the mirror. Jess's eyes gleamed with panic. The panic transformed the face—now it looked more like her own, the features tensed into place. She'd only ever seen Jess briefly afraid, and then she'd swallow it back down, far under the layers of the visible.

As she watched Jess's reflection, her mind began unspooling the terrible possibilities. She slid to the floor, the cold tiles where the roaches skittered at night pressing into the backs of her legs. She folded over herself, eyelids against knees, trying to halt the sensation in her center of endless plummeting. It seemed less likely that Jess would attempt to simply assume Nina's life than begin anew with it. One scene after another intruded, lighting up the inner dark, of Jess riding her body into new timelines. She traveled; she sat in a train compartment, watching a blur of landscapes Nina would never see. She pulled strange men down into beds in dingy rooms, sunlight prodding the curtains. Nina's body grew leaner, forehead lined and sunburned, and she lived off what she made as she roamed. She picked grapes in a vineyard, maybe, or conjured bills like a snake charmer from the wallets of people in bars and airport lounges, disarming them with her soft innocent face, an incisive remark, an allusion to a larger plan. She was going places, and they wanted to be a part of her story.

Or Jess could have simply flown Nina's body back to New York, forcing her to follow it. Perhaps all she wanted was a few more days in the Glass family home, days Nina had snatched from her in childhood, days Jess believed she was owed.

Nina stood, legs stiff, and made her way to the computer to email her mother, to gauge whether Jess had made contact. *Just wanted to say hi*, Nina wrote. *It's been a while since we talked.* Her fault: she blamed the time difference, claiming that whenever her family tried to call, she was asleep or at work. She'd hoarded them away from Jess, only half understanding why, Nina saw now, in the light of the likelihood she would never be known by them again. If Jess ran away with her body, they would believe their only daughter had gone missing. As she typed, she floated away from the container of Jess's body, a balloon at the end of a string bobbing against the ceiling.

Her mother responded immediately. *All good but miss you like crazy. Can you talk now? Zachy's here too. We just finished dinner. Everyone wants to say hello!*

Her misery soared. She felt frantic enough to tell. She could have tried, many times; the decision not to had brought her here. It had sent her cascading down the tunnels inside herself, far from the lights of home.

***

There was a knock on the door. Nina ran, prepared to see her own face behind it, but it was Gregory.

"Nina here?" he asked her. Nina shook her head. "I've been texting her all day," he said.

This she did not doubt. The month before, her Japanese teacher had taken the students to a traditional restaurant to teach them about dining etiquette, during which Gregory had called her six times. Unable to focus, Nina had stepped into the hallway to answer the phone.

"Where are you?" he said. "Are you with someone?"

"I'm with my class," Nina said. "I told you." He had forgotten; at the other end, he chuckled and apologized. "We're learning how to pick up rice," she said. "That's it."

She had returned to the dining room, flustered—but there was a pleasure in so holding his attention. Nina imagined Jess reading all their messages now, watching the rising of alarm that she had summoned.

"Why don't you come in and wait," she suggested.

He hesitated, narrowed his eyes into the dimness of the apartment as though Nina might be hiding there. Then he stepped inside and took off his shoes in the *genkan*.

"Nina hates when I don't do this," he explained.

She thought of how Jess might respond, and the effort at panto-mime, as it always did, focused her. "Nina has a lot of rules," she said.

"Tell me about it."

"And they change all the time. I can't keep up."

"We contain multitudes," he said. "Did she say anything to you about taking off somewhere today?"

"No," Nina said. "But I think her feelings were kind of hurt."

They were standing in the kitchen. Gregory crossed his arms and leaned against the refrigerator. "I don't really see why."

Be Jess, Nina thought, the defender, the one who extracts loyalty slowly and painfully as fingernails. "You didn't exactly show us a good time last night."

Gregory exhaled, shook his head. She could see him gathering his resources. This was always the moment her heart would begin flutter-ing, bracing itself.

But he kept his mouth closed. The sunlight coming through the kitchen window caught the brown speck in his eye. He looked at her now the same way he had glared at the old man. He looked at her as he would a stranger, someone who might do him harm.

Nina told him, in a small voice, that she was worried.

"I'm sorry. I am too. Nina's never disappeared like this before," he said, forgetting, perhaps, all the times she'd stormed out on him and all the times she'd come back. "I have an idea of where she might be," Gregory said. "Do you want to help me look?"

***

It wasn't long before Nina could tell where Gregory was leading her, and she was moved by his choice: it was exactly where she would flee, if she had ever found the propulsion necessary to do so. The park was a twenty-minute walk from the apartment, bordered by a gray-green pond. Old men sat fishing from the slope-roofed gazebo. In the park's center, in a ring of forest, was a humble mountain. She had climbed it once, knowing nothing; Charles had mentioned the park to her and she had gone with her notebook, hoping a change of setting would prompt her pen forward—she was trying to keep a journal about her time in Japan—but the moment she'd found a spot on the grass a young man approached, sat down beside her, and began peppering her with questions in Japanese. Was she a college student? What was she working on, then? Why was she living here? Did she like Chikushino? Did she know that her Japanese sounded very cute? Did she have a boyfriend? He leaned forward, tapping her notebook with thick fingers.

Yes, Nina said, and in fact she was meeting him now, though at the time Gregory had been locked in his apartment and had warned her he'd be unreachable; he had come to an especially trying passage in his project that he expected would drain him of the energy to do anything else. She wondered if she made Gregory feel the way the young man had her, like he was being scooped out in small chunks.

Focused on walking away with an aura of purpose, Nina hadn't really noticed where she was going, and found herself at a trailhead. She began to climb a series of stone steps framed by moss-etched stone walls, which eventually gave way to gravel. The incline was moderate, and she wasn't particularly dressed for hiking. A family, geared to the gills with walking sticks, wide-brimmed hats, and sturdy boots passed her on their way down and stared. Their perplexed faces, their preparation almost persuaded her to turn back until she saw ahead the outline of a torii gate.

Beyond the gate was a small shrine that looked as ancient as the mossy walls. It was empty of people but full of feral cats that swirled in and out of the weather-blasted structure. Nina knelt and petted the ones that let her pet them, and stood at the little stone pool and ladled cool water over her hands. The shrine was encircled by statues of lion-dogs, but the cats were its real guardians. Later that evening, so as not to interrupt him, Nina emailed Gregory about the experience, and the next morning he responded, *A shrine full of cats! Haha. That's your paradise, isn't it?* After the shrine she'd climbed the rest of the way to the top, saw the spread of towns below, houses that looked flimsy as paper boxes clustered around the dark green hills and rice fields. This unexpected peak was crawling now with hikers, humpbacked old women, children sucking from thermoses of iced green tea, panting dogs. The world is big, Nina thought, and nothing much seemed worth worrying about.

It was one of those realizations that later, upon the plunge back into her life, seemed at once true and impossible to return to.

Gregory now informed her that Nina had come here once before and found it calming; he noted that there was a shrine full of cats around somewhere, forgetting the detail of the mountain.

Annoyed, Nina asked, "What would she need to calm down from?"

He looked away. "She's a very anxious person."

She knew what Jess would say, what she herself might say were she not preempted by his claims to monstrosity: "Do you make her anxious?"

They rounded the northwest corner of the park, where a playground stood, empty now; all the families were off visiting the dead. Gregory's hands started working. He had a nervous habit of picking at his cuticles. "Did she say something to you?"

She told him what she had told Jess once. "That it's hard to know how to talk to you sometimes."

"It's not that hard," he muttered. His phone buzzed; he flipped it open and read something there and his face loosened, the suggestion of a smile blooming around his mouth.

"Who is that?" Who did he speak to? There was only his brother, Charles, and her. "Was that Nina?" she asked him, and when he shook his head and didn't answer, she snatched the phone from his grip.

Next Monday is so far from here, she read on the screen. *How am I supposed wait this long to see you?* She didn't recognize the number, a local one. She handed the phone back to him. There was the knowledge of something approaching. There was the rumble of it inside her.

"Okay," Gregory said. He sighed deeply, a tremble in his exhale, and wiped his hands over his face. "This is what I'm scared of. That Nina found out and took off."

"Found out what?"

He looked around. "Let's, like, sit down somewhere." He walked to a bench a few feet away and she followed. He sat down and patted the space beside him and she obeyed. There was so much the body could do without your permission or even awareness.

His fingers were working like crazy now, shredding his cuticles, and she wanted to seize them. "I know how much you love Nina."

She nodded. Straight ahead was a narrow strip of street and the houses that faced the park with their dark, concave tile roofs, all cramped together. You couldn't have screaming fights in one of those without the neighbors knowing everything.

"I love her too," he said. "I think I always will. She's my best friend. Do you believe me?"

A light came on in one of the windows and within it, a woman materialized, ducked down, reappeared, pot in hand. She started filling it with water from the sink. Somebody's mother.

"But I've fallen in love with someone else. Someone at my school."

The words didn't mean anything to her. Someone at school? The coworkers who amounted to only stories, jokes, in this unreal place? When Nina was overwhelmed by it, its impenetrable systems of etiquette, its alien blare and beauty, Gregory reminded her that one day it would all be a memory.

"Jess?" he said.

She was watching the woman, who had dropped noodles into the boiling water. This was like the time in his old apartment she'd slashed her hand open on a broken bottle in the trash, when she had gone to take it out, and seen the blood brighten her skin and leak down her wrist long before she felt any pain; she thought if she could run to the woman now, she would stop it, pause time before it reached her.

He touched her shoulder gingerly, the way you would a frightened pet.

Nina couldn't turn to look at him. She opened her mouth, though it wasn't hers, it was wider, thinner-lipped, and said to Gregory, "Why don't you just fuck off?"

***

On the walk home she forgot the body she was in. She looked at her watch: it was now 3:00 p.m. here, which meant 3:00 a.m. there, in New York. She thought, in a few hours I can call my mother.

At home she fell onto the futon and lay there for what felt like many hours, until she was desiccated by crying. Then she stood and went to the bathroom to blow her nose and saw in the mirror Jess's face swollen and slicked with tears and snot. It stopped her. It was as though the devastation was not hers.

Doubly so; as Jess, there was no one for her to reach out to. Nina closed her eyes against the reflection in the mirror, mentally wiped it away, replaced it with her own. This was *her* fault—Nina's. Her jealous guardianship over her realm, when Jess's was so lonely; her intervention with Mr. Quinn, and how they had never spoken of it in the years that followed, the resentment simmering in their silences.

There came a sound like snoring through her front door. Nina swiped a hand across her face, which felt hot and inflamed, and opened it. The sound was coming from the landing below, between her floor and Charles's, and there Charles was, curled on the ground like a sleeping infant, breath clattering in his nose, blood pooling beneath his skull.

Nina found more of it as she descended the stairs toward him, spotting the walls.

Last week, Gregory had told her, Charles came to his apartment with a T-shirt wrapped around his head.

"What are you doing?" Gregory asked.

"Looking for insurgents," Charles said.

"Go to bed, Charles," Gregory said, and had followed him back to be sure he had returned to his apartment, rather than stumbled into the night to terrify locals.

Now Charles's head was turned to one side, resting in its puddle of blood. He was not snoring but wheezing, with great difficulty. Her first instinct was to simply return to her apartment and wait for another neighbor to stumble over Charles's body, to deal with it themselves.

Instead Nina called for an ambulance. She heard Jess's voice tell the stammering operator that she didn't speak any Japanese. There was a long wait while she was on hold. She listened to the crickets chiming. She continued standing over Charles, who did not awaken. Looking down at him, slumped like a felled elephant, Nina thought that this was what happened when you allowed yourself to become borderless.

***

As the EMTs loaded Charles's huge body onto the stretcher—and still, he did not wake up—she saw Gregory come onto his balcony and look down into the swirl of ambulance lights. She had tried, once, to tell him the story of Mr. Quinn. They were in their bedroom in Brooklyn. It was a Saturday morning, mild, and she hated to taint a pristine moment, the warmth and pleasure of lingering in bed, but Nina told him it felt like time for her to share something from her past. In high school, she had been—she guessed you could call it assaulted, by a teacher. She hadn't struggled or said no, but she thought it must have been clear from how her body responded to his touch that she was unwanting and afraid. She didn't think about it much now, Nina said, heart thrumming, but it seemed important to mention.

Gregory looked into her eyes, nodding, his features softened with concern. He said he was sorry; he petted her hair for a while. He said that he too had felt the shock of being selected for attention he'd never wanted. The group of boys materialized each time he began attending a new school, unique to each town and yet essentially the same. It was his unfamiliarity, Gregory guessed, or maybe that he'd been a late bloomer, or his lack of acquaintance with whatever the local sports franchises were; he was insufficiently boyish in the preferred ways. Or it was none of those things, because none of them quite explained why he could never master his arrivals whenever his family had to relocate, never figure out how to land with a splash of mystery and allure rather than an apparent invitation to swarm, attack. It began to feel inevitable, assigned, like his tormentors had no more choice in the matter than he did. The bullying didn't let up, he said, it only changed form, and it had whittled him down and twisted him. How much one's childhood dictated: who would he be, absent the terrorizing? Would he be here at all? "But I'm glad I'm here," he told Nina, stroking the inside of her arm the way he knew she liked.

By the time they climbed out of bed Nina felt warm again with the privilege of being welcomed so deeply into what it meant to be Gregory. But woven through the feeling, contaminating it, was the pressure she had expected to release by her own sharing. Though she had not told him the conclusion to the story of Mr. Quinn, she'd been waiting, she realized, for Gregory to say something that would exonerate her, that would scrub clean of guilt all the spaces she shared with Jess.

***

A knock on the door. Nina turned over, shook herself free of the cling-ing vines of sleep, saw the sun was up.

She stood, made her way to the door, opened it to find herself standing there in the hallway, a backpack slung over her shoulders, a blush of sunburn prickling over her cheeks. Jess smiled a little. Jess was inside the smile—Nina had been ransacked by her. A wave of horror swept upward from her knees. Nina raised Jess's right hand and it hung in the air, in place, and then it swung outward and came down, palm open, against the cheek of the woman standing before her, with such force that the impact traveled up her arm. Nina watched her body fall back against the concrete wall of the hallway and raise its hands to shield itself from more blows.

***

Jess had not been obliterated by a train; she had not been abducted, strangled, her body stashed in a cave. She had not become lost within a tangle of intersecting alleys and pulled into an ancient wooden bath-house, gone forever. She had not even had a particularly difficult time communicating with people—she had not needed Nina at all.

Returned to herself, her cheek still singing with pain, Nina sat hunched at the kitchen table.

"Where were you?" she said. Now that she knew she would not be marooned from her body, there was no sense of relief at settling back within it. It was late August. She had renewed her contract at the beginning of June. Another ten months here.

"Hiroshima," Jess said. She clutched an ice pack in her hand. "I took the bullet train."

"You couldn't have just told me that? You couldn't have texted?" She sounded to herself like a hectoring parent and for a moment her sense of righteousness wavered.

"It seemed like you needed to be on your own. Like there was something you needed to find out."

"You don't know shit about my life here." Jess's mouth twisted. A thrill vibrated through Nina, the thrill of being the wronged party. She remembered the blankness with which Jess had looked at her in the hallways of their high school after their rupture. Not anger, but blankness, as though they had never met.

"Do you understand," Jess said—shakily, Nina recognized, with another little charge—"why I did it?"

Nina said, "Revenge."

"Revenge? For what?"

"For Mr. Quinn."

Jess twitched a little at the name. "I was trying to help you," she said, "the way you tried to help me."

"So you knew? About Gregory and the teacher?"

Jess looked up, confused. A line of concern formed between her eyebrows. "All I knew was that you didn't seem happy."

"I'm so happy now," Nina said. "Thank you."

Jess had to turn away from her again. She began picking at her thumbnail, and the gesture so reminded Nina of Gregory's nervous habit that it propelled her to her feet and onto the balcony. She leaned against the railing and shut her eyes against the heat. Behind her the door slid open.

"I really didn't know anything," Jess said, "except that whatever was happening between you and Gregory looked familiar." She paused, and then added: "Like my mom and Rob."

A thudding started inside her. She remembered the dread provoked by Rob's tensed form beside her, that night in the hospital waiting room, and the dread of seeing Mr. Quinn's face, full of anticipation.

Nina turned around. "I need you to leave."

Jess's eyes filled. She shook her head. "Please."

She'd never speak to Jess again, Nina resolved. And then in the next moment felt the decision leak away through her fingers. "What do you even need me for?"

"I just do," Jess said.

***

Gregory, smoking a cigarette on his balcony, saw Nina and Jess leaving the *jutaku* the following evening and called down to them, as Nina had wished he would only nights before. In response, she spun and flashed two middle fingers up at him. The juvenility of the gesture, she thought, was the sharpest barb she could have sent his way; Gregory who had to cultivate the aesthetics even of their arguments, preferring to withdraw from the scene and craft email retorts in which every line break and semicolon was carefully considered.

They embarked that night on a tour of Fukuoka's theme bars, beginning with one the size of a corridor done up in the style of 1980s Japan, pop stars caterwauling from the speakers, walls bedecked with framed portraits of women with high ponytails and neon dresses.

"You know I talk to your mom on the phone sometimes," Jess said.

"About what?" There were a few men in the bar, carefully not looking at either of them.

"You, mostly. How much we miss you."

Jess was not, necessarily, forgiven. It was only that now there
was no one else: the friends she might have made among other foreigners, Gregory had steered her from. Or, more truthfully, she had
assumed she would not need. She watched Jess, whose face was tilted
down toward the glass and eyelids were heavy with silvery shadow,
for some twist of her features that might indicate what she'd really
been up to when she took off. Had she truly seen anything about
Gregory at all?

"Your mom's always saying how hard it is when her friends talk about
the things they're doing with their daughters," Jess continued. "So we
made plans to meet up for coffee, but it never happened. I think it just
wouldn't be the same."

Perhaps she had started on a journey, like the ones Nina had imagined. Started, until something pulled her back.

"She needs you," Jess said.

***

The next bar was designed to resemble a cave, complete with mottled,
moist walls. There, Nina checked her phone and found that Gregory
had filled her voice mail with tears.

"I know I'm a monster," he said. "I know I've ruined your life."

Jess let out a contemptuous laugh at this, one that drew over to them
some glances, like fireflies, from around the dark space.

"Ruined?" she echoed. "Doesn't he think highly of himself."

But then Nina's tears returned, not only for herself but also for him.
It must have felt natural, dismantling all they had together. His early
years had been a series of nullifications, each little life he'd built in each
little town undone. And so why not once more? How could he understand the value of being bound to someone?

"I promise your life's not over," Jess said. "It may feel that way, but
it's not. I've been there."

"With Khaled?"

Jess gave her an odd look. "No, not Khaled."

***

They missed the last train: Nina, bladder bursting, pulled Jess into the parking lot behind a *konbini* where she squatted and peed, the fluorescent glare from the store illuminating the damp blacktop, Jess laughing so hard she almost fell to her knees. This and other events—pulling Jess, stiff-legged in heels, through the love hotel district, explaining in disconnected snatches about how you could book a room without being seen, and then finding, finally, a capsule hotel, where Nina asked the clerk in what seemed to her remarkably fluid Japanese for a twin room to share with her old, dear, most loved friend—would revisit her, in the bright next morning, through nauseated haze.

The room turned out to have bunk beds and no windows. "Amazing," Jess said, and lifted herself to the top. Moments later, her jeans and shoes came clattering down. When Nina switched off the light it was very dark.

"It's like being in the grave," Jess said.

Though she could not see it happening, Nina sensed the room orbiting slowly around her. Jess's words struck her as bad luck, an Evocation, even, which the *Compendium* had taught her differed from an invocation, a request; it was a calling, to the land of the unseen, for the appearance of an entity.

"Before," Nina said, speaking into the underside of Jess's bunk, "were you talking about Mr. Quinn?"

Silence pressed down upon her. Perhaps Jess was already asleep.

"You know, when I look back, I think he really did love me," Jess said.

The dark leaned against her chest, making it hard to talk. "How do you know?"

"I don't know. It was in his looks. Khaled never looked at me like that." She could hear Jess breathing; she could hear the pacing of her thoughts. "I remember once he told me he'd never felt like this before. He'd assumed there was something defective about him. Some kind of deadness. Until me. I don't think it was just a line. Sometimes his face, when he saw me, was so happy I felt scared. But like, in a good way."

The darkness doubled and Nina pressed her lips together so as not to make a sound.

"We talked once after and he said he'd always known, deep down, that he just wasn't meant to find love. But he said I would, some day."

Nina swallowed until she was sure her voice would be even. "I didn't understand."

"I see that now," Jess said. "It probably would never have worked out, right?"

Nina pulled herself from the bed and stood, feeling for the edge of Jess's mattress, wavering a little on her bare feet.

"I'm here," Jess said, and Nina moved closer to where her face must have been.

"We can't do this anymore," Nina said to her. "Make these secret plans for each other. From now on, we have to promise to just say what we're thinking."

"I know," Jess whispered.

It was then Nina forgave her. She had used Jess, after all, to make the relationship happen, and even though she'd never know it, it was justice that Jess brought it to an end.

***

They would be careful the rest of Jess's stay, and then remotely, for many months after that, over the phone and video chat, stepping gingerly around what had happened. Nina would tell Jess about how Charles returned, after a week, from the hospital, head heavily bandaged, only to be fired by his school and sent back home to Hawaii, where, she could only hope, he would get some kind of help. Gregory, now without Nina or Charles for company, left the *jutaku* to move in with his girlfriend. Nina's supervisor, Kimizuka-sensei, perhaps believing she would feel vindicated by this, told her it was a scandal at his school, that they were overheard arguing by the tennis courts, an embarrassing disruption to staff harmony, and none of the other teachers would speak to them.

Later, in the autumn, she would find friends in the people she'd previously believed, when she was with Gregory, that she had no need for; they would organize a trip to an island in the Philippines where Nina would learn to scuba dive. Underwater you couldn't speak, of course; you couldn't share what you were experiencing with anyone, and she would see an octopus camouflage itself right in front of her, vanishing into a tangle of coral, and a school of jackfish that traveled in a tornado-shaped funnel, and a shark resting on its belly on the ocean bed. But her favorite were the sea turtles, who would peer at you as they swam past with ageless eyes. Her mother would tell her over the phone that she was sounding better every day.

But before all that, she'd take Jess back to the airport. They would both cry when they said goodbye. On the way back up to her apartment, now alone, Nina would find herself thinking, without really understanding why, *The first part of my life is over.* In a reverie, she would open the door to the shower room and flick on the light, and a giant cockroach would go skittering across the tile floor with a terrible papery sound.

14
GREEN GIRLS
(2000)

It was strange to think of teachers having first names. It was strange to think of them having lives at all outside the school, of taking baths, weeping at movies, laughing, their heads thrown back, silver fillings showing, at something a person they loved had said. Of loving people. Mr. Quinn was the exception. His first name was Joseph, and some of the *Eagle Eye* staff called him Joey, with affection, behind his back, and occasionally to his face. Jordan Applebaum, the managing editor, had seen him out one night at the sushi place. He was there with three women.

"Pimp," said Adam Fleischer, the sports editor.

Despite the strangeness—or perhaps, because of it—they scrutinized the teachers, digging for hints of inner lives that were vulnerable and without authority. Mrs. Ackerman, it was said, had a five o'clock shadow; Ms. Perez had evidently decided to quit dyeing her hair and embrace her age, and the result was a wiry gray halo at the crown of her head that slowly, over the course of the fall semester, pushed the false brown downward. She looked, in a word (Rachel Koenig's word, she whispered it to Nina in the back of the classroom), like a hag.

But Mr. Quinn evaded the murmured brutalizing, though they'd all noticed his habit of wearing the same sweater two to three times a week. He never sent a single student to the dean, never so much as raised his voice. On the first day of English class, he reminded them they would be heading off to college soon, which meant they were practically adults, so he was going to proceed on the assumption that they could handle themselves. And when one of the boys snickered while someone read aloud from *Heart of Darkness*, Mr. Quinn only had to look at him and say, "Dude," and he would stop. The girls didn't disrupt at all; they followed the teacher with the same hazed-over eyes, whether he was monologuing about Conrad and colonialism or in character as Macbeth, thumping the desks, climbing on chairs, thrusting with invisible blades.

***

The *Eagle Eye* staff accepted that Mr. Quinn's position as adviser was mostly ceremonial, an avenue for bumping up his salary, and he in turn accepted how they used the newspaper's dedicated room. Occasionally it served its intended purpose, as someone tapped out on the yellowed keyboard an op-ed on the school dress code or a review of the winter concert—Nina's purview, as entertainment editor, though she'd assigned that one out. The writer had devoted the bulk of the piece to a solo from his girlfriend, a tenth-grade soprano, deeming it "transcendent."

But more often the room, nestled adjacent to the soundless chambers used for in-house suspension, was a hideaway. It had a door that locked, and its only window faced a courtyard. It was the sole space in the high school beyond the reach of the roving eye of discipline.

Staff forewent lockers and dumped their textbooks in its corners. They napped and rolled joints and made out in there.

The *Eagle Eye*'s editor-in-chief, Vicki Gordon, became de facto gatekeeper.

"I went in during eighth period to do layout and there were like five random people there," she told them, perched atop Mr. Quinn's desk at their Thursday afternoon meeting. "We have to keep it staff-only from now on."

Nina and Jordan, in their usual seats in Mr. Q.'s classroom, glanced at each other. They both knew Jess was at that very moment dozing on the plaid love seat—which Vicki herself had snuck in one weekend—in the *Eagle Eye* room. Jess was the most abusive of the friends-of-the-staff perks, dropping by the room every day, dumping her copy of *The American Vision* on the floor.

And when confronted by Vicki about her presence, Jess would blink and stare as though she did not understand the questions. There was no response to this. Her incomprehension was a void; you might toss something its way and never hear the clatter of it hitting bottom.

Nina felt a bit sorry for Vicki. Nina, too, had encountered her friend's odd blankness in the face of uninvited inquiry, the bite of isolation such misfires conferred. Lately, it had been happening more and more.

That matter settled, inasmuch as it could be, Vicki surrendered the floor to Jordan, who handled the editorial calendar. There was a gap in the upcoming month's sports coverage; could anyone go to a Tuesday evening lacrosse game? There was a consensus among the students on Jordan, much as there was on Mr. Q., that he had his charms but fell short of desirability. He couldn't quite get out from under that thatch of dark red hair. Big Red, and so on—the nicknames were no less hurtful for being uninspired, he confessed to Nina, early one evening when they were ostensibly working on copyedits and had the *Eagle Eye* room to themselves.

"You're not even big," she'd said. "I mean, you're slim—like, in a good way," and he'd swiveled in his chair away from the computer screen and kissed her for the first time. Leo had been her previous boyfriend, and middle-school relationships, Jess told her, didn't count, erasing Nina's romantic history with a snort of dismissal. So then Jordan was her first, after a string of earlier hook-ups, disconnected as loose change, but somehow nevertheless uniform, endless make-out sessions that left her with chin rubbed raw by nascent stubble, the feeling of hands struggling like trapped animals beneath her shirt, the insistent prodding through jeans.

Jess was onto her. "What's up with you and Jordan?" she had asked in the girls' locker room that afternoon.

"Big Red?" Nina said. Guilt floated up from her guts. "We're co-workers."

"I don't understand why you would even talk to him, after how he harassed you." Jess had stripped down to nothing. None of the other girls did this; they faced the lockers, contorted themselves in such a way that at most, only a strip of lower back or upper thigh was visible at any given time. (The gym teacher, Ms. Todd, had pulled Jess aside early in the semester and demanded, "Garcia, were you running around naked in the locker room?" Jess had smirked at her, much the way she smirked at Nina's claims to a collegial relationship with Jordan. "It's a *locker room*," she'd told Ms. Todd.)

But Nina would admit to no more. It was hers, whatever was happening. Jess had her own secrets, she suspected, since they were barely swapping at all these days. Each time she asked, Jess had some excuse; there was something she was barring Nina from accessing. And the longer she was confined to her ordinary, rules-abiding self—who like the other girls changed clothes in the locker room as though the body beneath them was all wound, and to expose it was to die—the fiercer her longing to escape it.

***

Nina slipped out of the meeting early so she could return to the *Eagle Eye* room before the others. Jess was still sleeping on the couch, facing away from the door, curled into herself, hair spilling over the cushions.

Nina shook her shoulder, rousing her. "Vicki's cracking down," she said.

Jess turned over, yawning. "So?"

"We have to figure out a legit reason for you to come here all the time."

Jess grimaced against the late-afternoon sunlight that fell across the couch. Eyes closed, she said, "We could switch and then I could take naps here and you could take Physics for me."

"And what exactly is in that for me?"

Jess sat up, opened her eyes a crack. "You get to undermine the boss," she said. "And have double the opportunities to be a good student."

"Wow. That sounds so amazing."

Jess dropped her head onto Nina's shoulder, a bit gingerly so as not to risk brushing their foreheads together. She raked her fingernails up and down Nina's thigh, leaving pale tracks on her jeans. "Oh," she said. She straightened. "What if I became staff photographer?"

"I thought you decided you hated photography." Jess had begun taking the class that semester as an elective to avoid being pushed into something less palatable, like home ec.

"I don't hate photography. I hate the students in photography class. I hate the way they walk."

"The way they walk?"

"Like this." Jess stood and set her shoulders back, disappeared the expression from her face. She moved slowly, zombie-like, around the room, arms dangling, bumping into the wall, staring unseeing into the distance. "Like they're sleepwalking."

"They all do that?"

"It's such a put-on. It's like they're trying to prove, 'Oh, I'm such an artist, I'm in my magical artist dream world all the time.'"

"Let me try." Nina stood and imitated Jess, floating absently along the perimeter.

Jess clapped her hands. "Perfect," she said. She joined Nina and they drifted, true artists, lost in the dream, still in it when Jordan and Vicki returned from the staff meeting. The others tried to interrupt them at this new game, but quickly gave up. They'd all learned by now that Nina and Jess had something impenetrable, maybe even unnatural.

***

Jess wanted to know why she could not play Hamlet in their class reading.

"Well," Mr. Q. said. "You certainly *could*. But I already promised the role to Raymond." Their old cafeteria companion had stunned them all by appearing on the first day of twelfth grade hardened and polished, made handsome enough over one mysterious summer to risk finally coming out of the closet. "What's wrong with Ophelia?"

"No fucking way," Jess said.

Mr. Q. offered her Polonius as a concession. "He has some of the most famous lines in all of Shakespeare."

"Deal." Jess offered a hand. Mr. Q. shook it and there arose a soft rippling among the girls in response to this moment of contact.

As he braced them for the weeks to come, themes and plot points, Jess flipped ahead in the play, searching out her lines. She stopped at one and giggled, circling it, and passed the book to Nina, who read:

> *Affection? Pooh! You speak like a green girl,*
> *Unsifted in such perilous circumstance.*
> *Do you believe his tenders, as you call them?*

***

After class, in the hallway, Jess grabbed Nina's hand and held her from proceeding to Physics. "If you could swap with one other person," she said, "who would you choose?"

"I have to think," Nina said, a bit stunned. Jess proposed a world in which it was possible to cover a vast amount of ground. The idea had not occurred to her. Their power, she'd always believed, was specific to the two of them; and only as a pair, together, could it be unlocked. "What about you?"

Mr. Q. emerged from the classroom and gave them a little salute.

"Maybe him," Jess said, watching the teacher navigate the flooded passageway. Mr. Q. was wearing one of his signature sweaters, and its colors waned as he walked away from them. "I want to know what it's like to have a dick."

It seemed to her evidence of the poverty of Jess's imagination. "Do you think there are other people who can do it?" Nina said. The bell was about to chime, but she had never been late before and would be

forgiven. And what did she need to learn, anyway, of a science that offered no account of what they could do?

"There must be, right?"

"Why must there be?"

Jess shrugged. "What's so special about us?"

***

The abstract of *Between You and Me: Body-Swapping and the Ownership of
the Self*, by Dr. Irma Orlova, Department of Neuroscience, Weill Cornell
Graduate School of Medical Sciences, referred to a study of perceptual
illusions related to the physical body: experiments with prostheses and
mannequins, speculation on developments in virtual-reality technology,
pitiful approximations of the real thing. A current of electricity applied
to the appropriate channel of the brain created in subjects the feeling
of being outside themselves, hovering six inches above their bodies, or
standing slightly behind them. Most subjects found this "highly unnerving," Dr. Orlova reported, and requested that the current be shut off
immediately. One young man was particularly troubled. The fact that
something as simple as an electrical jolt sent through gray matter in-
stilled the perception of departing oneself, the way spirits were thought
to do at the moment of death—what did this suggest, he wanted to
know, about the notion of an everlasting soul?

Nina recalled the *Compendium* entry on astral projection, the il-
lustration of the dreamer ascending from his own sleeping form. But
why go hunting now for an old book when the entirety of the known
world could be summoned to the screen before her? She minimized Dr.
Orlova's paper and typed *astral projection* into the search engine. There
flitted through her mind the idea of someone monitoring all this, an
agent looking for new recruits into his classified task force of superpow-
ered humans. It was her old self, the reader of the *Compendium*, the
fearer of ghosts, the believer in God, a companion who still tugged at
her hand sometimes.

She came upon an account from 1967 of dropping acid and visiting

the oneiric plane; a dry explanation of the phenomenon of sleep paraly-
sis. The world was not imaginative enough to imagine what they could
do, and if there were any others like them, they preferred to remain
hidden. Nina returned to Dr. Orlova's paper. *The everlasting soul* . . .
well, there was something, wasn't there, that could be pried loose from
the body? But without another body to enter, would it be stuck in that
void she passed through each time, the void that lay between Jess and
herself? It troubled her more and more, the idea of being a nothing in
a nowhere. It troubled her that whenever she went looking for answers,
in the *Compendium*, on the internet, inside the sanctuary on the day
that she became a woman, there were none. That when she knocked
she was answered by silence.

***

Jess's first-period entrances to the *Eagle Eye* room often had an element
of drama. She came in wearing big sunglasses, coffee in one hand, hair
windblown and mouth hanging a little slack, like a celebrity in an airport besieged by paparazzi.

Vicki stood to block her entrance, but before she could speak, Jess
said, "I'm joining the staff. As photographer."

She removed her glasses. Vicki seemed to wilt under her stare. "I'll
print out an application," she said.

Jess smiled at Nina, walked over to the couch and sank down beside
her. Nina extended an open palm and Jess slapped it lightly.

Nina leaned toward Jess and whispered into her hair, "We *are*
special."

"What do you mean?"

The sound of the printer screeched over them. "I did some research
last night. Did you know people seriously electrocute their own brains
to have out-of-body experiences?"

Confusion like a cloud passed over her face. Then it cleared. "People
do all kinds of stupid shit."

Nina thought again of the subject who'd asked about souls, the young man thrust into spiritual crisis. If only he knew there was much beyond electricity. But there was no trace on Earth of what they could do.

"You know what my mother tells me this morning when she drops me off?" Jess said. Nina smelled coffee on her breath. "'Always get a prenup.'"

"Aren't those for rich people?"

Jess looked at the back of Vicki's blond head as she bent over the printer. "I'm never getting married." She said it loudly, for the whole room to hear, they might etch it for her into some permanent record. Anita and Rob were on the precipice of divorce, deadlocked over who would keep the house. It was Rob who had sunk his money into it, he argued; Anita countered that it was she who made it a home. In the meantime Jess avoided the contested place as often as she could. She'd joined the track team their freshman year, and lately had begun, on weekend mornings, going for long practice runs that terminated at the Glass family's front door, and Jess, flushed and perspiring, would shower upstairs and join them for breakfast.

"Here," Vicki said, handing Jess the application.

"Thanks." Jess gave it a glance before shoving it into her backpack. They all knew she'd never turn it in. "They kept me up all night screaming at each other," she muttered to Nina. Her eyes were bloodshot. She looked like she'd sprinted out all her life force. The sunglasses and coffee were for her, not, as Nina had assumed, for the rest of them. Nina could give her relief. She was the only one, probably, in the world who could, and here she was, by unthinkable coincidence, sitting right beside her, but Jess didn't ask.

***

Another point of contention that the students had with Jordan Applebaum—in addition to the red hair—was that he had been given, for his seventeenth birthday, a brand-new BMW. Many of the other seniors had their own cars, but more often they were hand-me-downs. (Nina did not drive; she terminated the lessons with her father after their fifth session ended in her weeping at the wheel and pulling over to a tear-blurred curb as he seethed and swore.)

Only Nina knew that Jordan's BMW was a gift more for his parents than for him: it spared them having to drive him back and forth to each other's homes. It spared them, too, with its newness and pedigree, some of their guilt. They had divorced the summer five years previous and it was why, he told her, he'd been such a little shit in junior high. "I'm so ashamed when I think of it," he said, and though it was not an apology it was the closest, Nina sensed, that he could come to one.

He told her this as they drove around town one November evening, uncertain of where to go. Neither was interested in any of the usual activities available to them, the suburban offerings of diners, bowling alleys, strip malls. They coasted down side streets, down hallways of il-luminated split-levels and empty lawns.

Nina wished she could give him something in return. A secret prof-fered wanted a secret in response; otherwise it got lonely.

"That sucks," she told Jordan. He kept his eyes on the road. "Really," she said, and placed a hand over his, clenched around the wheel. "Your parents should know better than to think they could just buy you off with a car."

Jordan looked at her a little too long for a novice driver. He turned down a street that terminated at a canal, pulled over to a strip of grass singed by dog piss, parked, leaned in, pressed his lips against hers. His mouth was slippery with spearmint; he'd been thoughtful enough to chew some gum first.

"I feel like I can really tell you things," Jordan said.

"You really can." A laugh bubbled up at the back of Nina's throat, as she imagined telling Jess what a sensitive soul her raunchy tormen-tor had turned out to be.

"You're different from how you seem at school."

"What do you mean?"

Another car rounded the corner, its headlights burning briefly through the rear window. "You and Jess Garcia are pretty bitchy to everyone."

"That's not true." Amid the rolling boil of bitchiness that permeated

EHHS, her own could have hardly stood out. It was Jess, anyway, who was the difficult one.

Jordan shrugged. "People are scared to even talk to you two."

"Why?" she said, not really wanting to know the answer.

"Sometimes it seems like you think you're too good for everyone," Jordan said. She stared at his profile. "And Leo Ferrera is always saying he had to kick you out of his band because you tried to take it over."

An odor of brine was blowing off the canal. She could smell it even with the car windows rolled up. She lived in a small place, and the smallness was contagious, its grudges, its own sense of woundedness, dispersing into the air like spores.

"Sorry," Jordan said. "I don't know why I listened to that guy, anyway. He's such a dirtbag." He poked at her shoulder, trying to prod her back into playfulness.

"It's fine," Nina said. "I should try to be more friendly to people."

"Hey. I like you the way you are." Jordan leaned in like he meant to kiss her again, but instead, perhaps in an attempt to soothe, he rested his forehead for a moment against hers, a sensation so familiar, but so private. It was like being seen masturbating in public.

She jumped, cracking the back of her skull against the passenger window, plunging into disorientation. For a moment she wondered whether he knew everything, whether Jess had put him up to this as a test to see if Nina's findings were correct, that they were the only ones.

"Jesus. I said I was sorry."

Her head was humming with pain.

"So that's it for tonight?"

She stared out the window, waiting for the reverberations in her head to end. The thought of doing with him what she did with Jess, she entering his body and he hers, was too terrible to bear. She swallowed, tried to speak, but her insides still sizzled with adrenaline.

Jordan sighed, breath scraping the back of his throat. "Fine. I'll take you home."

He'd given her no time to recover. He wanted in, and he wanted in right now.

"I can walk from here," Nina said. She climbed out and something cracked in her chest. "So you can take care of your blue balls right now if you want." She slammed the door, and the sound briefly flooded her with satisfaction. But walking home she realized what this rupture meant. Her short time with him would be like all her other little secrets, all the things she'd ever tried to keep for herself since knowing Jess: invaded, stolen, or simply vanished into air.

***

She kept to herself the incident with Jordan. Jess would have had little sympathy, having sworn off their male classmates long ago. She'd made the error of falling for one only once, their freshman year. His name was Michael Miller; he was a junior then, with a buzzed head and a prominent position on the student council. He ran track, too, the 400-meter, the most difficult, Jess explained to Nina, because it was the longest sprint, a lung-singeing feat of perseverance and one at which he excelled, despite his legs being not particularly long. Jess approached him one Sunday at a meet, as though indifferent or ignorant to the hierarchy of under and upperclassmen, to congratulate him on a win.

Her race was next. "Can I rub your head for good luck?" she asked, and then ran a hand over his dark stubble without waiting for permission. He laughed a little, impressed, maybe, by her nerviness.

The two began lingering after practice on empty fields (his parents, too, rarely showed up to watch him run), fumbling around on the damp grass beneath the bleachers, accumulating that strange invisible force that rewrote you somehow from the inside: experience. But off the track he showed little interest in Jess, in fact barely acknowledged they'd shared anything at all, offering her at most a vague uplift of the chin when they passed between classes.

This only made her pursuit of Michael more ferocious. She shoved notes through the slats of his locker, cut math to slink by his classroom. It was cruel to expect her to go a full day without a glimpse, she told Nina. She stopped his friends, though she was a stranger to them, in the halls, to ask if they knew what his problem was. Finally, one day it was he who approached Jess, as she sat with Nina at their regular spot in the courtyard during lunchtime. A strong autumn sun bore down. Michael shoved open the doors from the cafeteria. As he strode over to them, Jess's face took on an alarming glow.

He jabbed a finger toward her chest. "Stay the fuck away from me," he said. "Crazy bitch."

Nina saw it, an almost imperceptible tremor in Jess's chin, and threw herself unthinking between the two of them. "*You* stay the fuck away from *us*," she said, but he was already gone, disappearing back inside the cafeteria, her great stand carried away by the breeze.

Thereafter Jess vowed she'd never feel a thing for a high school boy again, a declaration Nina was certain would be reversed by month's end. But it held: Jess had not dated, had not kissed, had not evinced even a flicker of interest in any of their classmates in the ensuing years. The demonic urgency that possessed her then: where had it gone? Could such a fire be extinguished for good?

***

In early October Raymond invited them to a concert with him and his boyfriend. "I'll drive," he said, and it seemed this was perhaps the real reason for the outing, to show off his new skill. That, and Nina suspected he thought she and Jess were gay, too, and hoped to guide them out of their hiding place, show them it was safe.

They picked up Nina first. Raymond's boyfriend, Tim, had graduated the year before; he had a buzzed haircut with the stubble dyed in a leopard-print pattern. He was the sort of boy whose attention she'd dreamed of when she was a younger student, but in the school hallways she'd always passed just beneath it, unable, as herself, to float up into his regard. As Jess she could. Jess knew how to be noticed.

As though to prove this, when they pulled up at her house there was a police car in the driveway, its lights splashing across the vinyl siding.

"What the hell," Raymond said.

Tim turned to him from the passenger seat. "Do you think some-one died?"

Nina remembered the night in the ER, the bulge like a bony para-site of Anita's dislocated shoulder.

"What do we do?" Raymond said. Before she could answer, Jess emerged, tiny from their vantage across the street.

She opened the door and climbed into the backseat beside Nina. "It was just a big misunderstanding," she told them.

"Shit happens," Tim said quickly, though such shit had never happened, Nina guessed, at any of their own homes, certainly not at hers. Raymond drove down the otherwise quiet streets, made a right onto the turnpike. Nina kept silent, peeking over occasionally. She saw that Jess was leaning forward slightly so that her long hair fell over her face. Tim tuned the volume up on the car's sound system, played a song by Fiona Apple, whom they were going to see. "I fucking love her," he said, and Nina and Raymond rushed to agree; they began wondering in large voices what she might play that night, their discussion overheated inside the bubble of the car. Raymond merged onto the Ocean Parkway, into a river of cars all heading the same place, as the venue reared up before them from its perch over the sea. To their right, a teenage girl in a red Pontiac rolled down her window, releas-ing a skunk-smelling fog and the blare of heavier music. She looked over at Tim and smiled lazily. Extended her arm and offered the joint.

"We're good," he called.

She drew her arm in and sipped from it, leaning her head back.

"What the hell," Raymond said again.

"You're driving, dummy."

"It doesn't affect your driving."

"Oh, really?"

Jess's presence was like a dark throb beside her through their argu-ment, but when they finally reached the venue she was composed. She looked at Nina over the roof of the car. "You were right," she said, "to want to get far away from them." Across the expanse of the parking lot they could see a jittery line of bodies waiting at the entrance to the the-ater. "I don't know if I can do this," she said.

Tim had a fake ID. Nina had been looking forward to getting into some minor trouble as herself, for once. She tried to gulp back her impatience. "Let's go for a walk," she said. She told the boys they'd catch up to them.

They walked to the far end of the parking lot and over the grass median. They crossed the parkway, snaking between idling cars, and made their way through another lot and onto the beach. The lights from the venue reached out here, dimly, as they shuffled over the brine-smelling sand. Damp clumps of it wormed into Nina's sneakers. Jess was ahead of her now. She reached the lifeguard's mound and dropped onto all fours. It looked for a moment like succumbing to grief. But then she was scrambling up, and pulling herself into the great white seat where in summer the young men sat, sun baking their hard chests as they watched the sea. With effort, Nina followed and hauled her body into the chair beside Jess. Pieces of music, a scrap of guitar, a few keys of piano, were carried over to them by the wind.

"I've been thinking," Nina said, "about our dorm room. How we should decorate it." She needed to pull Jess's gaze away from wherever it was looking and into a future wholly under their control. They'd been talking since May about where they'd go to college, how they'd room together and become the gravitational center of whichever dorm was fortunate enough to have them. They'd swap and go to all each other's classes, double the number of students and professors and clubs and frats anyone else could possibly encounter, and thus achieve a mastery of the campus that would send them sailing through the four years to follow.

Jess looked at her with flat eyes. "Let's stop kidding ourselves," she said. "You're going to go to some JAP college I can't afford."

Something jumped inside Nina's ribcage. It was a word they'd used only for others, never for her. She thought if she pulled Jess in right now, if she wrapped her arms around her, her friend might crack open, allow herself to be consoled. But the sting of the word was high in her chest. She didn't move.

Jess stared out at the waves. "My mom said to only apply to state schools. Divorces are expensive, you know."

"I bet you'd get scholarships."

"Why? Because I'm Mexican?" Jess shook her head. "It doesn't matter," she muttered, "I have my own things going on."

"Like what?"

"Just a plan B," Jess said. One corner of her mouth turned up, briefly, in a half-smile. "I can't say what it is yet."

Nina didn't reply. It seemed a clear falsehood, a childish one, best to let go. As the waves crested, the lights of the venue danced briefly within their black undersides. They fell against the shore, fell apart and were laced with white foam. When they were sucked back out, made a part again of the whole dark sea, they left a gloss behind on the sand like snail slime. More music traveled out to them, uninterpretable, a series of sounds with no connective tissue.

A fear, an excitement, rose in Nina as she realized she had made a decision, the only one that could lift Jess from her gloom. She gave her a poke. "Let's switch tonight," Nina said. "A sleepover, like the old days."

Hope rose in Jess's eyes. "Really?" she said. "Are you sure? It's pretty ugly right now."

"I'm sure. You need a break."

The relief in Jess's face was the relief of a question long unasked, finally answered.

***

What had she imagined? Anita, dead-eyed before the television, its blue light exposing stress-worn crevices in her face, a Parliament sizzling between her fingers, a wall of hostility cast up before her. But instead the house smelled overwhelmingly clean, a lemon-scented beacon in the night. She found Anita in the kitchen, hair up, chugging from a bottle of water. When she saw Nina, she ran over and wrapped her in a tight hug.

"I am so sorry you had to see that, kiddo," she said. She sniffed her hair. "Mmm. You smell like the beach." The air felt pressed out of Nina's lungs. Eventually Anita let go. "You okay?" Before Nina could answer, she continued, "It was definitely Fried who called the cops.

That jerkoff. Fat Fried. You know how many times he's called the cops on his own son? For what, nobody knows. God forbid anyone disturbs his perfect suburban peace for one second. The only noise he likes to hear is the landscapers."

Nina grunted a little in response. Jess wouldn't want to give her mother much of anything.

"Don't worry," Anita said. She took another glug from the water bottle. "Rob's not coming back. He said he's staying at Joanie's until everything's finalized. Like I care."

Again, she saw Anita's silhouette in the car on the way to the hospital, the vivid bruise on her shoulder. Her stomach turned over.

"Mom," she said, "I really don't think I should have to go to a state school."

Anita's jaw untightened, and her face hung briefly, uncomprehending. Then it scrunched again. "We've been over this. I'm not paying thirty thousand a year when you don't even know what you want to study."

"I have plans."

Anita laughed, a few raspy syllables. "You can barely be bothered to pick up a book. You haven't even started your applications yet. I'm supposed to believe you're gonna go away and magically turn into some brilliant person?"

For the second time the air was knocked out of her. Anita turned to retrieve her rag and cleaning spray. "I'm not stupid," she managed.

"No, you're not," Anita agreed. "You want to go away to private school with Nina, be my guest. But you need a scholarship for that. You need to work hard like her, instead of running around with God knows who."

The suggestion unsteadied her further. "Who am I running around with?"

"Like I should know. When's the last time I made you do anything? When's the last time you listened to me? The only person holding you back is yourself."

Nina's legs stiffened. She felt the strength in them, the months of running, no one watching her, no one in her corner. What Jess needed was not to be left alone. The realization made her slam her hand on the kitchen table. The glasses drying there chimed together, and Anita jumped a little. Irritation curdled and rose within her, formed words. "How can you say that to me? Do you even know anything about me?" A note of shrillness had entered her voice, making it sound more like her own.

Anita chuckled again. "I pushed you out of my body," she said. "I know you better than you know yourself."

***

There was no pleasure, the next morning, in exploring Jess's body, as there usually was. She didn't linger as she gathered the long hair into a ponytail, or skid her fingertips down the gentle convexity of the belly, run a tongue over the gap between the front teeth (Jess had been encouraged, had refused, to wear braces).

Mercifully, there was no encounter with Anita before she left. A dingy mist still hung over the streets as she walked, quickly to insulate herself from the chill, to the strip mall where they had planned to meet. She got there before Jess and went into a deli and ordered a coffee, took it outside and sat on the curb, sipping from the blue paper cup. She hadn't slept much the night before. Nina felt like an older version of herself, a little life-wearied already.

She watched Jess approach, wearing her body. Though she always tried to see it as others did, as something that belonged to another person and had nothing to do with her, her regard still snagged on its flaws as only an owner's would: the bumps sprinkled across the forehead, the ill fit of the jeans, the way they sagged a little in the back.

"So now you drink coffee?" Jess said. Her lightness had returned.

"I'm really sorry," she told Jess, "but I got into a fight with your mom." Jess frowned. "Bad?"

"I'm not sure," Nina said. "I don't think so." She felt, in fact, that it might be kind of bad.

"Well, it was only a matter of time," Jess said. "It's impossible not to fight with her these days."

Nina said again, "I'm sorry."

"It's fine." Jess looked down with distaste at Nina's ragged nails. "Your mom told me something really sad."

"What?"

"A student at her school killed himself. A boy she was trying to help. I think she feels like it was her fault."

Nina's mother, a social worker at a high school much rougher than their own, rarely spoke to her of her job. It had not occurred to Nina that her mother might be, at any given time in their home—standing in her robe in the kitchen, stirring scrambled eggs over the stove, or curled on the couch with a book, or reading to Zachary in his room at night—carrying with her the pain of strangers.

"Why?" Nina said.

"Why did he kill himself?" Hearing Jess say it aloud made the question sounded idiotic. "Who knows? But you should be extra nice to your mom for a while. She's having a tough time."

Nina finished her coffee and set the cup down on the blacktop. A breeze took it, scuttling, away from them.

"She was so happy to have a heart-to-heart with me. You," Jess corrected herself. "I don't get why you don't talk to her more often."

"She's not always so great," Nina muttered. *She doesn't even know when I'm not there*, she wanted to add. What kind of mother carried you inside herself, fed you, grew you from her body, pushed you out of it, and had no idea when you departed your own, another daughter in your place?

"Fine," Jess said, "whatever." She stood up. "Let's get going. I'm freezing."

Nina got to her feet, pressed her forehead against Jess's, felt the pull that began in her core and emanated outward, an insistence that rang through her organs, that left no time to even consider resisting before it slid her back into her skin. As ever, there was, before she was folded once again inside herself, the fragment of time in which she was outside them both, in the vastness of no place. What if there were a way for her to stay there? Would her own body just collapse, leaving Jess stranded?

Was that where the boy had gone, her mother's student, had he thrown himself into that nowhere?

***

When she returned that afternoon her mother was in the kitchen, slicing vegetables. Nina came up behind her and wrapped her arms around her waist.

"I'm sorry about your student," Nina said.

She felt her mom exhale.

"Thanks, sweetie pie."

"I'm sure you did everything you could to help him."

"I wish I was sure." Her mother glanced at Nina over her shoulder. She put the knife down. "Nina, I just want to make sure you understand why we said no last night to Jess living with us."

Perhaps it was fair. Nina had not told Jess everything, either. They had both made their requests. She would not tell Jess that she had discovered hers. There'd be a cruelty in laying down between them, like a piece of evidence, her childish hope.

"Yeah, I get it," Nina said.

"You know we love Jess. Hopefully soon she'll be out of there and off to college."

Nina nodded. She wished the same for herself, to be free of the town, the tired geometry of its streets, the house from which she passed in and out unseen. Her eyes traced the perimeter of the kitchen, its ordinariness, trying to find within its corners the thing Jess craved.

***

Vicki Gordon, resigned to Jess Garcia's self-appointed position and her strange alliance with Nina Glass, gave them an assignment: as a photographer-journalist team, ask the teachers about their New Year's resolutions and take their portraits.

The portrait-taking would go on far longer than the interview portion, with Jess coaxing them into unconventional postures and squeezing a smile, even, out of a mirthless tenth-grade chemistry teacher better known for muttering curses whenever he tried to turn on the slide projector and found that the students, again, had stolen its lightbulb. She searched out the boundary of teacher/student decorum and then threw her weight against it.

"To lose ten pounds," said Ms. Donoghue, a social studies teacher, to Nina's question.

"Are you crazy?" Jess said. She lifted the camera to her eye and snapped before the teacher could ready herself. "You're already super skinny. And what kind of message would that send to the female students?"

Ms. Donoghue reddened to her bony wrists. "Alright," she said. "To finish my novel."

"That's more like it," Jess said, and snapped again. In the photograph, the teacher would be flushed and beaming.

During lunch they found Mr. Q. in his empty classroom, chewing a bagel and reading.

"What's that?" Jess said, by way of greeting.

He turned the cover toward them. *Zen and the Art of Motorcycle Maintenance: An Inquiry into Values.*

"You have a motorcycle?" Jess said.

He shook his head. "That's not really what it's about."

"So why is it called that?"

"Well, there is a long bike trip that happens. But the book's main focus is the nature of knowledge and belief."

"Fun," Jess said.

Mr. Q. smiled. "What can I do for you gals?"

"We need to know your New Year's resolution," Nina said. "For the *Eagle Eye*."

He put down the book, took another bite of bagel, looked toward the ceiling in a performance of pondering. "I'm reluctant to give you one," he said, mouth full, the words muffled. He swallowed. "To resolve to do anything implies that you don't really want to do it, right?"

"Most of life is doing things you don't feel like doing," Jess said.

"Jess," he said. "That's very dark."

"I keep it real," Jess said, and Mr. Q. pointed at her in confirmation. There was an itchiness in Nina's chest. They were playing some sort of game, one whose success depended on her exclusion.

"There's nothing you want to improve on at all?" Nina said.

"I think," Mr. Q. said, "I could be more generous with others. And with myself."

Nina wrote it in her reporter's steno.

"Ooh," Jess said. "Does that mean we'll be getting presents?"

"I think you'll find that studying *Hamlet* is a gift unto itself."

"Sure." Jess raised the camera. "Pretend to be reading your bike book."

Mr. Q. affixed an expression of earnest contemplation to his face, not so different from the one he'd been wearing when they came in. He read aloud. "The truth knocks on the door and you say, 'Go away, I'm looking for the truth,' and so it goes away."

"Heavy," Jess said, and took his picture.

***

Raymond was hosting a holiday party, but when he invited them, Jess demurred.

"I need some alone time this break," she told him during English class. Nina was sitting beside her and she imagined this message was intended for her, too.

But Jess hated alone time. It was why she always wanted to be in the *Eagle Eye* room, even if it was just her and Vicki in there, why, maybe, her chosen hobby was track, with its continuous nearness of bodies, why she could only fall asleep when she was alone in bed to the sound of talk radio. Inside her refusal of the invitation, there was something fenced off from Nina, something she was unwilling to share.

Nina went alone to Raymond's celebration, which to her surprise included the more conventional members of their class. They'd apparently heard that it would be a party where one might have an experience more sophisticated than the usual crowding in a den, the top-40 music, the hard lemonade, the puking into hedges in a backyard.

"Where's Jess?" they kept asking Nina, as they sipped the champagne Raymond's parents, mind-bogglingly, had left for them, pretending to be unstartled by the fizz filling their throats. She told them home. She repeated the line about alone time. She wandered from room to room hoping in one of them to find the antidote to her unease. Looking in on the coats, piled on Raymond's bed like people shot from behind, a premonitory feeling washed over her. Late in the evening, she was asked again by Vicki about Jess's whereabouts, and Jordan Applebaum, retrieving a beer from the fridge, called out in response, "I heard she's been hanging out a lot with Leo and Lars." He said it only to Vicki, as though Nina weren't there. Still smarting over her rejection. You held onto something long enough, it became a part of you.

"Lars Michaelson?" Vicki said. "The one who dropped out?"

"Yep," Jordan said, twisting off the bottle cap.

Vicki smirked at Nina. "And isn't Leo your ex-boyfriend?"

"It was middle school," Nina said. "It doesn't count."

"Says who?"

After all this time, did Jess still want him? After all this time was she angry at Nina for ending their sharing of Leo? She'd claimed she wanted nothing to do with high school boys. "Children," she sneered, watching them slink down the halls. Maybe that was why she was keeping it from Nina, the identity of whomever she'd been running around with.

Nina turned and wove through the crowded living room, pushed open the front door. A voice called out; it was Raymond, at the end of the porch, leaning against the banister and smoking.

"Want one?" he said.

They stood together, looking out over the still-green lawn. "I wish people would stop asking me about Jess," she said. One lonely car rolled past the porch, turned at the corner. "I'm a separate person."

Her words hovered for a moment between them. Raymond blew a smoke ring. "So what was up with the cops being at her house that night?"

"Oh," Nina said, "it's complicated." Casually, wearily, as though it were something she had seen a million times before.

Raymond accepted this vagueness without complaint. "You're a really good friend. She's lucky to have you." He ashed onto some hedges. "I'm a little tipsy, so I'm going to tell you something."

Her heart stuttered. She did not entirely want to know what Jess was hiding.

"You're the only one who ever stuck up for me in elementary school," Raymond said. "I mean, Jess did too, sort of, but not like you. I'll never forget that time in Mr. Vitale's class. You remember that, right?"

He was looking at her with such earnestness her face burned.

"It was so brave." He took a long drag and exhaled into the night.

It was the bravest thing she'd ever seen, too.

***

She waited for a bad day, a coffee and sunglasses day. It took time: Jess returned from winter break invigorated—by what, she wouldn't say. Maybe it was her new friends, the ones Nina had thrown away years before. It seemed to help, too, that Jess was busy now with photography as well as track; the window of time spent with Anita or worse, alone at home, further diminished. She hadn't asked about switching in weeks.

But finally, the bad day arrived. Jess entered the *Eagle Eye* room one mid-January afternoon in sweatpants, hair unwashed and gathered in a stringy ponytail. "I'm so late," she muttered. "What exciting stuff did I miss so far?"

Nina swooped in. "I can take Physics for you today."

Jess turned. Her sunglasses were mirrored; in them Nina saw only herself. The thought skittered across her mind that underneath were not eyes but deep holes.

"Can you go to track for me too?"

"Sure," Nina said. *Eagle Eye* staffers filtered in and out of the room, paying little attention. If they saw anything as Nina and Jess worked their magic, they saw another of the hundreds of small intimacies passed between two friends who were oddly close, too close. Perhaps to them there was something unhygienic about it. Some of them had asked Nina if it was true that she and Jess Garcia dyked out, but they were already decided; they didn't believe her denials.

"But make sure you go straight there after class," Jess said. "Coach is already pissed at me for missing practice last week."

Nina nodded. Inside Jess, she did feel at once a cellular-level tiredness. She had to pry her borrowed body out of the couch.

But she had a purpose: Jess took Physics with Leo. He tilted his chin at her as she entered, a hint of warmth in his narrow eyes. How long had this been going on? She sat two rows behind him, listening, for the second time that week, to a lecture on oscillations and waves. The class could drone by, easily, without offering her an opportunity to find out anything. Nina ripped a page from her binder and tried to approximate Jess's eccentric scrawl, the voluptuous curls of her a's and g's. She wrote, *What are you up to tonight?* Adam Fleischer sat in front of her. She tapped him.

"Pass this to Leo for me," she whispered.

Adam winced, glanced at the teacher.

"Don't be a pussy."

At this he obliged. It was a risk: Leo might swivel in his seat and stare at her, perplexed. They might have no kind of relationship at all. But the note came back, a few minutes later: *Lars's house. u wanna come?* Perplexity would have been better. Now she had to learn the precise boundaries of Jess's secret.

***

It was the final period of the day. Loosed into the hallways, Nina made for the gym in the south wing, wondering how to ask Jess without arousing her suspicion if she could stay inside longer, long enough to go to Lars's house. As she turned the corner, Mr. Q. caught her by the elbow.

"Slow down, killer," he said. In middle school the boys had called Jess *Psycho Killer*. They'd given her her own song. She used to smile despite herself when they sang it, at her unruliness enshrined that way; she couldn't conceal her pleasure at being seen.

There was something strange in Mr. Q.'s expression, the person he was, his outside-school life, swimming closer to the surface than usual. Scanning the flow of students, he said without looking at her, "Can I talk to you a sec?"

"Okay," Nina said. She followed him to the *Eagle Eye* room. He held the door for her, closed and locked it behind him. It was Friday and the space had emptied already.

"Did you forget?" Mr. Q. said.

It hadn't been this way in a long time, switching a wire-walk, having to do the work of being true to each other without knowing exactly what true was. It was best, at these times, to keep quiet, to wait for the rules to be revealed. He wanted something, for sure. His face was lit with expectation.

"Jess," he said, "you're killing me."

Nina looked down. Besides the black sweatpants, she was wearing a baby tee, the one with leopard print, one of Jess's standbys. *Mosquito bites*, she remembered Rob's friend Fred saying. They were only a little larger now, like small anthills beneath the shirt.

Mr. Q. sat on the couch and patted the space beside him. "Come here."

"For what?" she said.

He ducked his head, peeked up at her from under his eyebrows, bashful. "Are you going to make me beg?"

She sat. She looked ahead, at the *Eagle Eye* door. Maybe Vicki would come soon. Mr. Q. stretched and draped a heavy arm across her shoulders and breathed deeply, a slight shudder in his inhale. But it was Friday, and Vicki had choir practice on Fridays. She was an alto; the rest of the staff found that funny and called her Man Voice behind her back. They were needlessly cruel, Nina realized. Vicki just wanted to put out a halfway-decent paper, something they could be proud of. Something they could look back on, as adults, and remember how they'd tried. She never stood up for Vicki, only stood aside and laughed from the edges, just as she had stood aside and watched as Mr. Vitale humiliated Raymond years before, and so not Vicki, not anyone, was coming to bail her out now.

Out of the corner of her eye, Nina saw Mr. Q. watching her, waiting for her to finally face him. In the waiting there was, exposed, all his performing cast aside, tenderness. It appalled her. Who was it for? Whomever he was seeing was a figure conjured only by himself and projected against the curvature of his eyes; it was not Nina, and not Jess. His mouth hovered for a moment, then floated forward and pushed hers open. Her English class had discussed his age and pegged it at early thirties, but he didn't kiss much more expertly than Jordan. Mr. Q.'s stubble ground against her chin. Nina found she could respond physically in an automatic, unthinking way—it was like breathing, only more abrasive— while a part of her split off to wonder if this had happened before, how many times this had happened before, how far she was expected to go. The wondering voice was shriveled and shrunken, like a dehydrated pea rattling deep down inside the husk of her body. He brought her hand to his crotch, drew it back and forth over the swelling there.

"See what you do to me?" Mr. Q. said. But she wasn't doing anything. It wasn't even her own hand. "I wanna make you feel good," he said. "It's your turn." Her pants and underwear were pushed down. Jess had put on one of her Days of the Week panties, which Nina bought her as a gag gift for her last birthday. Jess delighted in always choosing the wrong day. Today's said Sunday. Nina wondered whether these were selected because Jess thought they might tickle Mr. Q., or because she had hoped they wouldn't be seen at all. Mr. Q.'s fingers were jammed inside her, rooting around like blind worms. Nina understood that this sightless probing was supposed to call forth pleasure—she recalled, from Hebrew School, the story of Moses striking the rock to make water spring from it—but felt only fullness. So it was true: Jess was finished with boys. But shouldn't, then, Jess's body respond to this, welcome it? The fingers scraped clean a section of her consciousness, and in rushed scenes from the past, Jess beaming as Nina's mother bent over and whispered to her that she was a good girl; a bright, windy June day at the picnic tables, Jess trying not to react when Nina told her they couldn't have sleepovers anymore; Jess crying in the back seat of Raymond's car, and Nina had not comforted her.

Mr. Q. leaned back and extracted himself. He let out a long sigh. Nina pulled up the Sunday underwear and sweatpants as he got to his feet.

He smiled down at her, his eyes now infused with sorrow, meltingly sad. "You know I have to go," he said, as if she were begging him to stay.

Nina stood. The room's walls seemed to be dissolving. If she tried to lean against one for support, she would fall into the next world.

"That's okay," she said.

"Till next time," he said, as he opened the door.

***

The track pummeled the soles of her feet. Still dizzy, Nina felt her guise as Jess begin to slip. The coach waved her over to ask what was up.

"I'm a little lightheaded," she said.

He crossed his arms over his chest. "You eat enough today?" The coach, in the past, had only worked with boys; this was his first foray into the injurious rituals of girl athletes. He'd had a talk with them, Jess told her, about an outbreak on the team of diet pill abuse. Food was fuel, he'd explained; didn't they want sufficient fuel to compete? His confusion went too deep for them to do anything but agree that of course they wanted that. Meanwhile they continued to starve. Nina told him maybe she was coming down with a cold. Relieved, he sent her inside.

In the locker room, she removed Jess's gym clothes and left them in a heap on the floor. She stepped into the shower and stood under the lukewarm spray until the other girls returned. He'd left behind a smell: a campfire smell that was inside his sweater, now embossed on her skin. She asked one of the girls to throw her a towel. She couldn't, like Jess, prance nude through the space, indifferent to their darting glances.

"Jess?" she heard her own voice calling.

"Here, Nina," she said, summoning herself. Then she saw herself, grinning broadly. Jess lifted her hands; the nails were painted crimson.

"I got you a manicure," she said, "as a thank you."

"Oh," Nina said. Once they switched back, everything inside her that had been stirred, like the muck at the bottom of the lake, would settle back down.

Jess peered at her. "What's with you?"

"I'm just tired."

"It's tiring being me," Jess agreed, but there was suspicion in her eyes. They switched, and the look traveled with her. Nina wondered if Jess registered the twinge in her vagina from his too-long fingernail. She stared back. Surely now she would be able to see the evidence. The glow of it inflaming Jess's face, rising from the hidden, crackling fire. Mr. Q. a parcel she carried with her, turning it over and over as she went about her days. But if the evidence were there, she missed it again. It was shoved aside by the afterimage of Mr. Q.'s tender, waiting gaze, floating before her.

***

The following Monday, Jess was murdered in English class.

"For this, you need to come up here," Mr. Q. told her and Raymond, and Rachel, who was playing Queen Gertrude. "I'll be the curtain," he said, and stood facing Jess, his arms extended, his face blank as fabric. The class laughed. Behind his back, Hamlet berated his mother for her wicked tongue while Jess, as Polonius, paced near them unseen, eavesdropping, placing her ear close to Mr. Q.'s chest.

She frowned deeply, as though concerned, her cheek almost brushing the teacher's body, but she might only have been listening for Mr. Q.'s heart.

When her final lines came, she seemed to Nina possessed by a genuine fear, calling hoarsely for help, beseeching each of them, eyes unfocused and urgent, an inverse of the first time she'd stood before them, remote, imperious, in Ms. Brandon's classroom, leveling her judgment. Now, at last, she needed them. Raymond, armed with a ruler, thrust; Mr. Q. shifted his hips aside to allow it through, to plunge into Polonius's heart. "O, I am slain," Jess said. She said it softly, a ghost of a pronouncement, already yearning for her drained-out life. She sank to the floor and remained there in a puddle before Mr. Q.'s loafers until the scene ended. Then he reached down, took her hands, resurrected her to her feet.

"You didn't feel bad about killing me at all," she said to Raymond.

"Well, you did keep getting in his way," Mr. Q. said, and Jess turned to him, hands on hips like an aggrieved child. How hadn't she noticed? How hadn't any of them? Nina watched her classmates for signs of knowing, but each of them was elsewhere, in conversation with each other or writing listlessly in notebooks or half asleep, lids heavy, dreaming of themselves. How easy it must have been for him to swoop in and pluck her out. And how right it must have felt, for Jess, to let loose again with that violent urgency that had possessed her once with Michael. She believed it made her powerful, but in fact it made her a target, Nina thought, and there would always be men who took aim. By now he could be preparing to claim her for good. They were almost free of this place, most of them bound for more classrooms, more hours craned over books, but Jess would be spirited away by him somewhere. She remembered the campfire smell of his clothes and imagined a hideaway, deep in a forest.

Nina was coming to a decision. It grew larger as the hour went on, blooming like droplets of blood on tissue.

***

Nina remained at her desk when the bell rang.

"I just have a question about the final paper," she told Jess, who rolled her eyes and left, no suspicion now. As the room emptied she scribbled in her copy of the play, etching grooves in the margins of Jess's death scene.

When at last she was the only one left, she stood and approached Mr. Q., who sat at his desk flipping through the grade book. Feigning again, maybe—did he even keep grades? Was he, right now, actually standing before Jess's tiny figure in his humid fantasy of the *Eagle Eye* room?

But when Nina said, "I need to talk to you," he looked up with a face unmistakably adult, forehead striated with the beginning of authoritative lines. He smiled at Nina the way a good teacher smiles at a student, kindly and patient and slightly humoring. He would never let the mask drop for her. She scrambled for something else to say.

"So," Mr. Q. said, as the seconds transpired. Eyes so devoid of wanting she could almost believe the face she'd seen yesterday, when he believed she was Jess, was her invention.

She had only to utter two sentences, so she opened her mouth and spoke the first. "I know about you and Jess," Nina said.

The effect of this first sentence was so immediate, its power so evident, that Nina wished she could reach out and retrieve the words from the air and shove them back down her throat.

"I don't know what you mean," he said.

A laugh escaped her, more like a goose's honk than a human sound, and she began to flush. "If you stop now, I won't tell anyone," Nina said, and that was all, the phrases released, so she turned and fled the classroom. The bell for the next period had already rung, though she hadn't registered it at all, and she trotted down the vacant hallway and into the bathroom where she spent the following hour hiding from the security guards and listening to the other girls come and go to the stall beside hers, the private sounds their bodies made.

***

They'd had plans to meet after school that day and go back to Nina's to finish up their college applications. In unison, they would lick the bitter backs of the manila envelopes and press them shut; as one, they would open the mouth of the mailbox and drop them in. In this way they would seal their futures together. But when Nina stepped out the front entrance to the school Jess was not among the hordes boarding buses or climbing into cars idling in the horseshoe driveway. She stood in the whipping wind for a while, then walked the building's perimeter, past the whistle of the soccer coach in the back field, past the cracked window of the rehearsal room from which floated the pounded-out piano notes of a song from *Brigadoon*. Already knowing, but telling herself that Jess did this sometimes: she retreated, she made Nina go looking.

Jess needed now and then a confirmation that her absence had weight, that without her, Nina's life was incomplete.

She walked home. A break, then. Perhaps it was time to remind Jess that her life had a hole in it, too, without Nina. Perhaps even now Jess was with Mr. Q. and they were running away. They were in his car, speeding toward wilderness. Jess rolled down the window and her hair fluttered in the breeze. This was her destiny, she believed. It was what she would think as he swung open the door to his hideaway and invited her in, as she gazed up at the wooden ceiling beams pointing to heaven. But soon she would start to feel a squirming within, an unreachable itch, her organs trying to fight their way out of her, her skin tightening in response; she would be locked inside. The denial of her power, their power, a terrible confinement.

And she would come back. She would turn up at Nina's door and tell her that she understood completely.

***

If only she had waited, maybe in time the revelation would indeed have arrived. But as soon as Nina got home, she called Jess's house.

Anita answered. "She is in a *mood*," she said, and Nina's throat went dry. "Maybe you can snap her out of it."

An eternity passed in the moments between Anita shouting for Jess to pick up and the click on the line as she did. Nina sat on her bedroom floor, the knobs of her spine pressing against the dresser. Jess said nothing, but Nina knew she was listening.

There was a clogged sensation in her chest that was difficult to speak around. "Jess?" she managed. "Are you there?" The clot in her heart expanded, spreading dark wings. "It wasn't right, what he was doing," she said.

"Stop it," Jess said. "Just stop." It wasn't the malice she'd been expecting. The voice sounded, mostly, tired. "You couldn't let me have even this one thing."

Nina looked down at her hands, at the manicure Jess had gotten her, paint beginning to flake off her fingertips.

"It's not wrong," Jess continued, "to be in love."

Now what she heard was pity of her unknowing, of poor Nina in her passionless ignorance. How could Jess have stumbled this far from her into delusion, when they'd been so closely tethered? "Are you kidding me?" Nina said, and she might have chosen her words differently, had she known they would be the last she'd say to her friend for years.

Another long silence, until finally, Jess spoke again. "Why don't you just fuck off?" she said.

There was a click on the line as she hung up.

15

THE NOBODY SHOW

(2013)

New York was dead, and they were living in its ruined, dried-out husk: that was what Khaled would have said, Jess was fond of telling her. It had been stripped by wealth, more astringent than paint thinner, of all that had once made it dirty and alive.

Where, Nina would ask, would she rather live?

Maybe out West, or upstate; maybe in rural New England, somewhere green, a place in which you weren't being slowly murdered just by breathing its air. What about Nina?

"There is nowhere else," Nina would say.

Jess was disgusted by this response. Typical New York snobbery, she said. New Yorkers think they're worldly but they have no idea how big the world is.

She hadn't seen or spoken about Khaled in years, but had recently learned, from a former coworker at the studio, whom she saw occasionally at openings, that he had died. It looked like a heart attack.

Wasn't he a bit young for that, Nina wondered?

"Forty-five," Jess said. "So, yes."

Jess guessed it was drug-related. Nina wondered how she'd feel if

Gregory died. For a long time she'd dreaded running into him—she had heard from Charles, with whom she emailed occasionally, that he'd moved back to New York with the Japanese woman from his school. And for a couple years she did see him: leaning against the railing of the overpass at the Astoria Boulevard station, gazing down at the BQE; studying face wash in the aisle of a Duane Reade near her office; sitting a few rows up in an overly air-conditioned cinema on Houston Street before a screening of *The Third Man*, a film he'd once recommended to her. Of course, on none of these occasions was it really him. She was spotting only the phantoms cast by her own subconscious—seeing, in painful flashes, herself. And after a while these sightings stopped. She barely thought of him these days. Time took everything away.

But now Khaled was back, having breached Jess's mind once again. She was disturbed, especially, by the similarity of his passing to that of her father: both heart attacks, both unexpected, both not found for days.

To die alone like that and have no one notice—she shuddered. "Don't you think I've experienced a weirdly high number of tragic deaths, for someone our age?" she said.

Nina didn't think it was that weird. They were thirty years old, which was old enough to have recovered, as much as you were ever going to, from heartbreak, old enough to have friends now dead. She expected the preoccupation to pass.

But it only strengthened. Jess abandoned self-portraiture—"Let's face it," she said, "the art world only has room for one Mexican chick's pictures of herself"—in favor of taking up Khaled's mantle. She went out on hunts for the ordinary, the sort of people who took the bus to Rikers or bought stale rolls for breakfast from corner coffee carts. Chasidic women in ugly wigs, cabbies on break smoking outside a Pakistani deli, a postal worker dozing inside an open mailbox. She'd come home and tell Nina, "Stole some souls today," and flip through the furtive snapshots on the little screen of her camera.

She had expected the gallery show, years before, to lead to something, to her surfacing as an artist. But whatever that membrane was separating the unknowns from the knowns, Jess had never been able to puncture it. (That this brought Nina a feeling like relief, she hoped she never showed.)

Still, Jess had her eye. They were headed to Astoria Park one morning when she stopped and pointed out a group of old men at a taverna across the street.

"I'm obsessed with these guys," she said. "Every day they're here, smoking, drinking. Where are their wives?"

"Doing the housework," Nina guessed.

"When do the ladies get to hang out and bullshit?" Jess raised her camera to her eye, clicking away, not stopping when it was clear they'd noticed her.

"Hey. Little girl," one called, and gestured them over.

"Let's just go to the park," Nina said, but Jess shook her off and crossed the street. Nina followed, bent her head beneath the awning of the restaurant where the men sat around a table covered with a blue-and-white checked cloth. They were looking at them not with hostility but curiosity. The man who had called out asked Jess what she thought she was doing.

"You have an interesting face," she told him, and his friends laughed. "Yes, he could be model," one said.

"And what about you," said another, nodding at Nina, "do you think he's handsome too?"

"She's the interviewer," Jess said.

"Interviewer," the first said. "Ask us a question. We have many stories."

Jess said, "I bet you do."

"Sit, sit."

They sat. "Where are your wives?" Nina said, and they laughed again. Their faces were soft with wrinkles; they reminded her of the man who had once paid to worship at the feet of Simone, Jess's old roommate, years before.

They spent the morning with the men, who bought them coffee and pastries. The first one's wife was dead. He still worked, as a math teacher at a Greek Orthodox high school in Whitestone. It took two long bus rides to get there, which wearied him but also gave structure to his days. It was about breaking up the hours, he said, once you were his age, and your house was so empty.

He winked at Nina. "Maybe you come keep me company some time."

Jess took his photograph there in the shade of the awning. In the picture, one could see on his face a little smirk of pleasure at humoring some nice young girls, his pale eyes, a thick-veined hand on the handle of the smoky coffee mug, the blur of a waitress passing behind him. Nina recorded the conversation on her phone.

Later, listening to it in their living room, Jess shook her head in amazement. "People love talking about themselves. They'll tell you anything if you just ask."

"People want to be seen," Nina said. It did not seem such a surprise to her.

"We should really do something with this," she said, flipping through the images on her laptop. "Khaled would be proud." But Nina thought they had drawn upon something more ancient than Jess's ex-lover's work: their old *Eagle Eye* assignments, their aborted high school photojournalism.

"We should," she agreed, expecting nothing. All their years of collaboration, of tampering—what had it added up to? Once they thought they had the keys to the universe.

***

Their encounter that morning with the old men was the genesis of *New York Nobodies*, tagline: "A glimpse into the lives of the unspectacular millions who make this city what it is."

They updated the blog intermittently, their posts—a photo or two, a choice quote—offerings cast into the ether. It was only for them, as their old radio show had been; it was just an outlet for creativity otherwise smothered almost to death by day jobs. But months into the project, it was their first entry that led to sudden exposure: one of the old man's math students, an aspiring DJ with a wide network of followers, stumbled across it and shared it on social media, and then classmates from college were reaching out to say they loved this new project of Nina's, and then a reporter from the *Village Voice* was emailing to request an interview with the women behind the poignant new paean to the unseen, near-perished New York.

Was it a schadenfreude thing, Nina wondered, his solitude making everyone else feel better about their own lonely lives? Why were these admirers drawn in by him rather than by the teenage subway acrobat, or the lady cabbie from Martinique?

"There's nothing more palatable to people than a sad old white guy," Jess said.

But they agreed they'd always be thankful to him, their unexpected breakthrough, who all along had been waiting for them at the table in the taverna.

***

Thirty had a taste that was fresh and bitter at once. "Like broccoli rabe or something," Jess said. "Don't you think?"

They sat in crappy folding chairs on the roof of their Astoria apartment building, where they went in the evenings to work on the blog when it wasn't too hot. The roof was unfinished, its integrity dubious, but from it they could see, across the river, the lights of the Empire State Building.

"I think it's time I told you," Nina said. "I don't have synesthesia."

Jess's lips parted in a smile. "Oh, I know. But I like how you always pretended for me."

It was fitting, though, Jess continued, that their thirtieth year was bringing achievement entwined with ugliness. Maybe the two could never be separated. As *New York Nobodies* grew in popularity, as the *Village Voice* story about the blog passed from inbox to inbox across the country, far-flung relatives and long-discarded friends reared up to say hello, to ask for favors. Copycat accounts materialized in a gambit to claim some advertising dollars for themselves, and finally a writer for the *Observer*, disgusted, penned his polemic: "A sepia-toned, romanticized fantasy of New York and New Yorkers . . . one that views the down-trodden and the marginalized as mere objects for consumption, worthy only of a snapshot and a hundred words, perhaps a tear or two shed, and nothing more."

They were reading it again; they'd read it already at their day jobs, and now quoted bits of the screed to each other, mounting their defense.

Jess began typing furiously, slamming her fingers into the keyboard.

"What are you doing?"

"I'm sending this fucker an email," Jess said. "Did you look this guy up? He looks about twelve years old. He doesn't know what he's talking about."

"Do not send anything without showing me first."

Jess handed over her laptop. *Dear Aaron*, the email began, addressing the writer with a formality that in no way presaged the bile that followed.

"You can't send this," Nina said. "He'll just run it as is."

In the other realms of her life she had no authority. At last she'd become a journalist, sort of. She wrote for a luxury lifestyle magazine that was published quarterly as a slim, slippery insert in the *Wall Street Journal*. Her coworkers joked about how their beat was M&Ms—Maseratis and Monaco—while they struggled to cut back on weekly grocery bills. Nina's days were measured out in interviews with real estate developers in Abu Dhabi and efforts to pretend she knew what it was like to forget how many vacation homes one owned, the reward for which was forty-three thousand a year and a healthcare plan with an altitudinous deductible. Maybe it was too much to expect anything more. Jess still waited tables and freelanced for pennies in her off hours.

Jess said, "So then what?"

"We have to prove him wrong with the blog itself. I could start writing longer entries?"

"No one will read them. It works because it's short."

"I don't know, then. Maybe we just take it as a compliment anyone's even bothering to criticize us."

"Fuck that. We can do better."

Could they? The sound of traffic on the Triborough Bridge carried through the night air to the rooftop. They had turned out very ordinary. Their power had failed to propel them anywhere beyond themselves. They were a closed system.

***

It was Zachary who gave them a solution. He had turned out very clever. He graduated directly into the recession but managed to skirt its destruction by living at home, bartending locally, waiting it out, and now he had landed a job at a boutique financial firm downtown. What he did with his days might as well have been, for Nina, encrypted. She'd meet him after work for a drink, her baby brother now broad-shouldered and sipping bourbon. He drank so slowly he must have hated it. Nina imagined he'd gotten the idea from a senior colleague.

More often than not Zach picked up the tab. He nevertheless retained a younger sibling's awe of Nina, oblivious to her flailing. He had deep faith in *New York Nobodies*. Once onto his second bourbon, he was likely to hail the blog's capacity to heal the city's divides.

"What if there were a way for people to hear your interviews?" he said. "That way they'd know there's nothing cynical about what you're doing."

"By posting videos or something?"

"Or do a podcast. With like, longer conversations with people. You could call it *The Nobody Show*." Zachary sipped his drink and winced. "Didn't you and Jess used to make your own little radio shows when we were kids?"

"Yeah, we did." Nina still had the cassettes in a shoebox beneath her bed, though no way, now, of listening to them. And Jess had made it clear she never wanted to hear their old shows again. But their tiny voices remained, embedded in the dark loops inside the tapes, chattering forever about occult things.

"I used to think you two had superpowers or something," Zachary said.

Nina looked into the mirror behind the bar. "Like what?" she saw herself say.

"I don't know. Mind reading maybe? You were just so inside your own little world. I thought you must have some kind of magic going on."

They still did, she supposed, though it felt less magical now. Their jobs were dull, they were both single, knew all each other's friends, spent most of their time together. They had run out of things to discover, the once-foreign territories surveyed and mapped for good.

***

At first, before they could afford to rent studio space and buy decent recording equipment, they held their interviews in Nina's bedroom, because it was in the back of the building and faced an air shaft, and the only sonic interruptions came from sparrows.

In that tiny space, the difference in how people responded to each of them was palpable. Nina was gentle, soothing subjects with small talk, identifying points of connection, coaxing them into the belief this was only a chat between friends rather than an excavation. But Jess hacked through all that. Her dark eyes held the reassurance there was nothing you could say she would find objectionable. Her inquiries disarmed in their bluntness. Subjects might have been put off by her irreverence, her interruptions, but by the midpoint of interviews all their awareness flared toward her, Nina only a faint murmur near them, wind in trees.

What did it say, Nina wondered after one of their first interviews, that here they were again in her bedroom, recording a show as they had when they were children?

"That people don't change," said Jess. She looped the cord around their microphone and put it away.

But weren't they really performing for one another, Nina thought, each playing to the vision the other had in her head? Jess was bold, Nina cautious; Jess savvy, Nina naive. These were strictures that could only be lifted by a slide into each other's bodies, their roles now calcified by shared history.

"I still have the tapes, you know," Nina told her.

Jess sank into Nina's office chair and began twisting it from side to side. "I still have the radio."

"Your dad's?"

"Yeah."

"Why'd you hang onto it?"

"It felt too full."

"Full of history," Nina said.

"Sure," Jess said, "I guess you could say that."

Usually when they remembered their old selves it was with laughter: at their own perversity in sharing Leo, or at their daring in how they'd fucked with people, their teachers, their family, the guests at a fancy party, everything they'd gotten away with.

"Why didn't you ever want to listen to the tapes?"

Jess sighed and then spun the chair hard, her face flashing in and out of view. "I felt sorry for her," she said finally. She got up and left the room. Nina listened to the old floorboards creak as she crossed the apartment. It was not clear to her whether Jess had meant she pitied Nina or her own childhood self.

***

Nobody was a nobody, was the show's unspoken thesis. Not the cashier at the produce market on Thirtieth Avenue or the bartender at the dive on Crescent or the kid stopping pedestrians on the sidewalk, hectoring them about Greenpeace donations. Not a novel concept, but something people were hungry to be told again and again, she thought, especially the people still adrift in the wake of the recession, the ones who never recovered.

Madame Janelle, who claimed to be a medium, was initially a disappointment. "I don't know," she kept saying to their questions: What was the afterlife like? Did everyone go to the same place? Were the dead always trying to reach us? There were dozens like her in the city, peddling their incense-scented bullshit out of bleak storefronts with blinking neon signs—hers was wedged between a Key Food and a Verizon store—and Nina and Jess had expected at least a stream of colorful nonsense.

"Why do you think you have this ability?" Jess said.

"I don't know."

"Well, what does it sound like when the dead talk to you? Is it like a voice in your head?" Her questions had taken on an urgent vibration. She was digging for something, Nina realized, and it wasn't what they discussed when they passed Janelle's shop and agreed an interview with a psychic would make for a hilarious episode.

"No," Janelle said. "It is not in language. It is like a second pulse in my body that I translate into words."

The stiff diction, the trace of an unplaceable accent reeked of fakery to Nina. They, not Janelle, were the ones with the power.

"Is there a dead person hanging around everyone who comes in to see you? Like does everyone have some ghost just waiting for the opportunity?"

"No. Many clients I turn away."

"How do you know when there is someone wanting to communicate?"

"It is just a feeling."

"How much of it is really more like close observation?" Jess said. "Picking up cues from people's body language and stuff?"

Janelle sat rigid in Nina's office chair. "None."

"I think what Jess is asking is whether a kind of radical empathy factors into your readings," Nina said.

"I communicate with the dead," Janelle said. There was a time, in her childhood, that her parents worried she had paranoid schizophrenia, she told them; what other explanation was there for her insistence that through her spoke invisible people? The disbelief ended, finally, when she told her father something that only he and his late brother, who had committed suicide as a teenager, would know.

"What was it?" Jess asked, but Janelle only smiled.

"What about other abilities?" Nina said. "Like, I don't know, lucid dreaming, or telesthesia, or—"

"Telesthesia?" Janelle echoed.

Jess looked at Nina like she wanted to kick her. "Is there anyone hanging around either of us?"

Janelle smiled again and pressed a business card into Jess's hand.

"Aha," Jess said into the microphone, to their unseen, theoretical audience, perhaps the same invisible assembly they'd addressed as little girls. "Nothing in this life is free."

***

Jess was the one who brought in Adrian, a child psychologist, the brother of Albert, the maître d' at the West Village bistro where she worked. She found them sharing a cigarette in the alley behind the restaurant after closing.

She was annoyed. It was where she liked to go for a few quiet minutes, she told Nina, before catching the subway, inevitably full of drunk kids that late in the evening. It was her spot to air out after hours surrounded by intoxicated clatter. "What's this guy's deal?" she asked Albert.

Adrian laughed. "No deal."

"Would you say you're a nobody, then?"

"Yeah," he agreed, "definitely a nobody." His geniality annoyed her too. He was a happy idiot, she told Nina, the sort of person who probably never thought about the fact that they were all going to die. She invited him on the show to see if she could get him to crack.

Adrian's handsomeness was like the flash of some sea creature moving beneath murky water, there and then gone. Nina kept looking for another glimpse of it glinting off the angles of his face. He seemed gently amused by the makeshift studio, by being interrogated by them, as though all of life had been contrived to entertain him. Jess immediately attempted to tilt their talk toward doom.

"How formative is what happens when you're a kid?" she said. "Like, is there a certain amount of shit that can go down before a kid is fucked for life?"

"Um," he said. "You want me to calculate?"

"You have a PhD, right?"

"Doesn't that technically exempt someone from being a nobody?" Nina said.

"No, that's only a medical degree," Jess said. "That's only if you're an actual doctor."

"Ouch," Adrian said. It was difficult, sometimes, to keep the show from attenuating back into the little queendom they'd crafted as children, to restrain themselves from riffing and one-upping until their subjects vanished entirely.

Jess reached over and paused the software recording them. "Hang on a sec," she said. "We forgot to get you a drink. Excuse us for a minute."

She pulled Nina into the kitchen, pulled her close. "He's interested in you. I can tell."

"No. He's just one of those people that has a twinkle in his eye."

"For you. Let's switch and you'll see."

It was true that outside her body, sometimes, what once was hidden came abruptly into view. Now she watched herself animated by Jess's unthinking fluidity, as she took a mug from the drying rack and filled it with tap water. She followed her back into the room, watched her hand it to Adrian, watched him watch her.

"Adolescents are sort of this reviled group, aren't they?" Jess said, affecting what she must have decided was Nina's signature move, a smart self-consciousness, heightened language punctuated by qualifications, by nervous little gestures, a tug at her earrings, say. "What made you want to work with them?"

"That's a good question, Nina," Adrian said, and one of his hands hovered for a moment as though he wanted to tap her knee, close to his in the small bedroom, but then he thought the better of it. "I think they're not really so difficult if you just treat them like people." He smiled at them both but at Jess, Jess-as-Nina, for longer. There it was. Inside herself she may have written it off. But from here she was no longer the subject of his attention, and its sudden absence was unmistakable. "Do you remember being a teenager, what it felt like when an adult you looked up to took the time to really listen to you?"

"I do," Nina said, and Jess looked over at her. Nina saw her own eyes narrow.

"To go back to Jess's question," Adrian continued, "I think having just one positive adult in their lives can make the difference for kids who've seen a lot of shit."

"Absolutely," Nina said.

"I'm not saying that's me. The number of patients who'd say I made that difference for them is probably pretty low."

"I don't know," Jess said. "It sounds like you're a great therapist. I wish I'd met someone like you when I was that age."

Was Jess still speaking as Nina, or as herself? Her face was turned away and closed to Nina now, latched on instead to Adrian, who looked back at her with a focus Nina would have found unnerving.

***

Around the same time that Nina and Adrian began dating, Jess started visiting Madame Janelle. Her first appointment was an evening in mid-April; earlier that day a bomb had been detonated at the finish line of the Boston marathon. Photos of a young man, corpse-gray, legs mangled below the knees, made their way around the newsroom, and in the subway stations policemen circulated like blood clots.

All afternoon her coworkers had spoken in murmurs, a forest of reverence. Adrian sent her a text; Jess must have given him her number. *Hey Nina, it's me, your interview subject,* he had written. *Can you believe this?*

I know, she wrote. A strange entrée to asking her out, which he ultimately did, after they exchanged a few requisite remarks about the ever more frequent intrusions of chaos. That must have been why, Nina thought, there was a droplet of dread coloring her excitement about their upcoming date.

By six thirty it was still sunny and mild, a breath of summer in the air. When Jess blazed in, Nina took her intensity to be a reaction to the tragedy. She dropped her purse on the floor and stared at Nina, who was standing in the kitchen, stirring scrambled eggs on the stove.

"Madame Janelle is the real fucking deal," Jess said.

"What?"

"I went to see her." Sheepishness started to curve her lips, but she fought it down. "She wasn't bullshitting."

Nina extinguished the flame on the stove. "What did she say?"

"The first thing she asked me was if I said hello to a dog on my way in. Which I did," Jess said. "I said hi to this pit bull I saw tied up outside Key Food. And Janelle goes, 'He says hi back.'"

There were dogs everywhere in their neighborhood. The odds of Jess passing, even greeting one, on her way someplace weren't that small. Nina said nothing. Jess's enthusiasms were infrequent, but when they arrived they came hurtling in with planetary force. At these times, it was best to stand aside.

"And she said right away that I had lost someone recently, and someone long ago. And I said, not *that* long ago, it was eight years or so, and you know what she says?"

Nina's eggs were growing cold in the frying pan, but she left them to join Jess on the couch. She shook her head.

"She said, 'But you *really* lost him in childhood.'" Jess watched Nina, scanning for her reaction.

"Oh, weird," Nina said. She rubbed her arms as though banishing goosebumps. Certainly, communing with the dead could be possible, another power one might be overtaken by, as Nina and Jess had been by theirs. But she didn't believe Janelle was anything like them, with her lacquered talons and cheap storefront.

"And that's not all," Jess said. "Janelle told me it was really hard for her to get a clear connection to the people I know who've passed away."

Of course, Nina thought.

"She said it was like when there's static on a phone call. Like the flow of my energy has all these interruptions in it."

Nina's energy was interrupted, too. A part of her had broken off from the conversation to consider her upcoming meeting with Adrian, how to present herself and at the same time read him for the sort of portents she'd walked right past in succumbing to Gregory.

"Doesn't that sound," said Jess, "like she was picking up on what we can do?"

"Maybe," Nina said. "But, I mean, who isn't kind of scattered? Couldn't that apply to anyone?"

"Interrupted," Jess corrected. "Like I'm there and then I'm not."

"Janelle said that?"

"Why are you so skeptical? People have picked up on it before. That little girl you used to babysit, she sensed something."

"You mean Scarlett? Is that really what happened?" Nina said.

The blaze of excitement was out, Jess's face turned sour. "I'm going back next week," she informed Nina, and stood from the couch, headed for her bedroom. She said over her shoulder, before closing the door behind her, "I'm going to talk to my dead."

Nina understood she was deliberately withholding the reaction Jess wanted, pulling back and pelting her friend with doubt. She was, in a way, being Jess. But why should she be envious of them, Jess's ghosts, and her faith that they were reaching out for her, out of the void?

***

Adrian was from Peoria, Illinois, the sort of place New Yorkers might refer to when what they meant was some distant slice of America so incomprehensibly bland they would never set foot there. (And he was not, in fact, even from Peoria itself, but from a small suburb outside of the—apparently, it was one—city.) Of course, he was not a Jew, had not so much as met one until he went to college at the University of Illinois.

"But don't worry. I broke out of the Midwest after that," he reassured Nina, from across the small table in the cocktail bar. They'd needed to be buzzed in—he'd made a reservation. The bar was tiny, ten tables, with servers in bow ties and a man with manicured eyebrows preparing drinks. Adrian seemed in a rush to persuade that he himself was not bland, even though from the outside Nina knew there was nothing much to her: a youngish woman from Long Island, middle class, medium pretty, head just above water professionally.

"I'm not worried," she said. He smiled, maybe taking her reserve for a sign of some buried wonder to dig for. After U of I, he said, he'd joined the Peace Corps and taught English to elementary students in The Gambia—"Don't forget that *the*"—where he discovered his interest in developmental psychology. When his term was up, he moved to New York to get his degree, and had been living here since, mostly in the Bronx, working out of an elementary school clinic with kids already steeped in trauma.

"How so?" she said.

"No, let's talk about you for a while. Like, how'd you get to be a such a good interviewer?"

Of course, it had been Jess who interviewed him. Nina sipped her concoction of a drink, sweetness and smoke coating her tongue. What was special about her was all sealed within her, she could never communicate it, it could never amount to anything beyond her entanglement with Jess. This was the trouble she ran into on every first date, the ones from which she slunk home half-drunk and shamed by the absence, in her chest, of any feeling at all; the ones where the men monologued at her all night, so desperate to convince her of their merits they failed to ask a single question and thereby discover she had nothing to give. Last month, to avoid another lopsided conversation, she'd agreed to a man's suggestion they skip the drinks and go straight to the loft where he lived—with his parents, yes, but who would turn up staying rent-free in SoHo?—where they fucked in a bedroom with floor-to-ceiling windows overlooking Houston Street. "What do you like?" he had asked, and Nina, racing through her preferences, finding none that seemed sufficiently lurid, returned the question to him. "Rough sex," he answered immediately. Soon after they heard someone come into the apartment. "Bryan?" his mother called. Nina took the opportunity to flee. On the long subway ride home she told herself this did not make her disgusting. Jess did things like this all the time. Was she disgusting?

"Interviewing's easy," Nina told Adrian. "All you do is show a little interest. Everyone loves talking about themselves."

"Oh no," he said. "I guess I proved that."

"It's okay. I'm genuinely interested."

He smiled, and the handsomeness returned to his face.

"I guess I first learned how to interview when I started writing for my high school newspaper," Nina said.

"On Long Island, right? Did you like growing up there?"

"God, no. It was terrible."

"Tell me more," Adrian said. "I love hearing about terrible things."

***

Where were they now, Jess's dead? Where in the cosmos did Madame Janelle's theology locate them? Nina imagined a waiting-room world, borderless and full of gray mist, through which they shuffled, on occasion calling out to their living loved ones, out of which they might be summoned if only you were to ask in the right way, as she and Jess had tried to do as children.

At her second session, Jess reported, after Nina pressed her to share, Madame Janelle said that once Jess's father had tried to reach her but was unable to get through. Something cut him off.

"The radio," Jess said. "That has to be it."

Once she'd wanted only to exorcise him, but now Jess was hungry for answers. Why Khaled had removed himself from life, why her father had removed himself from *her* life. There were people who could smell such hunger to *know* on you, and then they would pounce, Nina understood; Avi had taught her.

After that revelation, the channel of communication had again closed to Madame Janelle. But come back next week, Jessica, the medium said. We'll keep trying.

***

For their second date, Nina and Adrian took an extended ferry ride, zigzagging from borough to borough along the East River. As they passed Roosevelt Island, she found herself telling him, as she had once told Scarlett, the story of Nellie Bly.

"It used to be called Blackwell's Island, and it was nothing but hospitals and lunatic asylums," Nina said. They stood on the upper deck drinking canned beer from the concession and she wondered, hair wild in the wind, how she looked. "But they were locking up all these women who were perfectly sane, most of them poor immigrants who couldn't speak English, and so Nellie Bly feigned mental illness to go undercover at the asylum and write an exposé on it."

Adrian watched her, chewing on his lips a little—a habit he had, Nina would learn, when he wanted to focus on something. She told him how once inside the asylum's walls, long after she'd dropped the charade, Bly could not get out. The staff had become immovable on the matter of what she was.

"Joseph Pulitzer, her publisher, had to come and rescue her," Nina said.

Adrian watched the island as they shuttled past. "A lot hasn't changed since then." He looked back to her and smiled. "I liked the way you told it, though."

There was something he had to tell her, Adrian now said, as the ferry pulled away from Roosevelt Island and groaned its way toward the tower-lined shores of north Brooklyn. He hadn't really grown up in Peoria; that was just where he finished out his youth. In fact, his family had moved several times when he was young, pinging from hamlet to hamlet for his father's work as an education consultant, summoned to revive one ailing Midwestern school district after another. (Nina was struck by the similarity to Gregory's own peripatetic childhood. What drew them to her, these wanderers, and her to them?)

A few weeks after one relocation, when he was about seven years old, Adrian had approached his mother with a strange question. He wanted to know why Adrian Two had not moved with them. Adrian Two, he explained to her, was the boy who lived in the attic of their previous home, with whom he would speak whenever he went up there.

His mother was unnerved, she would tell him; she told him this story several years later, when he was fourteen. Upon hearing it, Adrian found he had no memory of a boy in the attic. The name, he said to Nina, if he were to analyze it now, suggested his double, perhaps a projection of himself, a sturdier version to serve as a companion amid all the flux of his young life. That he stashed this secret self in the attic, a hidden, unlit space, seemed fitting. In Jung's conception of the house as a reflection of the psyche, spaces like basements and attics were the seats of the unconscious.

That was the sober explanation. But Adrian wasn't so sure that was all there was to it. The following year, his family had made its final move—his father retired thereafter—to Peoria, where he had significant trouble adjusting to the new school. That Thanksgiving, while visiting cousins in one of their prior towns, the one that had been his favorite, Adrian fantasized about injuring himself in such a way that he would be forced to stay behind to recuperate. All through dinner the fantasy bloomed. He had never been a complainer; his little brother, Albert, was the emotional one, and Adrian had strived to be stoic through all their moves as a model for him, but now it seemed imperative that he communicate to his parents his despair, through the breaking of a limb, the gashing of his head. In the pause between dinner and dessert, as the rest of the group watched football, Adrian had slipped into his cousins' backyard where they had a small shed, climbed onto its top via the tree that leaned against it, and stood there, waiting for the nerve to jump to rise within him. To his surprise—some part of him was convinced he would not, in fact, go through with it, that this was all posturing, if only to himself—he finally leaped. As he fell through the air, amazed, already regretting, there was a flash of light against the grass just before his body met it, and after a few moments passed, he realized, picking himself up, that he had not been hurt at all. What were the odds? The light, he thought then and now, had served as a cushion somehow, and though he did not recall with any clarity Adrian Two, it seemed to him that his childhood friend was connected with the light—had protected him.

"I don't know why," Adrian said, as the ferry pulled into the station at Greenpoint, "but I just felt like I should tell you that."

Adrian's double reminded Nina of the *Compendium* entry on Psychopomp, the entity that could look just like you and appeared to escort you out of this life. Where was her copy of the *Compendium*? She'd searched her parents' house and the internet, and found no trace of her childhood guide to the universe. But it had been real, solid, of that she had no doubt; an offering cast to her from somewhere in a time of need, to bind her to Jess. What was to guide her now?

"I'm so glad you did," she said to Adrian. For the first time she thought she could imagine a future in which she might one day share her own story. She couldn't tell whether the desire that flared was to confess or to take him to bed; the urges were twinned, inextricable.

***

The Nobody Show began to get sponsors. A laundry delivery service reached out, then a mattress company. A fan, unprompted, began a fundraising campaign on their behalf, after Jess apologized on one episode for the howl of sirens in the background, explaining they couldn't afford better soundproofing. Zachary came over to look at their income and advise them how best to manage it. He was astounded by how little they knew but did his best to hide it, inhaling deeply before explaining how to pay estimated quarterly taxes and register as an LLC.

It wasn't quite enough money yet to quit their day jobs, but the show was clearly growing into something beyond mere hobby. In July they began renting a studio at a rehearsal space on the north side of the neighborhood. It became increasingly difficult to manage the influx of requests from people who believed they should be featured on an episode, all the messages detailing how they, too, were nobodies.

The criticism continued, too, with each new episode. It bothered Jess far more than it did Nina; she spent long stretches of time gazing into her phone screen and tapping furiously.

It was Adrian who taught Nina to float above the online skirmishes. It made people feel safe, he explained, in bed in his studio, to point the finger, jab it at every wrongdoing. They believed that by doing this, they themselves would never err, or never be caught at it, anyway. What she was living now was an adult's life; he spoke to her as an adult, and she tried to perform in kind, despite her sense of unpreparedness, of incompletion. Nina began to look down with benevolent comprehension upon her detractors, and upon Jess, still enmeshed in petty squabbles, in her little power struggles.

***

Jess didn't complain about the growing frequency of Adrian's visits to their apartment, nor did she offer anything in the way of congratulations when Nina came home one evening and told her that they had said *I love you* to one another for the first time. They were up on the roof, wind licking off the East River. Across the river, in her mind's eye, Adrian was unlocking the door to his place, smiling, remembering the moment when he had said, *There's something I have to tell you*, and Nina's face had lit up. Soon she would move in with him.

"Wow," was Jess's only response. "Things are moving fast."

Adaptation had become the way she fed Adrian's curiosity, skirting, in her storytelling, the borders that contained the power she shared with Jess. She could still speak at length of the closeness of their bond, the heartbreak of their high school rupture ("over a boy," Nina explained, with an eye roll at their folly). For the other eras of her history—her travels, the lessons of her relationship with Gregory, her meandering career path, her family—she discovered that it was surprisingly easy to omit Jess entirely.

The glow of the day began to sizzle away. What she'd wanted and imagined was for Jess to run over and embrace her, to see at long last that Nina had found someone who could see her, the triumph of it.

"What have you been up to?" Nina asked.

"Khaled finally came through," Jess said. "He said what happened was no one's fault but his own."

She could see the lights around Astoria Park, their vaporish glow, and the red oval of the track. Even now, some people were running. Khaled had seemed to Nina ancient history, his death unlikely to unsettle Jess for more than a few days. But of course nothing was ancient history. "Did you think it was your fault?"

"No," Jess said quickly. "I just felt kinda bad I never reached out.

Remember that time he came into the restaurant last year? He looked like shit. I knew something was up."

It was very simple, what was happening. Madame Janelle would make vague presentiments, coax clues from Jess, and then tell her what she—what anyone—would want to hear. All the medium needed was attunement, not her own personal tunnel through the membrane of the visible to the land of the dead. A charlatan was being granted greater significance in their lives than Adrian, and Nina's blindingly good fortune in finding him.

"I don't know," Nina said. "I don't see how she's any different from Avi."

"Well," Jess said. "She's not a cult leader, first of all. She can actually do what she says she can." The tectonic plates beneath her face were shifting again. She turned away to peer over the lip of the roof, and an image flashed absurdly though Nina's mind of Jess charging forward, shoving her, her body tumbling to the street. "And she's the only person who's ever been able to give me any real information about my dad. Or give enough of a shit to listen."

I give a shit, Nina thought. So much so she'd raided Jess's diary for intel, twenty years before. Nina said, "She's a grief vampire."

Jess shook her head slowly, in wonder. "You can't stand me having anything for myself."

It was an echo of what she'd said about Mr. Q. Both times the same ungenerous interpretation of what was really, Nina thought, an urge to protect Jess from predators. If there was envy, too, entwined with that, if she also wanted to keep Jess to herself, was that so wrong? Was a feeling ever unalloyed, ever only noble or self-serving? Jess walked past Nina and disappeared into the roof's bulkhead, a little breath of warm air following in her wake. Nina looked down at the street and after a few moments saw her emerge onto the sidewalk, purse over her shoulder. She watched as she went down the block and around the corner and out of sight.

***

For several days Jess treated Nina as nothing more than a colleague, addressing her only when it was necessary to the planning and execution of the podcast. Nina was certain listeners would notice something was askew when they heard the newest episode, but only Zachary did.

They interviewed a canvasser for Greenpeace. "Yes," Jess said in her opening, "one of those dudes you brush off when they try to stop you on your way to the train."

He was young and a bit frightened of them and Nina had done most of the talking, trying to put him at ease, trying to project her own. They talked post-college aimlessness, shit jobs, the flattening hours of temp work.

She recalled a gig stuffing envelopes for a nonprofit's annual gala. "You look at the clock and think an hour has passed and it's been eight minutes," Nina said.

The Greenpeace kid nodded. "And I'm like, is this really it? Is this just life now?"

Jess spoke for the first time since she introduced him. "What were you expecting?"

The kid glanced at Nina, eyes jumpy.

"Did you think," Jess said, "the world was just waiting for you?"

"What happened?" Zachary said on the phone that night. "Where was the banter?"

"I know," Nina said.

"The banter is a big part of the draw for people. The connection the two of you have."

"Is that really what they listen for?"

"Do you know how many people wish they had that?"

"It's not like what you think," she told him.

"No," he said, "I guess it never is." But he sounded unconvinced. Though he'd become a de facto adviser to them, Zachary was still a little bit the boy allowed into Nina's room, if he sat quietly and didn't interrupt their games and left when he was asked.

After hanging up, Nina went to Jess's room and suggested a swapping experiment.

"Like the old days," she said.

Jess nodded, no hint of a smile.

Nina continued with her proposal, that they switch and Nina go to Jess's usual appointment with Madame Janelle in her stead. If she was authentic, Janelle would surely notice that the woman she was speaking to was not, in fact, Jess. Nina could be reassured her friend was not being taken advantage of, and Jess would have confirmation that Janelle truly was offering her a portal to the other side.

"I don't need to have anything confirmed," Jess said, but she agreed to the plan.

***

It was startling, upon entering Madame Janelle's storefront, to find that beyond its New Agey anteroom—crystals, candles, a love seat upholstered in furry, jewel-toned fabric—the space where the medium gave her readings was not unlike a therapist's office. Only a few of the books lining her shelves were psychic-specific (*Explaining the Unexplainable, Conversations on Life After Life*), while the rest were mostly novels. Nina had her choice of couch or wooden chair across from Janelle, who was seated when she entered. She went with the chair. She couldn't picture Jess reclining.

"Hey," Nina said.

Janelle's eyebrows were shaven, replaced by fleet black pencil lines. She raised one at Nina, then closed her eyes. Janelle took a deep inhale and unleashed an intonation that began low before pitching upward into a high, long note: *om*. Was Nina to follow suit—did Jess usually? There was a torsion in her guts she recalled from their first days of switching, when she was convinced she would give them both away and ruin the game forever. Jess would say the *om*, Nina decided, even if she thought it was stupid; certainly, self-consciousness would not hinder her. She chanted along.

"*Om* is the sound of the universe," Janelle said in a monotone that suggested to Nina this was part of an opening ritual. "Today I would like to add one additional incantation of *gum*, the sound of Ganesha, the creator and remover of obstacles."

Nina joined her. There was pleasure in the vibration of Jess's voice rolling out of her throat, its deeper register sounding in her ears.

"So," Janelle said in a chattier tone, and Nina opened her eyes, "did you give any thought to what we spoke about last time?"

Nina shrugged one shoulder, in a way she'd seen Jess do before, a way that communicated not caring about not caring.

Janelle's smile deepened. "What's this?" she asked, mimicking the shrug. "Did you come up with any ideas," she said, "about what it might mean to have enough? Enough to feel safe, to feel stable in yourself?"

This *was* therapy, Nina realized. The medium was familiar, almost maternal, a presence to unclench into. After everything, she had grasped little of what Jess needed.

She closed her eyes and tried to dissolve into the darkness beneath the lids. She tried to speak in Jess's voice.

"I don't know," she said. "I'm so alone."

"You're not. You already have everything you need."

"That isn't true. Other people—Nina—" She was falling deeper into pretending, into the absences inside Jess's body.

"We imagine that other people have exactly what we want. But if you could actually step into someone else's life, do you really think you would find what you need there?"

***

She knew—she thought she had known—that Jess always stashed her sorrow far within herself. But there had been a faltering in her imagination. Nina felt her body pressing into the chair, but really she was back in Jess's childhood house, rummaging around inside it as she had many times when they were small, feeling her way down the hallways, pushing open door after door onto the blackness of unlit empty rooms. She was the only one home.

"I just," Nina said. She opened her eyes. "I want to know when I'll get to talk to my dad."

The smile lines vanished, and Janelle's face went smooth as stone. She listed forward slightly in her chair.

"Jess?" the medium said.

Her gaze went in, Nina realized, as Janelle's eyes dropped from her face to her chest, past breastplate, incising heart.

"Yeah," Nina said weakly.

Janelle broke her stare, shook her head. "Something's wrong here."

"Bullshit," Nina tried to say, with all Jess's usual bravado, but the sound stuck somewhere down her throat. "I'm sorry," she said, "but I'm just not feeling well." She stood, made for the door, certain she'd find it locked, certain that Janelle was crouching down, gathering the energy to spring, inhuman, upon her. But the door opened easily, and Nina saw over her shoulder Janelle still in her chair, only watching her exit in a quizzical way.

***

Jess was waiting in Nina's bedroom when she got home, ostensibly editing the podcast. Doubt had crept in, of course. It always did in the aftermath, even of their switching. How could it be, these powers of intervention, this access to something so much more than herself? But it didn't matter, Nina decided, whether Madame Janelle was authentic, because she was providing something her friend needed, something Nina herself couldn't give, not even in allowing herself to be possessed.

"I owe you an apology," Nina said. Jess turned to her, face blank—Nina's own face, expressionless, closed to herself. She had her headphones on, but Nina knew she'd heard. "Janelle is the real deal. I guess we're not the only special ones."

Jess removed her headphones. "I guess not."

"I guess I just was worried about you being taken advantage of."

"When will you learn," Jess said, "that I would never let that happen?"

Not like you, Nina supposed was the subtext, and it was strange to see this declaration come from her own lips. It seemed to her the moment you announced something about yourself was the moment you were doomed to prove the opposite.

"Let's try something," Jess said. "Have a seat." She positioned the microphone between them. Her mouth twisted into a half-smile, all hers, and Nina could see briefly Jess's spiky energy throbbing under her own skin. "Let's a do a show, just the two of us, like the old days. You be me, and I'll be you, and we can interview each other."

"I assume we're not going to hit each other this time?" After that show, the one where they compared their pain thresholds, she had taken a bath and watched the red welts on her thighs waver like snakes beneath the water. Some went black-and-blue, lingered. Some she pressed on, from time to time over the ensuing days, waking the tender spots, feeling thrills traveling up inside her at how they'd marked one another.

"No, no." She folded one leg beneath her, crossed her arms over her belly—a Nina posture. Jess was always looking so closely, even if she didn't feel it. "Jess, we've been friends a long time," Jess said. "But is there anything you've always wanted to know about me, that you were afraid to ask?"

The game was materializing. "What do you think are your best qualities?"

"My best? That's what you're afraid to ask about? Wouldn't you rather hear about my worst?"

"Give me a minute to work up to that."

"Try again."

"You know, generally, Nina, the interviewer dictates the flow of the interview," Nina said. "I would think you knew that."

"I know that the subject is the one who really has the upper hand. I'm the one you're trying to get something from."

"That sounds weirdly sexual."

"Information can be very sexy," Jess said. They stared at each other, into their own eyes, trying not to laugh. And it *was* like old times. It was what she loved most about the friendship, the current that ran between them, the steel-cable feel of it, holding something in her hands that was permanent and unbreakable. A tether to the outside. "Alright, you suck at this. I'll ask the questions. Jess, why do you think you're such a difficult person?"

Was it what she thought Nina wanted to know about her, or was she really seeking self-knowledge? "I don't know if that's totally fair. I mean,

I can be nice. But I'm not just *nice*. I think people who are just nice are boring. You need more than that. Like a little grit, a little edge—"

"Do you think I'm nice?"

Nina tongued the inside of her cheek, Jess's cheek, which felt bumpy; maybe she was clenching her jaw at night. "I think you're good at seeming that way."

"Ouch. Jesus."

"I'm just saying it's complicated."

"Everything is. You ever think about all the shit that's happened in the past ten, fifteen years? September 11, the recession, global warming. The Boston bombing a few months ago. And don't you get the feeling that there's much more in store? Like it's all disintegrating toward—"

"Entropy?"

Jess blinked. Nina could tell she didn't know the word. "There was a time things maybe seemed to make sense. Before we graduated from high school. When we had a plan." She was thinking, maybe, of Mr. Quinn. Dread began creeping over her skull.

"But it wasn't a simpler time, right? It was a simpler us."

Jess seemed to remember her role. "When were you simple, Jess?" she said. "Although actually things are going pretty okay for me." She smiled. "I'm in love."

"Congratulations, Nina," Nina said. "I'm really happy for you about that." If Jess wouldn't say it to her of her own volition, she could say it to herself.

"But are you really?" Jess said.

"I think so." Nina tongued the chewed-on cheek again. "I just wish I had someone."

"Is that what you want?"

"What do you think I want?"

"I'm asking the questions right now."

Nina looked at the computer screen, the peaks and valleys their voices made on the recording software. "Maybe I want to start over again."

"Like in a new career?"

"No," Nina said. "From the very beginning." She closed her eyes and saw again the empty rooms of Jess's childhood home. "From when I was born. Start over in a whole different life. Be a baby again, a fresh start, in a new city, with new parents . . ."

Jess looked away. "But then what about me? What if we never met?"

"Maybe then we wouldn't need to. Maybe we'd be okay on our own." Jess put a hand over her eyes as though to conceal tears, and it occurred to Nina she'd only seen her cry once or twice before in the lifetime of their friendship. "Are you still pretending?" Nina said. "Nina, don't cry. It doesn't mean I don't love you."

"I'm not." Jess slid forward and grabbed Nina and placed her forehead against hers. Returned to herself, she stood and left the room. Nina looked at the closed door, doubled and tentative in her vision.

***

The following Thursday Nina waited, in the apartment, for Jess's return from her weekly appointment with Madame Janelle. She would, she told herself, be attentive and nonjudgmental as Jess recounted what had come to light.

But by midnight Jess still hadn't returned. Nina cast a few text messages into the void before giving up and going to bed. At first a wriggle of worry that Jess had not come home because, beneath Janelle's probing gaze, she had been forced to divulge all, from the first swap in her bedroom until today, kept Nina awake. But perhaps that would mean a kind of clearance to tell Adrian, too. Adrian Two: Nina drifted away thinking of him, the double in the attic.

A slam awoke her at 3:00 a.m. She swam out of humid sleep, climbed to her feet and cracked open the bedroom door. An assault of light from the kitchen, where Jess was digging though cabinets, pulling down boxes of cereal. She opened one, plunged a hand in. Her face under the high beams of the humming fluorescents was white and severe as a ghost's. Discarded on the countertop was a familiar black box: the once-haunted radio.

***

She'd been unable to stop thinking about it, that they'd destroyed the only chance she'd had to hear from her father once more, Jess explained to Nina the next night. She was still in her pajamas, on the couch, when Nina got home from work.

"I took a sick day," Jess said. "I'm disgustingly hungover."

Nina did not say that she had not destroyed anything, that she'd only done what Jess asked her to do, eight years before.

So Jess had brought the radio—which had been stored in a black trunk slid beneath her bed—to Madame Janelle, to see if the medium might lay her hands upon it and feel within its tubes and circuitry a space where her father once dwelled, where he had pitched his voice across the unknown topographies of the beyond into her bedroom. And Janelle had placed her fingers, tapering to painted points, upon it. And her penciled eyebrows had risen slightly for a moment, then drew closer together.

What she felt, Janelle told Jess, was what one might call *residue*. It was said there were such things as intelligent and residual hauntings. An intelligent haunt was closer to the traditional ghost mythology with which Jess was likely familiar: a shade reaching out with intention, with a message or warning to the living. Whereas a residual haunt was much like a tape recording, played again and again; an impression left behind that did not, could not possibly, interact, for there was no soul behind it.

Of course they knew this already: the *Compendium* had taught them, Nina had brought that knowledge into their lives.

Inside the radio, Janelle said, were perhaps the dregs of Jess's father, but nothing more. (Nina imagined if she picked it up and shook it, she would hear the rattle of bone fragments, teeth.) She was not one for proclamations or prophecies, Janelle said, but she felt it highly unlikely that Jess's father had attempted to make contact through the device.

Device, she called it, as though she came from another world where there was no need for such things.

So if and when her father *had* tried to communicate with her, Jess had missed it entirely.

Was there any chance, Nina asked—to show just how seriously she took this all—that Jess might speak to him now, through Janelle?

Jess shook her head. "Janelle says he's moved on. She says that's a good thing." The corners of her mouth turned down. Nina felt afraid for her. Adrian joked that he appreciated those rare moments when Jess was sleepy or hungover or coming down with a cold, when she was docile, but this was something else.

If Jess had known, Nina wondered, that what filled her radio was merely an echo, would she ever have come looking for her?

"Did Janelle say anything about me?" Nina said. "I mean, did she have any idea what was going on last time?"

Jess shook her head. She looked down and picked at the pills on her sweatpants. "It didn't come up," she said.

***

Out of concern, Nina invited Jess along to Vermont. She and Adrian had planned the long weekend as their first getaway as a couple, and when she told him over the phone that Jess would be joining them, she could hear within his pause the disappointment.

"I thought this was a thing just for us," he said after a while.

"I know," Nina said, pulling clothes off the floor of her bedroom, straightening books on their shelves, busying away her unease. "But she's having a hard time right now, and I just feel like she could use a change of scenery. And I figure," she said, flooding her voice with suggestion, "that we're going to have plenty of opportunities to go away together."

Adrian sighed. "Well," he said, "it's sweet how you look after her."

***

That evening Nina and Jess followed their usual Thursday night ritual, ordering Indian takeout and drinking cheap wine on the couch. Under the hum of Jess describing the man she was seeing— older, a photography professor whose paunch was undercut by his steady gray-eyed gaze, the softness with which he shared with her his seemingly bottomless knowledge of art history—Nina felt her body settle into the cushions, muscles slackening. They were back where they were supposed to be.

The professor's serenity, Jess was saying, wavered only when it was confronted by the future, in the form of her occasional questions about what he envisioned for the two of them.

"And he's almost *fifty*," she said. "At what age do guys finally grow a set of balls?"

"I don't know if it's a matter of balls. By now, he must know what he wants."

Jess did her half-shrug and then shook her head, clearing something from it. "What about you and Adrian?"

The opportunity to speak about him rarely presented itself, and Nina did not want to squander it. "It's going really good," she said.

"How good? Like marriage-level good?" Jess was watching her closely, almost as closely as Janelle had.

"I'm trying not to get ahead of myself," Nina said. "It's only been a few months."

"Fuck." Jess swallowed some wine. "So this is it. This is, like, life for you now."

She spoke as though meting out a sentence. And with her words, Nina felt a calcification within her of what before had been only a whisper through her system. Her future, unrolling before her so naturally she might have suspected it was a lie. The leveling of her life.

***

The rental car broke through the haze of the city at it crossed the Westchester border, black pavement swallowed away beneath its wheels. Sitting beside Adrian in the front, Nina kept sensing a pair of eyes drilling through the leather seat, her spine, webs of muscle, into the dark red throb of her heart, but whenever she turned, Jess was watching the green blur of trees lining the parkway.

Hours later, as they neared the cabin, Nina and Adrian rolled down

their windows. Sweet air poured in, washing them. Jess pressed her forehead against the glass.

"I feel kind of hot," she told them.

***

When they arrived, Jess dropped her bag in the threshold and went
directly to the bathroom; soon after, they heard her vomiting. Adrian
looked at Nina, wordless, eyes speaking, knowing: now she would spend
their romantic weekend playing caretaker. Surely, he had his theories
about their devotion to one another. Maybe he'd name it codepen-
dence, insecure attachment, protracted adolescence. Nina could smell
the theories brewing, but he never verbalized them to her. He might
just have been waiting for the right time, but she suspected that rather
it was a kind of grace Adrian possessed, that of finding satisfaction in
sitting alone with his awareness, not needing to prove it to anyone else.

"She can take care of herself," Nina assured him. She remembered
how Jess had vomited the first time they switched, right on the floor
in her bedroom, all her insides stormed with the power of it. While
Nina had sat there, frozen, every rule she'd known thrown out, every
entry on magic and myth in the *Compendium* now alive and crowding
around them.

***

They left her at the cabin and went to dinner without her, and at first,
the car swooping over the hills, the trees just starting to turn blurring
green-gold around them, Adrian occasionally reaching over to give her
a teasing squeeze at the pressure point above her knee, it felt like the
private getaway they'd planned. But once settled in a dark booth at the
back of the restaurant, Jess began popping up again in their conversation.
It was like Nina was a new parent, loosed from the confines of home
and expecting to relish her freedom only to find she didn't want it, she
missed the kid, what she liked best was the constant tugging at her hem.

She tried to focus on Adrian. There was still much to uncover. They were going to meet each other's families soon, and there were the trouble spots, the inevitable knots in relationships, to acquaint one another with ahead of time. He was warning her about his mother's politics, about Albert's tendency to needle her. It was all sufficiently interesting; two people alone, no matter how close, no matter how deep their history, could find enough opportunities to misunderstand, to clash, to reconcile, to sustain their whole lives.

But none of these others could hold her attention. "What," he finally said, resigned.

She was only thinking it made perfect sense Jess should fall ill now that she had a chance to pause. There were years of grinding work behind her, and unacknowledged grief over her father and Khaled. Finally she had stopped for a minute and it had all overtaken her. Didn't it often happen that way?

"Well," Adrian said, "stress really compromises us." When annoyed he rarely said so, but his speech tightened, and it was clear enough.

She didn't know how to explain that Jess had no one to attend to her but her, or how hard it would be to let that go. But she would have to find a way, for him.

***

Nina went to check in on her the next morning. The room was dim, curtains over windows pushing off the sunlight. Jess lay in bed, like a child with the covers pulled over her throat. Against the dark knots in the wood-paneled walls, Nina saw again Jess as a child: skinny, defiant, unfussed over, ready to poke out the eyes of anyone who posed a threat. She sat at the foot of the bed. She felt a surge of tenderness for her.

"You're welcome," Jess said, with a thin smile.

"I'm welcome?"

"For Adrian," Jess said. "You know I got the ball rolling there."

It was true, actually, about nearly all her relationships, Jess's imprint everywhere. "I owe you." Nina patted her feet through the blanket. "How are you feeling?"

"Like garbage." She closed her eyes. The lids looked translucent, as though Jess's dark regard could pierce right through them. She opened them again. "Do you think we could switch for just a little while? I want to go for a walk. You know I've been thinking one day I could live somewhere like this."

Nina was getting ready to leave her behind, they both knew. But who else was there? Even Jess's dead had moved on. Nina was, had always been the only one who could offer relief. She was the only one who had ever bothered.

"Of course," she said. She placed her cool forehead against Jess's fiery one and felt the old pull, still thrilling, and the soaring through the void, which was maybe where they would both end up one day when they were dead, and then the entry into Jess, the possession of her.

***

She sank into Jess's skin and felt immediately the coursing of sickness. A rawness in the ears and throat, fire stretched across the face. Stomach floating on an uneasy sea. It was strange that she'd always thought of it as a switching only of bodies, their minds remaining intact and entirely their own. As though the mind could be cleanly severed from the body, when really the two were perpetually whispering to one another, Jess and Nina leaving a residue on each other with every visit, becoming ever more ensnared. Already Nina could feel Jess's fever coloring her thoughts. There was no telling now where she ended and Jess began, which of them Adrian truly wanted. With this realization an alarm began sounding, but faint and far-off, like the long, lonely moan of the Long Island Rail Road trains she'd been able to hear, on some nights, from her childhood bedroom. The alarm was smothered by the fever, which tugged Nina, with a pleasant insistence not unlike the kind she felt when they switched, down into sleep.

***

Heat sat atop her skull like a hat. Something was tickling her toes.

Nina opened her eyes and saw herself standing pale and ghostly at the foot of the bed. *What am I doing over there?* she thought. The pain in her throat was immense.

"Nina," her double said. "Wanna switch back now?"

Nina sat up in the bed, understanding slowly returning. How much time had passed? It could have been an eon, or none at all. She nodded her pounding head, pressed it against Jess's. And maybe it was the fever, but it seemed she hung in the in-between a fraction longer, and in that fraction found that her terror of it was also her longing for it, the gray nowhere, for in that place there was no longer any wanting or worrying about having enough, or of feeling incomplete; outside the cell of a body she would disintegrate into space.

***

Some of the fever did seem to return with her, an ache inside. In their room, Adrian was in bed, waiting. He stretched out his arms to her. Despite the drag of whatever she'd brought along from Jess's body, Nina leaped playfully into them. They closed like a gate over her back.

"Cutie," Adrian said into her hair.

The ache was their secret, hers and Jess's, Nina decided. It would slowly sicken her to keep it buried, far beneath the warm weight of Adrian's arms. She had no choice but to tell. The truth of this sounded deep within her, and Nina dropped into sleep again.

***

But the ache was still there the next day. Nina woke to Adrian nuzzling her between her shoulder blades. She smelled his musty morning odor that she had come to like, to miss when they were apart.

She stood up and went to the hallway bathroom to pee. What she felt was not really an ache, but a presence. Something was residing inside her, the same way they were residing in the cabin, as visitors. Nina cupped cold water over her face. In the mirror she watched herself dripping and waited for it to subside.

She went to the toilet. Sitting there, urine draining out of her, she felt it coming, the understanding of what had happened yesterday after they switched. Nina looked down between her legs into the bowl for confirmation there.

It hit not all at once but in waves, as the nausea and the visions had when Avi poisoned her in the gymnasium. And then two more memories, overlaid, like when a teacher in elementary school mistakenly placed one transparency on top of the other on the projector, turning sensible language and lines into cryptograms. Jess, on her couch in the East Village apartment, suggesting they find out which of their boyfriends was better in bed. And then her mother, in the kitchen, explaining to Nina why Jess couldn't come live with them.

She had been invaded, and it coated every corner of her system. It was worse, far worse, than what Mr. Quinn had done. Nina heaved into the toilet, but nothing came up.

"Nina?" Adrian at the door. "Don't tell me you caught whatever Jess has."

She stood and with one numb hand opened the bathroom door. Adrian stood there with his concerned and intermittently handsome face. He reached out and cupped her cheeks with his warm hands.

"Adrian," Nina said, and tried to stiffen all her muscles to hide their trembling, "did we have sex yesterday?"

He tipped his head over slightly, like a dog. "Is that a serious question?"

"I'm feeling kind of weird. I honestly don't remember."

A smile started around the corners of his mouth. "You wanna rehash it, huh? Our walk in the woods?"

Nina could see it: as she lay febrile in the dark room, Jess, in her body, a witch coaxing him into the forest. He was still there. He would never emerge, come back to her.

"I can help you remember," Adrian said. He laughed, floated his hands over her hips.

Nina said what she knew. She identified the presence within her and felt it stir with the words. "I got pregnant yesterday."

"Come on," Adrian said. He reared back to take more of her in. "There's no way you could know that already. It wouldn't even show up on a test yet." He planted his lips on her forehead, feeling with them for heat. "Are you sure you're okay?"

***

She sent him away to have breakfast alone, promising she only needed to sleep a little longer and then she'd be ready to take on the day with him. Once Adrian closed the door behind him, her trembling increased to what seemed to Nina an unsustainable intensity. She would be torn apart. In the kitchen, blindly, she pulled open drawers. From one, she extracted a carving knife. Its rough brown handle transferred the knife's stillness to her hand and up her arm, into her chest.

Nina's body crossed the living room without her awareness or consent; she found herself outside the door to the room where she'd slept, innocent, the day before. With her free hand she turned the knob and pushed it open. Jess lay there on her back, dark hair fanned out against the pillow, shut safely in her slumber. Was she dreaming? What was she seeing right now, against her closed eyelids?

I've been wrong, Nina thought, for all these years. I have never known this woman.

"Wake up," she said, and Jess's eyes fluttered open.

"Morning," she mumbled, and then she saw what Nina was holding. "What are your plans for that?" Jess said, the words mixed with grit as they came from her raw throat.

Nina had no intention of harming her. It was only that the knife gave her a sense of stability, absorbed all her trembling.

"I know what you did. With Adrian."

Jess pulled herself up into a seated position, stuffed the pillow behind

her back. She took her time. When she was finished there was a suggestion of mirth around her lips. "So you're going to stab me?" she said.
"Jesus. I didn't think you'd be this dramatic."

"What you did," Nina said. "It's like rape."

"Of who?" Jess's skin was pale, the hollows beneath her eyes as dark as
fingerprint smudges. "How is it any different from the ways you use me?"

Nina's stomach turned upside down. It was the new being inside
her, spinning.

"Why don't you just calm down, Nina. Take a few deep breaths."
Jess pulled her knees up, rested her chin on them.

"How have I used you?"

"Come on. I need to tell you?" Jess laughed. "And now you're ready
to settle down, so you don't need me anymore."

The knife handle was growing slippery in Nina's hand.

"But you'd never have gotten to where you are today without me,"
Jess continued. Her sickness lowered her voice an octave, so that it
sounded like it belonged to someone else. "And you've never been will-
ing to share with me the way I shared with you."

"I've shared everything." Nina put the knife down on the dresser,
ran her wet palm through her hair. The vibrations returned; Jess looked
at her, waiting, as though for proof. "My entire life. My family—"

"Your family? Are you kidding? You ended our sleepovers exactly
when I needed them the most."

There they were again, sitting during recess at the picnic table behind
the elementary school, Nina telling Jess she wanted a break from their
switching. Jess—she saw it now—looking down, biting back tears, knowing
she was trapped. The still June air, the silence enrobing them, recording it all.

"I was just a little kid."

"But this is who you are," Jess said.

Nina had understood even then, picking at the cigarette burns on
the table, that her decision could not be taken back. "I know it was bad
for you," she said.

Jess's face, rigid with righteousness, seemed to slip a little. She bent
her head and coughed into her hands.

When she was finished Nina said, "I know you asked my mother once if you could come live with us."

Whatever softness had been materializing on her face fell away. "You wouldn't share even a little."

"So you just took what you wanted?"

Jess did her half-shrug, a tiny movement. Behind it was an ocean of contempt. It had been churning in her since they were ten years old. "It's only sex, Nina. It's not like what I had with Mr. Q."

It had been so easy for her to believe they'd left all that in the past. "I got pregnant," Nina said.

It was the first time Jess looked startled. Then she shook her head. Echoing Adrian, she said, "There's no way you'd know that already."

Nina knew. Far inside her something was splitting open, pulling itself from nowhere into existence. The vibrations dropped away, replaced by a sadness that ran through her marrow, the outline Jess had filled in for her.

"I'm going for a walk," Nina said. She picked up the knife. "When I get back, please be gone."

She turned from Jess's pale face, her dark eyes. In the moment before she turned she saw its whole semblance drop, exposing the child at the picnic table, the new girl sitting beside her in Ms. Brandon's class on the first day of their friendship, terrified.

"Nina," Jess said.

***

In the woods beyond the cabin Nina found an abandoned seat from a chairlift, half-covered in weeds. The nearest ski resort was a town away; she couldn't imagine how it had gotten here. She placed the knife gently down on its peeling leather. Most of the leaves had not turned yet but their green was less vibrant, draining away. Within their whispering she felt sheltered, untouched by what had transpired. She had stepped out of time.

But when she emerged from the trees she began thinking, *Maybe there is a way. If Jess didn't listen to me, if she hasn't left yet, maybe . . .*

The cabin was empty. There was no trace of Jess on the gravel road leading back to town.

Nina walked around the rooms. Something was rising in her; maybe she had caught Jess's flu after all, one last bit of sharing. Maybe she was about to be sick.

But that wasn't it. She went into Jess's bedroom. The bed still bore the imprint of her shape. The pillow was still slightly damp from her perspiration. Nina took it in her hands. She held it to her face and screamed into it.

16
THE BEAUTIFUL VOYAGE
(2018)

What had Jess said four tasted like? Had she ever said? It must be a strong flavor, bitter and sweet, like dark chocolate. The age was over-powering, laden with discoveries but also with the burgeoning sense of one's own helplessness. Mommy had to take the laces from your thick unwilling fingers to tie your shoes. She had to help you with your sweater, tugging first one arm and then the other through tunnels of fabric until your hands, wriggling like fish on land, emerged at the end of the sleeves. And then she lifted the bulk of it over your head and you were submerged for a moment in a strange, dim world, like being inside the fur of an animal, until the drama of dressing was over, and you were reborn to the light.

Then you were back in the apartment in Jackson Heights. You knew that name but not its borders. It might have rolled on forever. Jackson Heights was always full of the smoke from street carts where tall fig-ures turned over meat, vegetables, dumplings, with wide silver spatulas and peered way down at you, sometimes with their faces cracking open into smiles, sometimes not. It was a sort of game you played, with only yourself, to toddle up to them and wait for their noticing, and while you waited, to guess which expression would come. In either case you would tell them, "Hello," before returning to your mother's reaching hands.

Maya did not yet suspect (Nina hoped) that there might be anything unusual about their family of two. She had friends, of course, who lived in apartments full of people, but those people she seemed to perceive as incidental. There might be a sister or an auntie or a daddy the same way there might be a dishwasher. She had never asked Nina where her own sister or daddy could be, but she had asked why they couldn't have a dog.

But who knew what Maya wondered? That morning, before it was time to leave for preschool, as Nina was pulling on her boots, she glanced over and saw Maya lying on the living room floor in a pool of weak winter sunlight. She was on her back, staring at the ceiling.

"What are you doing, My?" she asked.

Maya said, "I'm thinking."

"About what?"

No answer. Maya's concentration on the ceiling, rimmed with its ancient moldings, did not flicker. The apartment had been updated not long ago, clean tiles in the bathroom, new appliances in the kitchen, but the molding, a dark oak braid tracing the perimeter, remained, holding the rooms in place in the past. Nina would never know what, in that moment, were the shapes of Maya's unsharable thoughts. She housed, already, many mysteries.

They had entered the world with her. When Maya was a newborn in a bassinet, Nina would look over from the bed sometimes and find her daughter awake and silent, secrets roaming behind her half-seeing eyes. While she was pregnant she felt it: Nina a house for Maya, Maya a house for her own self, a strange doubling within her belly that sometimes made Nina feel dizzy but also, perpetually, accompanied.

***

It wasn't as though she'd discovered some kind of new serenity. Once, when Maya was an infant, Nina had been reading a book with the baby on her lap and dozed off and dropped the paperback directly onto her tender face. Long after Maya's howling stopped, it went on sculpting eddies inside Nina's chest. There had been hundreds, probably thousands of mistakes like that. Later, when Maya was two and a half, Nina's mother had called to let her know that Zachary was engaged. He and his girlfriend, Ashley, helped out with the baby a lot. She should have been happy for them.

Maya, from her booster seat, where she was eating rabbit-shaped crackers, watched Nina through the phone call.

"Mommy sad?" she said, after Nina hung up.

The thought that had snuck past all the others—about wedding plans, about how families, like certain amphibians, regenerated themselves (her grandmother had recently died)—was the kind Nina was usually vigilant for, guarded against. It was that she must call Jess and tell her the news. "I guess Zach finally got over you," Nina would say. "Remember how you used to bribe him with kisses to leave us alone?"

Nina nodded at Maya, who doubled in her vision. "A little," she said, and Maya's mouth turned down to mirror hers. A two-year-old was not supposed to be your confessor; sadness was the sort of thing adults were to conceal from children, or it might sink in too deep, wound them in some way that did not become apparent until many years later.

And now it was as though, years after her final rupture from Jess (and it was final, there'd be no reappearance of Jess this time, turning the corner and walking down her block), that Nina had mislaid an entire mythology. They had created their own compendium of the universe, but to sustain it required them both, and so gone was their hall of nobodies, their candle rooms, their haunted radios, their sleepovers; gone was the closest she would ever come to seeing and being seen, from the inside out.

***

After work she retrieved Maya from pre-K and they went to visit Zach and Ashley, riding the 7 train over dense neighborhoods, foreign alphabets beaming up at them from storefronts and restaurants. Maya, face pressed to the window, repeated the names of everything she saw until

Nina acknowledged that yes, there was a bus and there a church and there, in the distance, a skyscraper. Maya had her quiet thoughts, but then there were times that her desire to make her insides visible flamed up with searing insistence. How much of her bore Jess's imprint? She had been inside Nina's skin when Maya was conceived, and it seemed possible—as possible as two girls, for decades, switching bodies unnoticed—that at least some of Jess's spirit had been transferred to her.

They changed to the G train. Maya did not want to be carried at all, and so Nina joined her in gingerly stepping down staircases and through tunnels into the underground and back up into the light.

In Williamsburg the construction sites she had once observed with Gregory, the maternal cranes bent over nothing, had bloomed into silver towers, and in one of these Zachary and his wife now lived. The security guard at his post in the polished lobby greeted Maya warmly, let her venture behind his desk. She stood on tiptoe, to see what he was seeing. "May I?" he asked Nina. She nodded, and he lifted Maya onto his lap and explained to her about his screens, how they showed all the corridors and corners of the building.

"This one is for the elevator," he said, pointing, Maya's eyes following, "so when you take it, you can wave hello and I'll be able to see you."

"Wow," Maya breathed. The doorman smiled at the purity of her amazement. Around a child, people opened themselves with astonishing readiness; walking the world with Maya gave Nina such access to strangers it felt almost like a superpower.

In the elevator Nina pointed out the security camera and Maya waved at it, frantically, for the entire ride up.

The apartment bloomed with cooking smells; the booster chair for Maya was waiting there at the table. "It's good practice," Zachary told Nina once, of the time spent with his niece. He'd been married to Ashley for only a year. "Think they'll make it?" Nina had asked her father at their wedding, late in the evening, when she was very drunk. He said there was no way of knowing. Because what could they know of her brother's remotest interiors, or anyone of their own?

***

When Adrian returned to the cabin, Nina had still been curled on the floor in Jess's room, gripping the pillow. He reacted as a professional well-acquainted with emergency: minimally. He coaxed her out, sat her on the couch, poured her a glass of water, stroked her back for many long minutes. Then he asked if she was ready to talk about whatever had happened.

In retrospect, she could see, she should not have begun with *Jess and I are more than just friends*. After that he had not been able to really listen. It was all sewed up in his mind. But Nina could think of no other preamble to finally sharing her secret. *It started when we were kids* had not served her either, but how else to capture the duration of it? She spewed out the story in chunks, what she could rally from within herself, much omitted; she found she spoke mostly of their rules to swapping, how they strove to maintain fidelity to one another, to pass in and out of each other's lives unseen, and how it had always turned out that way, they alone capable of seeing the wreckage and rewards of their interventions. And now this, the worst one of all, this violation of both Nina and Adrian. *And the new being inside me*, she did not say, because it struck her as more unbelievable than anything else.

He'd gone rigid, a stone man with moving eyes.

"Adrian," Nina said. Her voice was a mewl. It sounded just like Giselle's. "Please tell me what you're thinking."

His lips hardly moved. "When a patient comes to you with delusions, you're never supposed to try to dispute them. But you're not my patient."

"I'm not—" Nina began, but he held up a palm to her.

"What I'm thinking is you're in love with this woman, and have been for years, and you've constructed this elaborate mythology to justify your feelings to yourself." He looked down. "Does she feel the same way about you?" Adrian asked.

Nina looked at the fireplace, closed and dead. If Jess were here she could prove it, switch with her, in her body tell Adrian things only they knew. But the small realm she'd made with him was narrowing, and in a few moments, it would blink out of existence. "I'm never going to speak to her again," she said.

"Well," Adrian said. He put his hands on his knees. "It doesn't have to be that way. You can be with her, if that's what you want." Then he raised his hands to his face, breathed into them loudly. "Fuck," he said. "I really thought we had something."

***

Zachary and Ashley never pressed her on the details of her love life, her social life. Nina wondered whether they congratulated themselves, after visits, for accepting her on her own terms, or worriedly parsed each moment she'd spent in their company for evidence she was okay. More likely, wrapped in each other, the newlyweds simply moved on with their day.

Nina wondered for a long time whether she should have let it slide. It was, as Jess had said, only sex. Could she have lived with that knowledge fuming inside her? But it made sense, she tried to decide. There had been something about the relationship with Adrian that was not quite real. It unfolded on the dream plane, like the drama of the candle room.

That night, Zachary had news. He and Ashley, he said, had gotten into the habit of watching travel documentaries at night, to wind down after work by imagining themselves into places their scant PTO days would never allow them to visit. Last night they'd been watching one about Greece and then, during a scene in Athens, against the backdrop of blindingly white buildings, guess who he had spotted, unmistakably herself even as she was weaving so quickly past the tourists in khaki shorts and old men drinking coffee in cafés?

Funny how he posed it to her this way, as if it would be a great surprise.

"Jess," Nina said. She thought of the old men who had called out to her from across the street as she took their photograph, who had to speak to her, sure she had something they needed.

Ashley looked annoyed. Perhaps they'd discussed this already and decided not to tell her. Nina had declined to explain why she'd returned from Vermont without a boyfriend or a best friend, the apartment already emptied of all Jess's things. She let everyone draw their own conclusions.

Zachary shifted a little in his chair. "Maybe it was dumb of me to bring it up."

"Maybe," Ashley said.

Nina told them it was fine, that she was glad to hear Jess was seeing the world. She glanced over at Maya, unsure what she was expecting, her face illuminated, maybe, by sudden recognition, but her daughter was only scooping mashed potatoes into her mouth with great focus.

For the rest of the evening she engaged with her family, laughing in the correct places, exhorting Maya to eat more carrots because they brightened her eyes. The left one is really shiny, Nina told her, but the right one still has a way to go. But she was operating as an automaton, occupied wholly with watching Jess as she drifted through blue distances.

She never told Adrian that she was right, she was pregnant. For a while she worried she might run into him, when she was eight months along and enormous, or when she trudged down streets with the infant Maya strapped to her chest or buckled into a stroller, but she never did. He might as well have been as far away as Jess. The city had a way of swallowing people. If she hadn't already had so much practice at it, New York would have made keeping her secrets easy.

***

Nina left carrying Maya, asleep or pretending to be, in her arms, her warm density easing the tension in her chest. She remembered as a child how she would drift away on car rides home from somewhere, through her dozing half-dreams feeling the familiar blacktop of their driveway beneath the wheels and knowing she could rouse herself but electing not to, her limbs so heavy and the darkness behind her eyelids so pleasantly encompassing, letting her father lift her from the seat, the perfect security of his arms around her.

In the lobby the doorman wanted to talk again. He looked at Maya's face and shook his head. "Is there anything sweeter than that?"

Nina was tired. "I need a cab," she told him, and he nodded. She leaned against his desk, her biceps beginning to hum with the ache of holding Maya.

"Hey," the doorman said. She turned to him. "You're doing great with her," he said.

***

How had he known it was what she'd been waiting to hear, when she hadn't known herself?

She put Maya to bed, the child's eyes remaining closed even as Nina tugged off her shoes and socks, puffed up the pillow beneath her head, laid the blanket over her. She'd been wrong, Nina thought, looking at her daughter's face, in sleep soft and unguarded. Maya was not a repository of secrets; she was open. Nina could almost see dreams pulsing beneath her skin.

The living room window overlooked busy Thirty-Seventh Avenue. A fallback activity she could always undertake with Maya was to perch her on the sill and have her describe everything she saw. A lady with a pink scarf on her head. A man walking three dogs, all different sizes. A little boy being yanked along, crying. Now it was dark, and lime-green taxis were sliding up and down the thoroughfare, bearing people home.

The child monitor lit up and through it came a stream of unintelligible sounds, Maya's sleep babble. Nina knew she was stalling. She was afraid of what would come slamming into her. But there was no way to brace for it—there never had been.

***

It didn't take long for Nina to find the documentary. She lay on the couch watching, the voice of the British narrator lulling her almost to sleep, the sunlight-flecked water of the Aegean flashing through her half-closed eyes.

The scene shifted, the camera leaving the islands behind, hovering over the Parthenon and swooping down into the cramped passageways of the neighborhoods below. And then, for a second, there she was, Jessica Garcia, the creator and remover of obstacles.

Nina sat up and pressed pause. She missed the moment that Jess walked right by the camera, when her profile was visible, so now the view stilled on screen was of her walking away, up the road, dark hair streaming behind her, arms caught midswing. There was no question it was her.

What would it amount to, all they had done to and for each other, if it could be weighed on some universal scale? Had they, as they passed into each other's flesh, left behind more than they had taken?

She thought of what Janelle had asked her—asked Jess, really—about when she would have enough. The medium had been speaking about satiety, what it took to find it. Was there an end to wanting, to incompletion, to groping within yourself and feeling your hands brush up against absence?

A sigh again from the child monitor, a murmuring. Jess continued to hover on the screen, walking away forever. The image recalled Jess's old sketches and photographs, her strange surveillance of herself. That distance—had she managed to shrink it all the way down, climb back inside herself and be contented there, alone in her darkness? Nina could gaze at her for as long as she wanted and imagine that she had—that she was free.

And if Jess could look through the television screen into the apartment, watch her as she stood and walked away, follow with her dark gaze as Nina went down the hall and into Maya's room, knelt on the floor and leaned over to breathe in the scent of the little girl's hair, she might imagine the same.

ACKNOWLEDGMENTS

First, thanks to Nanny, who plied me with great literature and taught me that in a pinch, the dictionary can make for good reading. And to Opi, who loved wordplay and understood endurance better than anyone. Thanks to the Schubach clan, whose vocabulary is colorful, teasing, affectionate, and support unwavering: Omi, Shelley, Mom, Dad, Julian, and Lisa. Thanks to Charlie and Nancy Kilpatrick, and to Connor and Megan Kilpatrick; may our chats never go public. Thanks to my writer friends who read this book, some parts multiple times and in grotesque incarnations, and whose insights were essential: Libby Boland, Austin Grossman, Helly Schtevie, Lisa Gordon, Christine Meade, Sarah Simon, Patti Affriol, Seth Sawyers, and Jé Wilson. Thank you to Danielle McDonaugh and Greg Travis for showing up to readings and just being "nicies," and to Katherine Hill for all the advice on this strange endeavor. Thank you to my teachers, especially Aileen O'Connell, Kathleen Hill, David Hollander, and Elizabeth Gaffney. Thank you to my agent, Robert Guinsler, for truly being in it for the long haul, to Dianca London for connecting us, and to everyone at Blackstone. Thank you to my editors, Meg Storey and Betsy Mitchell, for all you saw in the manuscript that

I did not. Thank you to the Center for Fiction, the New York Foundation for the Arts, the Vermont Studio Center, and the Virginia Center for the Creative Arts. Thank you, Lynn Gold, for many years of wisdom. Thank you to Kelly Caldwell and the staff and students of the Gotham Writers Workshop. Thank you to Jeanette Duffy and Crista Scaturro, with whom I collectively share over fifty years of friendship and who are my cheerleaders, humblers, and sisters. Did we find each other or create each other? And finally, "thank you" does not suffice for Scott Kilpatrick. Writing this book and embarking on a life with you are two adventures inextricably entwined. The first I completed because of you. The second is happily ongoing.